I0819670

YOU'RE DEAD TO ME, REED WALKER

You're DEAD to Me, Reed Walker

GWENYTH REITZ

ROARING BROOK PRESS
NEW YORK

Published by Roaring Brook Press
Roaring Brook Press is a division of
Holtzbrinck Publishing Holdings Limited Partnership
120 Broadway, New York, NY 10271 • fiercereads.com

EU representative: Macmillan Publishers Ireland Ltd, 1st Floor,
The Liffey Trust Centre, 117–126 Sheriff Street Upper, Dublin 1, D01 YC43

Library of Congress Control Number: 2025028013

First edition, 2026
Book design by Abby Granata
Printed in the United States of America

ISBN 978-1-250-40417-6
10 9 8 7 6 5 4 3 2 1

TO MY MOM, WHO SHARED THE JOY OF LOSING YOURSELF IN A REALLY GOOD STORY. AND TO MY DAD, WHO SHARED HIS PASSION FOR WRITING THEM.

AFTER

The crumbling floorboards creak as the house shifts on its aging foundation. Gusts of wind howl against its bones, rocketing the shutters back and forth, sending ice-cold breath slipping through the crevices. Each sound a new note in an orchestra of decay—rot blooming, a rustle of wings, the scampering of mice. I should feel cold. I should feel spooked.

But I don't.

Old houses make noises. And if anything is here to press frozen fingers against the necks of unsuspecting victims, it's us.

CHAPTER 1

Tessa
BEFORE

LONG LIVE BEER AND BROS

My feet skid to a stop as I stare up at the large block letters rearranged over our high school entrance. *Are you kidding me?* Every senior prank day the graduating class tries to outdo the year before. Last June, they toilet papered the halls and stole all the furniture out of the teachers' lounge; before that, all the classroom doors went missing—until the janitor found them on the roof. I'm sure beer and bros is just the beginning.

Students are already starting to crowd the entrance, gawking at the sign, snapping photos, and smacking one another on the back. Apparently, a lot of dudes are going to miss a lot of other dudes. It's hard being a bro on the brink of graduation.

I sigh, standing on my tiptoes to peer over the heads in front of me. What other horrors are waiting inside? I knew we shouldn't have scheduled the Marjory Fieldman Honor Roll luncheon for today. I begged Principal Evans to postpone to next week, but did he listen? No. And now sensible-shoe-wearing, church-choir-conducting Marjory Fieldman herself will probably turn around with her giant custom-made scholarship check, declaring a full ride, and hightail it out of here in moral outrage over "kids these days." Goodbye, scholarship. Goodbye, financial aid. Goodbye, all hope for my future.

"Your strawberry milk tea with boba, milady." Brandon, my longtime boyfriend, stops beside me with my morning fix of tapioca pearls.

"Are you seeing this?" I gesture dramatically at the word scramble above, foot tapping in righteous indignation. Brielle van der Born, our high school namesake, must be turning over in her grave. Or maybe not. She was Dutch. I'm pretty sure they like beer.

"I got a photo when I parked my car. Only one spot left at the back of the senior lot. You're so lucky you get a reserved space with the teachers. The perks of being student body president." He sighs wistfully. Brandon isn't ambitious, but he's happy to live vicariously off my ambition. I'm not entirely sure why we're still together—except he's always so sweet with the boba.

I take a pull off the straw and get a delicious hit of chewy tapioca goodness. "That's why I ran for president, for the perks.

And the tea." I give him a quick peck on the cheek. "Why did you take a picture?"

"I don't know. It's funny. I wanted a memory of our wild high school days." He pumps his fists in the air while headbanging like we're at a concert, then almost loses his balance.

"No offense, Brandon, but there is nothing about me, you, or our high school days that is remotely wild."

Brandon's more . . . dependable, like a warm sock. He's mildly cute if you catch him in the right light, when his shaggy, sandy hair is out of his eyes. But he's about as wild as a potted plant. Brandon likes tea. And jazz. Not to play, just to listen to in his car. His idea of a fun Friday night is to swap calculus notes . . . and listen to some jazz . . . in our warm socks.

My life is so depressing.

At the edge of the parking lot, Donika Chaudhari and her boyfriend, Davis Miller, are taking selfies as they kiss with the sign in the background. I wish Brandon and I did that more often, but it's like we've forgotten what it even means to be a couple. Trying to resurrect whatever spark we used to have, I give him my most sultry and smoldering expression wondering if he'll do the same, but he's busy tugging a string loose from his shirt.

"What? Is there something on my face?" He rubs his chin when he catches me staring.

So much for romance and excitement. I return my attention to the sign, trying to will the letters back into place. How long until Janitor Bailey can get a ladder up there to rearrange them—unless he's dealing with something far worse? My stomach tightens around the thought.

Teetotaling Ms. Fieldman once huffed out of a church fundraising dinner for Habitat for Humanity after they served wine to the adults in attendance. I can't chance her getting offended now and storming off. Neither of my parents attended college, but my dad especially is counting on me to finish what he couldn't. *Life has a way of derailing you, so don't let that happen, kid*, he said, and I don't plan on it. My life's mapped out perfectly, my course charted. I know exactly what I want—two years at SUNY Albany so I can remain close while my father gets back on his feet after losing his job, before transferring to NYU to study chemistry and eco-friendly textile design. Then, I'll be ready to wage my one-woman war against the fast-fashion industry.

Which is why things cannot go sideways today, not when I'm so close to seeing my plans through.

"So . . . there's just one beer for all those bros to share?"

"There's only one *S*." I squint at the sign, running all the letters that would normally herald the entrance to Brielle van der Born High School through my head.

"Why not *long live beers and bro*, then? Isn't it better to share many beers with one good bro than one beer with many bros and only get a sip each?"

A laugh flies out of my mouth, startling me. "Brandon, you made a funny."

"I didn't say anything." He shrugs.

What? Who've I been talking to? I turn to Brandon, standing next to me, gazing at the entrance sign, and that's when I realize there's someone standing next to him. That someone leans forward, a smirk lighting up his face.

Reed Walker.

My nemesis since the sixth grade, when he moved to our upstate New York town from wherever evil spawns. Denver, apparently. Valedictorian to my salutatorian. Stealer of spelling bee trophies and science fair titles. The smile drops off my face faster than Ms. Fieldman dashing out of here in her sensible shoes clutching my giant check.

Reed arches an eyebrow at me. "I mean, with all those letters at their disposal, they could have been more creative and gone with . . ." He takes a moment to consider. ". . . *neighborhood hellraiser*?"

What is going on right now?

"Or . . . maybe . . ." He points at the school entrance. ". . . *doing believable horrors*."

"How are you word scrambling these so fast?"

Reed winks. He enjoys rubbing his stupid hyper-computing robot brain in my face.

I glare at the sign. Then the letters start to shift in my imagination and take shape. "Wait. Um . . . *alien* . . . um . . . *slobbering alien . . . overlord! Slobbering alien overlord!*" I jump up and down, proud I found onc. Brandon high-fives me.

As Reed taps his chin, determined to best me, I catch the fraction of a dimple I never noticed before. "How about . . ." He looks me right in the eye. "*Horrible Brandon*."

He's arrived at the idea like it's obvious. So rude.

"Hey, my name's in the sign!"

I roll my eyes. I have no time for smug, entitled pricks. "Don't you have other people to torture?"

"So, Reed." Brandon moves the conversation along, oblivious. "You ready for your speech next week?"

"Pretty much." He shrugs. "Will you be accompanying the ice princess to graduation?"

"Who?"

"He means me." I sigh.

"Oh, Tessa? Yes." He half mumbles it, distracted by something across the parking lot.

I shoot Brandon a dark look. I guess I'll have to defend my own honor. But I don't get a chance: Reed's music friends are running over. Kira's all tats and piercings and purple hair. She's nonstop energy. Santiago's more chill. He's rocked the same orange knit beanie since ninth grade. Either he's cultivating it as a look, or he's too stoned to remember he still has it on.

"The English hallway is sick," Kira shouts, tugging Reed across the parking lot.

Oh God. What now? "Why? What's happening?" I race to catch up. The scholarship luncheon is supposed to be held in the library—which is next to the ELA classrooms.

Kira turns to speak with me, but neither of us can see past Reed's enormous guitar backpack. He brings that ridiculous instrument wherever he goes. Pretentious much? I don't think I've ever heard him play, but that doesn't stop him from reminding us all that he *does* play by carting it around everywhere.

"It's like a troll doll army threw up in there," she says.

Oh hell no. Not on my watch. "Brandon," I call.

"On it." Brandon whips out a notebook, awaiting further orders.

Kira does a double take, surprised we're still following.

I race ahead, shoving past students still gaping at the entrance sign to throw open the double doors to the English corridor. It's way worse than I thought. Blue shaving cream is smeared over the lockers, dribbling into puddles of goo below. Multicolored Silly String dangles from the fluorescents overhead, creating a forest of impassable sticky vines, while the floor is coated in a two-inch-thick moat of glitter slime. I'll probably need a hazmat suit to enter.

"Oh shit," Reed mumbles on a laugh as they arrive behind me.

I knew something like this was going to happen. I swear if I lose my scholarship over this BS, I'm going to haunt this school for eternity. A mounting anger bubbles and froths inside me. So many of these students, Reed included, don't need to stress over money for college. But some of us have to work extra hard to get out of this town. And that's just what I'll do now. Like always.

I hand Reed my bubble tea. "Hold my beer, bro."

CHAPTER 2

Tessa

I always wondered how I'd behave if oxygen masks dropped from the ceiling of an airplane as we plummeted in altitude, careening toward the earth below. Would I put mine on then calmly help my neighbor? Would I prepare to grab my seat cushion in case of a water landing? Or would I unbuckle my seat belt and race through the aisles screaming, "There's no hope left! We're all gonna die!"

I think I might be the kind who panics.

My stress and anxiety become my own personal jet fuel. Which is a useful trait, since I'll need all that jet propulsion to give the teachers' lounge a makeover. I scan the site of today's new luncheon location. Armed with fabric from the drama department and a bag of past spring fling dance decor,

I've had to make quick work of the space. I run over my to-do list. *Rearrange the chairs around the perimeter.* Check. *Hide any random boxes of copy paper in Principal Evans's office.* Check. *Call Ms. DelVino, PTA president, and inform her that we'll now be stationed far away from the English hallway disaster.* Check. If I throw a few more decorations up and arrange the flowers, my work will be done. I set out some donated bouquets, hoping a particularly tall vase of sunflowers can somehow disguise the vending machines.

"How do you do it, you radiant goddess you?" Tilly, my best friend since kindergarten, dashes in during passing period.

"Tills, thank God you're here. Principal Evans has been sending me volunteers all morning, but it's like herding cats. We only have an hour left. Tell me it looks okay." I gesture to the buffet tables draped in purple fabric, each covered with colorful confetti that I've spent my morning hole punching.

She puts her hands on my shoulders. "Only you could convert the teachers' lounge into a thing of beauty."

"Thanks—wait. Hang on, Tills." Across the room, Brandon's precariously balancing on a chair as he hangs crepe paper from the ceiling. "Brandon," I shout.

"Yeah?"

"You have to twist the colors together to create each bow. You can't just tape it up and call it a day. Grab Jenny Chu, she did the other side." Jenny shoots me a side-eye, annoyed I'm doling out commands. Tough luck, J Chu, I have no time for your feelings.

I bet she's only here because she thinks she can sway the scholarship results at the last second. But last month, Principal Evans pulled me aside to tell me I'd won the Marjory Fieldman

Scholarship for Outstanding Moral Fiber and made me swear to keep it on the down-low. Not only am I in charge of the event, but I desperately need the money. And Jenny's family doesn't. It's as simple as that.

Tilly spins me around. "You did the braids! And check out your gorgeous threads!" She knows how much this day means to me.

"Yep, it's a braid day." I turn to show them off. I always wear my long black hair in two messy buns at the nape of my neck, but when I'm really trying to make an impression—and today I am really trying to make an impression—I braid my hair into the buns.

"And I'm loving this sea-foam color and fifties A-line cut. Is your suit from Second Place?"

Second Place: my apparent lot in life *and* my favorite vintage store. "I made a quick trip to Albany last weekend. The cherry blouse was hard to pass up, too." I smooth the blouse out and rebutton my jacket. I buy and alter almost all my clothes from secondhand shops. Part of it is style, part is funds, and part is a commitment to upcycling. I have a good eye. I can find a diamond in the rough. "Besides, who are you calling gorgeous, goddess divine!" I say as Tilly struts across the room in her lemon jumpsuit, a splash of sunshine against the dark tones of her skin. She always dresses like candy. "You, my love, are as effervescent as a sunrise after a storm at sea."

"Well, you're the mist rising off the ocean on a cool spring morning."

"Oh stop!"

"No, you stop!"

"Could you both stop? I'm going to be sick." Jenny sneers,

teetering on a chair as she tries to help Brandon finish up the bow he was having so much trouble with before.

My phone vibrates in my pocket with a text.

> **MOM**: Sweets, I got the graduation tickets you sent but didn't realize it's the same day as Michael's piano recital. He's been working so hard this year. I don't think we can miss it. Let's celebrate together when you visit Phoenix this summer instead.

I stare at the message, a lump forming in the back of my throat.

"Oh no, what is it?" Tilly's brow crinkles in worry.

I pivot the screen around for her to read. When our eyes meet, her look says it all. Tilly knows. We've helped each other through a lot—my parents' divorce and our financial hardship, her mom's breast cancer, which is thankfully in remission now. Tilly is that kind of friend. We can laugh together, but she's not afraid to face the hard stuff.

I shake my head. "She does this *every* time." My mother hasn't set foot in town since she ran off with Kino, her physical therapist, five years ago. Of course, she doesn't mind if my sister Jillian and I visit her. When my breathing picks up speed, Tilly rubs my back in slow, gentle circles; she knows how quickly my anxiety can avalanche. "God forbid she return for my graduation. I'm only salutatorian. I'm giving a speech and everything. Michael's twelve. He'll have plenty of other recitals." It figures she'd make time for my stepbrother. We're her discard family. They're the ones she's trying to get it right with.

"You know my parents will be cheering you on. And my

aunts and uncles, and the entire cousin army." She squeezes me in a side hug.

"Thanks, Tills." I lean into her for a moment, before I feel like I'm neglecting my duties and peek at the progress across the room. Brandon flashes me a thumbs-up, then drops his crepe paper roll and has to scramble down from his chair while it unspools across the floor.

"That boy." Tilly tsks. "Have you talked to him yet?"

"What? I can't hear you. I need to get back to my checklist." I turn to grab my clipboard from the chair by the door.

"Stop, Tess." She steps in front of me, dropping her voice low. "You have to tell him. If your heart's not in it, then it's not fair to string him along."

I sigh. It's pretty rich of Tilly to give advice—her relationships always end in disaster—but I know she means well. "I will. I know. It's just . . . he *is* a good guy, and honestly, better the bland sandwich you know than—"

"Did you just compare your boyfriend to a sandwich?"

"Um . . ."

"To a *sad*, tasteless sandwich?"

"I mean, okay, I did, but . . . after my mom left—" The bell rings, saving me from having to explain how even a little kindness is better than nothing.

Tilly swings her backpack onto her shoulder. "Look, you and I are the type of people who are meant to thrive in college. I'll find the sexy-studious, dark-academia boy of my dreams and you will, too."

I quirk an eyebrow at her. "I'm *also* finding the dark-academia boy of your dreams?"

She rolls her eyes. "No. Smart-ass. Of *your* dreams. Because you and I both know he's not over there." She nods toward Brandon, who's still chasing his crepe paper across the floor. "And when we trek through Nepal after we graduate, you can bring him." Ever since freshman year Tilly and I have been planning the perfect post-college adventure, which involves lots of hostels, cute boys, cozy sweaters, gorgeous vistas, and each other.

Tilly squeezes my hand. "Tell him, Tess. He deserves someone who loves Miles Davis and Earl Grey as much as he does."

"Yeah. You're right. I know."

As she heads out the door to class, I glance over at Brandon with his shaggy hair and freckles, with his Jazz at Birdland T-shirt and his near-constant need to please me. As he's determinedly trying to respool the crepe paper back together, making a disastrous, crinkly mess, it hits me. Just because someone's a good person doesn't mean they're the right person for you. Brandon is sweet and safe . . . and kind of boring. But maybe he's actually someone else's perfect cup of tea. And who am I to hold him back from love?

Though I'm not sure where that leaves me.

Because if Brandon's not my cup of tea, then who is?

"Reed."

"What?" I stare blankly into the face of Mr. McKeen, my economics teacher. It's possible he's been talking for a while, but my mind's still distracted over the luncheon setup.

"I said, why don't you work on your graduation speech with Reed since you've already completed all your other assignments. You can give each other feedback." He gestures toward the small vestibule off the back of his classroom, where he keeps a few computers for the yearbook students.

My stomach drops. I should have found more puttering chores to do before the luncheon started, rather than catch the last fifteen minutes of fourth period. Resolved, I shuffle past my classmates hunched over their notes—half of them discreetly texting under their desks—to the yearbook office, where Reed is reclining in his chair, legs kicked out in front of him.

For a moment. A. Very. Brief. Moment. I'm distracted by the light streaming in from the windows casting a warm summer glow over his olive complexion and bouncing off his sleek black hair. He wears it chin-length and tucked behind his ears; today, there's a pencil stashed back there, too. But when I catch his smug expression the spell fades, and I'm reminded why I avoid him. He's far too pleased with himself.

And why am I even staring at him like that? Bleh.

I clear my throat, but Mr. Have-I-Mentioned-I-Got-Into-Harvard-Yet-Today ignores me. He doesn't move his outstretched legs, either, forcing me to step over them if I want to enter the room, because what would the last days of high school be if we didn't find something to compete about? In this case, square footage.

"Excuse me." I wave at his feet, but he won't budge. When he finally glances my way there's a sparkle in his eye. Like he thinks it's funny.

"Well, well, well, if it isn't Tessa Sinclair." Reed leans farther back, his self-satisfied dimple mocking me.

Oh, so now he can see me?

"Whatever." I don't have time for his BS today. I sling my loaded backpack down to heave over him first, making sure it knocks into his knees.

Except the weight of it sort of . . . takes me with it.

Suddenly I'm sprawled across the lap of my nemesis, the contents of my bag spilled everywhere: pens, folders, tampons.

Could this day get any worse?

CHAPTER 3

Reed

Tessa pretending she didn't just collapse on top of me is the funniest thing I've seen all morning. I'm not sure what's more quintessentially Tessa, that she is always in such a frantic hurry to achieve something she couldn't give me a second to put my feet down or that she's now primly settled in her chair as if she hadn't brushed herself off, then vaulted the remaining distance like an Olympic gymnast.

"Are you okay?" I slyly rub my aching knee where her backpack nailed me. "Maybe next time you could make more of an entrance."

"Mr. McKeen said to come back here and work on speeches." She stuffs her belongings into her bag with a look that says we will never speak of this again.

"Did you need some coaching?" I bat my eyes innocently.

"I think you have that backward. I'm here to give you pointers."

"Since you're my warm-up act, I figure we should make sure you set me up well."

Her lips press together tightly while she sifts through a folder, probably for her speech. "Can't ever let me forget you're valedictorian, can you?"

"Oh, am I?" I tap my chin, feigning confusion, then snap my fingers. "That's right. It's all coming back to me. How you fought tooth and nail and still walk in my shadow."

"You're such a dick."

"But I'm growing on you."

Wait, did that sound like a weird innuendo? Blood rushes to my cheeks. She always throws me off my game. "Come on. Let me see it." I reach out a hand.

She glances over and catches McKeen watching us. "Fine, I'll show you mine if you show me yours."

I lift an eyebrow but don't say more as we exchange papers, curious how her speech stacks up against mine. She's my first test case.

We're both quiet for a while, flipping pages. Somehow, Tessa's gone with the bright idea of interviewing local business owners, like she's writing a town book report. I can't help my loud snort-laugh at the exterminator's advice to "Do away with the metaphorical pests in your life." Why exactly are we listening to this guy?

She clears her throat, shooting dagger-eyes at me. "Okay. I have some notes."

"Yeah, me too. And they are: Are you kidding me right now? Is this what you're really going to say?" This must be a prank. I'm on camera now, right?

"What's wrong with my speech?" She crosses her arms and sits up higher in her chair.

"Um . . . life lessons from famous local business leaders?" I shake my head, laughing again. I think my eyes are actually watering.

"What's wrong with that? I interviewed local leaders for the secrets to their success."

"Do you honestly think anyone is going to want to hear what the head of Hyperion Realty thinks? Or"—I flip to the next page—"Mikey Jones's Pest Removal? Oh my God, I'm dying right now. Tell me this is a joke."

She blows out a hard breath. "Mikey Jones had some really nice things to say about believing in yourself and taking risks! It's just like you to dismiss someone putting in a hard day's work, something you've probably never had to do once in your cushy life."

"Stop. I can't." I grab my gut, almost falling out of my chair. "You're killing me."

"You're one to talk. Your speech is a dumpster fire. Of course you worked your Harvard acceptance into the first line, but after that, it's chock-full of vague graduation platitudes. Nothing's personal, it's just a bunch of drivel like 'We'll always remember these times we shared together' and 'They'll tell you it can't be done. Don't listen.' It's full of ideas that make sense by themselves but strung together are total nonsense. No offense."

Okay. That stings. Did she not read to the end where I explain how I created the speech? And why? It took half a year of late-night coding. "No offense taken. I didn't write it. Or, rather, I wrote an AI algorithm based off the work of some MIT students that pulls from all the graduation speeches on the web and generates a new one out of the most common phrases." I thought she of all people would be impressed.

"Wait. *What?*"

It's a hell of a lot more work than talking to the local plumber for life advice. "You need to give the people what they want. And on graduation day, all they want is some basic 'keep it real, stay strong, we are the future' BS."

"So . . . you cheated." She tosses my speech back at me. "Using AI like this is banned at our school."

"No, I didn't cheat. The AI generator re-forms sentences, rearranges content. And I built it myself." It was hard, and I did it around my regular school load because I plan to do something with my life. And I'm not talking about making money, my stepdad's sole motivation. I'm going to change the world. Help people. Keep the planet from burning up. Technology will be on the forefront of all that.

"*I built it myself.*" She mimics my voice back at me. "Like that gets you off the hook for cheating. Is that how you write all your essays, too? You're unbelievable." She snatches her paper out of my hands and begins packing her bag.

"Well, if you'd read to the end of my speech, which you clearly did not, you'd see that I mention it was created by an algorithm, we should embrace the AI revolution, and that we all have an important role to play in a changing world."

Tessa grabs her backpack and stands. I do, too: The entire classroom is cleared out. Did McKeen forget we were back here? The clock on the wall says we're already ten minutes into lunch.

"I was so distracted by your absurd bot-generated speech I lost track of time. Principal Evans is going to kill me. I'm supposed to emcee." She marches toward the door. "Hurry up. You don't want to miss your Cheater of the Year award."

"Is that why you're all dressed up today? The honor roll thing?" I hoist my guitar bag onto my shoulders and follow her out. "Who cares if some ancient crone hands over a check and some thanks-for-playing participation awards?"

The hall is oddly silent, a ghost town.

She races toward the teachers' lounge. "Not all of us are legacy students at Harvard, bankrolled by dads who are loaded."

"Stepdad. And no, I'm not a legacy. I worked very hard to be where I am." I keep pace with her.

"And I didn't?"

"I never said that."

She rounds on me under the flickering fluorescents. "You know what your problem is, Reed?"

This should be good. "Please." I wave my hand. "Enlighten me."

"Everything gets handed to you. Your life is perfect—"

"Oh, is that so?" That hits like a gut punch. It's just like Tessa to assume she's the only person in the world with problems. For all her brains, she can be so self-centered sometimes.

"Yeah. And you think it always will be, but I have news for you, mister. Today is as good as it gets for you. Ever. You're the kind of guy who peaks early. It's a tough world out there, and you won't be ready to face it."

I laugh mirthlessly. "And I suppose you will? Are you serious right now? Everyone fawns over you at this school, and you eat it up. You love being a big fish in a small pond, but try finding your way when that's not the case. I think that's really why you chose the state school down the road, because you and I both know you could have gone for the Ivies. But you know what you didn't have? The balls."

"Anatomy tip: I wouldn't have those."

I ignore her smug expression. "You're scared out of your mind. You can't stand the idea of being the small fish. You can't stand not being *special*."

"God, you're insufferable. Just leave me alone."

"Oho. You can dish it out, but you can't take it."

She storms down the hall, casting an annoyed look over her shoulder.

"Excuse me for trying to give you some advice," I call after her.

"I don't need advice from you. I'll use AI for that instead," she tosses back.

"Or maybe ask your boy, Mikey Jones. I'm sure you'll be working alongside him setting out rat poison any day now. It's a promising future, Sinclair." It takes only a few long strides to catch up with her again. "Or, who knows, maybe you'll follow in your dad's footsteps and end up unemployed. I'm surprised he didn't make it into your speech. I'm sure he has great advice to share about the job market."

As soon as it's out of my mouth, I regret it. I got too caught up trading zingers. But why did I go there? Even I know that was a low blow.

"Shut up. Leave my dad out of it." Tessa quickly wipes her eyes, like she doesn't want me to see her cry. But it's too late. "You have no idea what you're talking about." Guilt twists deep in my stomach.

I didn't mean to be so casually cruel. Or maybe I did, but regret washes over me. "I shouldn't have—" I reach for her to apologize, but she shoves my hand away.

"Don't." She turns for the teachers' lounge, but before she can grasp the handle, Principal Evans yanks the door open.

"What the hell is going on out here?" he scolds us under his breath.

I want to answer, but I'm too distracted by the guest of honor herself, Marjory Fieldman, who's appeared out of nowhere dragging her massive scholarship check, probably lost after the location changed for today's luncheon. She reaches out a frail hand to tug on Tessa's arm.

Tessa's body pulses with fury as she yells, temper flaring, "I *said* don't touch me, and shut your stupid face!" As she swings around, fist held high, I catch her eyes widening when it's clear it's not me behind her. But there's no way to halt her momentum, only enough time for Marjory to squeak out "Where can I find the—" before Tessa's fist connects with her jaw.

BAM.

Spit flies from Ms. Fieldman's mouth as she stumbles back against the lockers. Evans rushes to steady her before she crumples to the floor from Tessa's knockout blow. My body's frozen in shock. Curious students and horrified faculty stare aghast from the lounge.

Holy shit.

Tessa just clocked that old lady like some mixed martial arts fighter. She went full Justin Gaethje on her, like she was in the UFC championships. I wish I'd had my phone out to film it.

Then realization dawns—she meant that punch for me.

Damn.

"Oh God, Oh God, Oh God. I can't pass out in Principal Evans's office." Tessa leans her head between her legs. Beads of sweat run down her forehead, even with the air conditioner on. "Why did I wear this constricting suit jacket? I've already achieved peak humiliation. I can't go any lower. Can I?"

"Don't be so dramatic. You'll be fine," I say from my perch on the small mahogany bookcase near the window. I pull the vertical blinds aside so I can spy the parking lot. Flashing red lights splash the back wall, illuminating smiling family portraits and awards for educational excellence. "Looks like the ambulance is here."

"I think I'm going to be sick." Her breath comes rapid and shallow as she rocks back and forth. I thought she was being a drama queen before, but she really does look like she might hurl.

"Yikes." I wince, trying to distract her with the action outside. Evans and the rest of the office staff have escorted Ms. Fieldman out front in a wheelchair. "Oh, that is not good."

It works. Out of the corner of my eye I catch Tessa lift her head by a fraction, tracking me. She's so predictable. Nothing irritates her more than being kept in the dark. She needs all the answers immediately.

"Are you being purposely vague to annoy me?" She waves her blouse a bit, trying to get a breeze flowing against her overheated skin.

My mouth goes dry.

Quit staring, dumbass. Get a grip.

"I wouldn't dream of annoying you." I place a hand over my chest, affronted. "I'm too afraid of your right hook."

"Very funny. Just tell me what's going on out there."

I lift an eyebrow, bristling at the command, and she begrudgingly amends through gritted teeth, "Please."

I pull the blinds aside again, preparing to give my report. "Well, Evans looks like he's apologizing profusely . . . and . . . wow, she's hit him with her purse."

"What?"

"Your violence must be rubbing off. To think you've corrupted poor Ms. Fieldman." I shake my head in mock disapproval, then turn back to the window.

"And now?" she prompts.

"Now they're strapping her down and wheeling her into the ambulance. Oh . . . and look." I can't help chuckling. "A disgruntled EMT is shoving your giant scholarship check beside the gurney. I think there might be a little blood on it. You slammed her pretty hard."

"I'm doomed," she groans, head back in her hands. "No college. No future. My life is over."

I can't believe I'm feeling pity for Tessa. "It was a misunderstanding." I hop off my bookshelf perch and sit in the chair beside her. When I stretch my legs out, she eyes them darkly. Thinking of our moment back in McKeen's classroom earlier, I shuffle them farther forward, reclining as far as I can, then wink at her.

She does not look amused—though that's always been part of the fun with Tessa. And the challenge. Can I get her to crack a smile, let her guard down for a second, and take things less seriously? It's something I've been trying and failing at since moving here in the sixth grade.

I still remember our first conversation at recess when she insisted that gallium was the best element because who doesn't love liquid metal and then challenged me to a cartwheel competition—which she promptly won, clocking in at fifty-seven. She's always been smart and fearless and beautiful—if a bit high-strung.

But she has never, not once, been interested in me. She likes bland-as-toast guys like Brandon, I guess. Though why, I'll never know.

"This is not the reputation I want to end senior year with." She waves at the hallway outside.

I tilt my face toward her. "What? That you were the asshole who punched Grandma?"

Her glare is piercing.

"Look, I saw out the window. She's fine." That doesn't seem to appease her. "Tessa, I promise you, this is not the impression you're leaving high school with. It's a footnote. An epically funny footnote, but that's all it is."

She bites her lip, so I know she's at least considering what

I'm saying, just like she does in debate when someone scores a point on her and she needs to craft a rebuttal.

This is not the catastrophe she thinks it is. I know what it's like to have your life implode. When the tectonic plates shift underneath you and you realize something foundational—which you thought you could always count on—has vanished in a blink.

And the world seems like it's over . . . but it's not. Day by day, you discover you're still here. You crawl back.

"I know it feels super important right now," I say slowly. "But it's really not, in the scheme of things. It's all going to work out."

"Why? Because things always work out for you, Reed? Not all of us are so lucky."

And there it is again: the guy she thinks I am. Some golden boy whose life is perfect. I'm not sure how she got that impression. Besides valedictorian, which I pushed myself hard for—mostly thanks to her—my life is a complete shitshow. But Tessa doesn't look. Or ask. No, to her I'm just some guy she wants to slug in the face.

And that was no lightweight punch. That came with the full force of hatred behind it.

All that anger, meant for me. How did we get here?

The door flies open and Kira and Santiago step inside.

"Why is no one in the main office?" Kira tucks a strand of purple hair behind her ear. "Is this because you got into a fist-fight in the hall?"

Tessa bolts upright in her chair. "Is that what people are saying?"

Kira shrugs. "Something about you two, fists flying, and some old lady getting tackled."

"Oh my God," Tessa groans again. So much for helping to snap her out of it.

"Dude, there's no one here. I should totally smoke this jay in the principal's office right now." Santiago makes himself at home behind Evans's desk, kicking his feet up as he pulls a joint out of his pocket. "I'd be a school legend."

"Yeah, you would," I say with a smile, and we air-five each other across the room.

"Are you crazy?" Tessa hisses. "They'll be here any second." The ambulance is already driving away, sirens blaring.

"You're right. I should save it for the graduation party." He stands, tucking the joint in his pocket. "You coming tonight?"

We all turn toward Tessa. It seems to take her a moment to realize who Santiago's talking to. "Oh, um . . ."

"She doesn't party," Kira answers for her, lounging against the doorframe, absently scrolling her phone.

"You can't miss the most kick-ass event in all of high school. We're seniors. We're gonna blow it up! Everyone's breaking into that old van der Born mansion on Route Twenty-Eight outside town." Santiago swings his hips back and forth, dancing over to Kira. "It's going to be lii-ii-ii-ii-it!"

Kira laughs as he twirls and dips her. So, I guess it's official. She's fully moved on from me. Is she into Santiago now?

The thought doesn't sting as much as I'd expect. There was a time when I'd hoped for more with Kira, but after one extremely awkward date, we realized we made better friends. Still, even though it didn't last long, I wouldn't mind her feeling a little jealous.

"Yeah . . ." As my eyes snag on Tessa's, my heart picks up speed. I can feel Kira staring at me, too. At *us.* I hadn't considered Tessa might actually attend, but what if she did? Now that the idea's out there, I realize this is what I want. One night before my new life starts and I move away to Boston for school. One final shot to prove to Tessa Sinclair that I'm not the guy she thinks I am. And hey, if it came with the added benefit of Kira regretting shutting us down, then I wouldn't complain about that, either. "You should go. I hear it's going to be lii-ii-ii-ii-it."

"She won't attend if it's not a school-sanctioned event." Kira rolls her eyes.

Tessa crosses her arms, clearly annoyed by Kira's assumption, but I can tell she's still about to make her excuses. Like always. I cut in before she has the chance. "We're pretty fun. Why don't you come find out? Or do you and that wet blanket you call a boyfriend have better plans? Is it bingo night with the other retirees? Big game of canasta you can't miss? Come on, Sinclair. I dare you."

"You *dare* me? What is this, sixth grade?"

"I dare you to live a little before your high school years are over."

"Live a little?" she scoffs. "You think you have me all figured out, don't you, Reed? But for your information, I was *always* going. Who do you think had the idea in the first place to party at the van der Born estate and arranged for us to use that mansion?"

The dancing comes to a halt. My jaw hits the floor.

What?

First Tessa hauls off and punches an old lady, and now she's throwing the party of the year? An uneasy knot settles in my stomach. Maybe I don't know her as well as I thought.

"So, looks like I'll see you there." Tessa shrugs, easy and nonchalant, though I clock the finger tapping rapidly against her thigh.

"Looks like it," I say just as breezily back.

Kira's eyes narrow, darting between us.

My smile is slow and victorious, because it occurs to me that I just got exactly what I want.

CHAPTER 4

Tessa

"Smells delicious." Dad pops into the kitchen to lean over the bubbling lasagna I've pulled from the oven. He gives me a peck on the cheek before heading down the hall to remove his tool belt. Maybe cooking his favorite meal was over the top, but at least it gave me something to do besides doomscroll in my room over the punching memes on my classmates' social media. Somehow, someone recorded the whole thing.

When Principal Evans returned to his office, he blasted Reed and me for our behavior and insisted I was lucky Ms. Fieldman only took her money and ran, instead of pressing charges.

And she would have had every right. I feel terrible about what I did. If Reed hadn't gloated over my dad losing his job, I wouldn't be in this situation. It still makes my blood boil. He should be the one with the black eye.

I can't wait until this party is over and I never see his entitled face again.

"It's not as good as yours, but I'm getting better every time I make it. I didn't even need to use the recipe tonight." I carry the lasagna to the kitchen table, breathing in a steam cloud of garlic and oregano, before hanging up my oven mitts. I thought cooking would help, but I'm still just as unsure how to proceed. How do I tell him? How, after his long struggle with unemployment, do I drop the bomb that we now need to scrape together my entire college tuition and expenses? Unless I can patch things up with Ms. Fieldman. Maybe if I get down on my knees and beg?

"That's the thing about those old family recipes," he calls from down the hall. "After a while, you sense them. It's like you carry the knowledge in your bones."

I pull out a bottle of Kraft Zesty Italian from the fridge to dress the salad. "How was the new gig?" I'll start slow and work my way to the bad news, that's probably best.

He grabs a beer, then plops down at the table with a heavy sigh. "You know me, I'd rather be building turbines than hired to deconstruct old ones, but it pays, can't complain."

"Not even about the commute?"

"Fine. I'll complain about the commute. Two hours both ways is killer."

"Or that it's temporary? You're allowed to say things are shitty, Dad." I place the salad bowl on the kitchen table. *Just confess already, Tessa.*

"Nah, not going to complain like that. I'm thankful for the work. When's Jillian getting here? I'm starving."

"She texted she's on her way. They kept her at the hospital to finish up some paperwork." As I'm saying this, my sister's car pulls up out front. Jillian's older than me at twenty-seven, but she lives nearby, and since my parents' divorce we've made Friday night dinners a habit. We both know Dad gets lonely, though he'd never admit it.

Jillian knocks but then lets herself in. We have the same pale complexion and jet-black hair, but where I look like Billie Eilish before her glow-up, she manages to pull off Snow White, even in her nurse's scrubs. If they were allowed in the NICU, she'd probably be surrounded by singing chipmunks and bluebirds. "I could smell that lasagna out on the lawn. Serve it up!"

I'm already plating our meals as she washes her hands and finds a seat. "What's that?" I ask.

"Oh." She flips over the box she's carrying to reveal a thousand-piece puzzle of a wizard battling several dragons. "Someone left this up for grabs in the staff room. I thought we could try it tonight."

Everyone digs into their dinner. It tastes amazing—gooey, cheesy comfort-food deliciousness. "I can't," I say through mouthfuls. "I'm going to a school party." That I lied and told Reed I was throwing. Oops. And for what? To save face? Who cares what he thinks?

"Really?" Jillian's eyebrow quirks in shock. "Who are you and what have you done with my sister?"

"I think it's great." Dad reaches for a second helping. "You deserve to live a little."

Oh God, he sounds like Reed. "Why does everyone keep

saying that to me?" I'm fun. Do I not seem fun? Even to my own family?

"You work too hard, kid—looking after me, focusing on your studies, you should go have a good time. YOMO and all that. Or is it FOLO?"

Jillian and I both burst out laughing.

"It's YOLO, Dad. YOLO. *You only live once*," Jillian corrects.

"And FOMO stands for *fear of missing out*," I add. "I think you told me, 'You only miss out,' which is kind of depressing."

"Well, don't miss out. Go have a good time. It's a student government thing, right?" Dad asks.

"Mm-hmm . . . yes . . . student government." I wonder how he'd feel about my breaking into an abandoned mansion for a graduation rager. Jillian catches my eye with a sideways glance, not buying my cover story, but not ratting me out, either. She's good like that.

The doorbell rings and I leap up to let Brandon and Tilly inside. Mostly, I'm happy for the excuse to avoid discussing the luncheon disaster. I'll tell Dad tomorrow. Maybe there's a way we can write a letter together pleading my case to Ms. Fieldman or bring her flowers. This is still salvageable. I will not allow my college dreams to slip through my fingers.

Dad beams as we enter the kitchen. "Hey, the whole crew's here." When Brandon peeks at the puzzle he adds, "You can start that if you like, we were going to tackle it after dinner."

"Sweet." Brandon joins him at the table. "I'm the puzzle master. The trick is to find the corners first." He pours the pieces out and starts sifting through them.

As Tilly's swigging from her water bottle her phone pings wildly. She pulls it out of her bag and almost chokes when she sees who's texting.

"Uh-oh. Another cousin crisis?" I ask.

She's frozen in place, hand shaking as she scrolls.

Something's wrong.

"Wait. It's not your mom's health again, is it?"

My dad and Jillian look up, eyes full of concern. But it's almost like Tilly doesn't hear me.

"Tills?" I try again.

"What? Oh, no. Cousin drama, like you said." She waves me off. I'm surprised I haven't heard who this particular crisis is about. Unless it really is her mom. I'm tempted to ask, but she'll tell me when she's ready. Like always.

"If you're upset, you don't have to go to the student government thing tonight. You can hang out here. Watch a movie or something," my dad offers.

"What student gov—" Brandon begins.

"Oh wow, would you look at the time." Tilly cuts him off, glancing back at her phone.

"Thanks, Dad, but we should really get going." I feel guilty lying to him, but I guess once you punch a sweet old lady, it's a slippery slope off the moral high ground. And the fact is, I can use the distraction.

"Are you sure you don't want to stay in and do the puzzle instead? We could listen to some Coltrane." Brandon's already opening his Spotify playlist, Jazz Greats.

I cringe inwardly, imagining the field day Reed would have

with this information—which only hardens my resolve. I will prove to him and everyone that just because I work hard doesn't mean I'm not all kinds of fun deep down.

"We don't want to be late." Tilly playfully shakes Brandon's shoulders.

As he scoops the unused puzzle pieces into the box, Tilly shoots me a meaningful look. *Did you talk to him yet?* I shake my head.

"Well, have fun, kids. It's the last week of school, after all." Dad leans back in his chair.

"That's right. Time to finish senior year with a bang." With a wave at my family, Tilly breezes out the front door, hoping the magnetic pull of her convictions drags us along.

After a quick goodbye kiss to Dad and Jillian, I grab Brandon's hand and follow her out, mind whirling. I could end things, or let our relationship fizzle out naturally before college starts in the fall. It doesn't need to be complicated.

We still have to graduate and there's an entire summer before us.

I have loads of time to figure it all out.

Besides, right now I need to focus on finding the van der Born mansion.

It takes over an hour scouring backcountry roads, so by the time we arrive, the party is in full swing. A towering stone wall surrounds the property, save an ornate wrought iron entrance gate that's flung open. We step over bolt cutters and a thick metal chain on our way in. Someone came prepared.

A deep pounding bass beckons from the dark turreted mansion up ahead, rattling the windows and drowning out the frogs from a nearby pond. People are everywhere. A group of guys have packed into a crumbling gazebo to create a pyramid out of beer cans, while across the weed-infested lawn someone hangs upside down to chug from a keg as the crowd chants. People lean out windows, spill down the front porch, or chase each other through the expansive grounds.

"Was that Kennedy Conway, first chair violinist, skipping in her bra through the bushes holding a candelabra?" Tilly asks, stunned.

"You saw that, too? For a second, I thought I'd dreamt it." I shake my head in disbelief.

"I think we just solved Clue. This party is wild. Is this what we've been missing for all of high school?"

I turn to find Brandon lingering at the gate, hunched over a commemorative plaque about the old van der Born mansion. On every field trip we've gone on, he'd stop to read each historical sign and the description for every work of art. It drives me crazy.

"Brandon, the party." I wave my hand in frustration at the three-story house up ahead.

"That was really interesting," he says, walking up. "Our town founders lived here for over a century until they fell on hard times and abandoned the place in the 1940s. The historical society began doing repairs but then ran out of cash and the project stalled. Now they're raising funds to convert it into a museum. Whoa." He stops in his tracks, as if he's noticed for the first time how many people are here. Or maybe he's caught sight of Kennedy in her bra.

I'm about to ask whether we should make our way inside when I'm lifted off the ground in a bear hug from behind. "Tessa, I thought I had you figured out, but man, you're my hero." Finn O'Connor, captain of the soccer team, puts me down as his girlfriend, Megan Blackwell, our yearbook photographer, staggers over.

"I know, right? I thought you were a goody-goody student guv'ment type, but then you were throwing punches today and now you're throwing the best party ever!" Megan's over-loud speech is slurred. She leans her forehead against mine, hot alcohol breath blowing in my face. "You're full of surpr'ses and I love that about you. Now, shhhhh, this is very important. I've been meaning to tell you . . ." Then she turns and throws up in some bushes. Finn runs over to help her.

I must be standing in shock because Tilly grabs my arm and ushers me away. "I think we can let her do her thing." We wander along the mossy stone pathway meandering toward the front entrance, Brandon tagging along behind us. "At least she didn't puke on you. That's the lace wedding dress you repurposed, right?"

"Thank God." I spin in a circle, skirt flaring, showing off my fingerless gloves and black Victorian grandma boots, too. "Best thing I've made." I found the dress in a discount bin while vintage shopping. Over the last few weeks, I've dyed the material black, taken in the long ankle-dusting hemline to hit mid-thigh, and even sewn in some pockets, because dresses with pockets are the best. "The earrings are from Aunt Betty's."

"Really? Way to support Black-owned businesses." Tilly gives my shoulder a playful nudge. "Especially my mom's."

I don't know if I should reveal that they were so highly discounted her mom practically gave them away. Instead, I sling an arm over her shoulder as we march up the path. "We're unstoppable. Chef's kiss."

"They should bottle us. How can you top this perfection?"

"Oh stop," I tease.

"No, you stop." She laughs.

"Come on, Brandon." I reach back and drape an arm over his shoulder, too. "Let's take this party by storm. Beer and Bros and all that."

When we reach the large crowd gathered outside the mansion's front door, people begin to cheer, call my name, raise their bottles in my honor as we pass.

"What is happening? Does everyone think I threw this party?" I whisper to Tilly. My small white lie to Reed has gotten completely out of hand. Between Ms. Fieldman this morning and breaking and entering here, Principal Evans will probably yank my letters of recommendation next. "I've somehow managed to completely ruin my reputation in less than twenty-four hours."

"Ruin?" Tilly laughs. "I think you mean you've cemented it in BVDB High School history!"

We push through the students gathered on the porch, making our way inside the grand foyer with its high vaulted ceiling and intricate compass rose inlayed in wood across the floor. The building is clearly in disrepair, with cracks in the siding and wall sconces shifted off their mounts, but the sweeping staircase is still impressive. With a little spit and polish and a hefty financial contribution from the historical society, the place could definitely be restored to its former glory.

The party is just as wild inside as it was outdoors. Rick Bonicelli is sliding down the banister from the second floor. I hope he doesn't fall to his death; the track team needs him.

Someone from my right screams, "We're doing shots in the ballroom," and a rush of people elbow past me. Tilly gets swept down a long hallway with the rest of the thirsty masses.

Brandon shrugs as we watch her disappear under a large ornate archway. "I guess she wanted shots in the ballroom."

"She doesn't even drink."

"Great party, Tessa," Eloise Mitchell, drama club star, shouts from the second-floor landing, and the entrance hall erupts in cheers.

"When's the DJ getting here?" A deep, familiar voice cuts through the noise. I crane my neck to get a better view of the people leaning against the second-floor banister.

Reed's there, smirking.

"Ooh, there's a DJ coming?" Olive Dingle bounces on her toes beside me. She's not usually this hyper in Model UN.

"You said there'd be a DJ," he calls down. What? No, I didn't.

The crowd whoops again, all eyes on me.

What's Reed doing? Is he testing me? Does he suspect I lied about organizing the party? Forcing me to come clean to everyone here or double down?

"Um . . . yeah." I pull out my phone, pretending to scroll

recent texts to buy myself some time. Out of the corner of my eye, Reed's smirk grows. Jerk. "Oh, here it is . . . the DJ said he'd be here in half an hour."

"Sweet!" Rick Bonicelli hops off the ground-floor banister to high-five me.

Just as everyone's turning back to their friends, Reed shouts, "And the keg?"

I glare at him. *Shut up.* His smile only grows wider. He's enjoying this, the little shit.

I try my phone trick again, pretending to scroll through more texts. I hope whoever actually broke us in here isn't anywhere in the vicinity to blow my cover. "Yep. Another keg's coming." My heart rate's flying. The panic mounts. "Woo-hoo," I add with as much gusto as I can muster.

People—some total strangers—smack me on the back with "Yaaaasss!" and "This is epic!"

But I'm not paying attention to them. I'm laser-focused as I march over to intercept Reed walking down the stairs. Of course, I have to wait for everyone to fist-bump him or pat his shoulder on the way down. Why do people like him so much? "What are you doing?" I whisper-growl when he arrives.

"Upping your notoriety."

"Well, could you not?"

"Why? It's a sick party, Tessa. Though, tell me, where exactly in the student president handbook are those tips for purchasing kegs?"

My eyes narrow to slits of fire. "It's in Appendix D, under Dick Moves. Why dare me to come just to give me a hard time?"

"Oh, but I live to give you a hard time. Someone has to. Or life would be so boring. Isn't that right, Brandon?"

We both turn to Brandon, but he's preoccupied by something across the room.

While he's distracted, Reed asks, "Actually, Tessa, could we talk?" He indicates a quieter corner of the room.

"Sorry. What?" Brandon's focus snaps back to us.

"Ignore him," I say. I have no patience for Reed's nonsense tonight. I grab Brandon's hand and meander us through the cavernous rooms of the ground floor, each filled with packed partiers. Eventually we make our way to a formal Victorian sitting room, by the looks of the high-backed couches and spindle tables. Large cracks zigzag the walls, with chipped plaster piling by the baseboards. I can see what Brandon meant about the restoration having only partly taken place.

I glimpse a flash of cherry-red romper cutting a path through the crowd. "Hide me," Tilly begs under her breath as she arrives.

"Why?" I glance over her shoulder.

She ducks behind me so she can't be spied through the doorway. "Remember Creepy Carl, that redheaded botany major I dated for like a hot second last January?"

I try to focus on what she's saying, to push Reed's dickishness out of my mind. "Uh—"

"The one whose plant pathology professor mentioned that lily of the valley symbolized everlasting love?" she presses. "Which made him think of us and how we were destined for each other, blah, blah, blah. That guy? Well, now he's here." She's almost hyperventilating by the time she gets to the end, peeking over my shoulder to watch the door: So far there's no sign of him.

But I nod because it's all coming back to me. "Right. The college guy obsessed with Venus flytraps." Weird dude.

"Didn't we all go to the movies together once?" Brandon peers behind us down the hall. "Do you think he's here because of you?"

"Either that or he's a perv who likes high school girls," Tilly replies. "It wouldn't surprise me."

"Gross." Now that I really look, there are several people here who don't go to our high school. Word must've gotten out.

"I feel kind of queasy." She does look off. Tilly's eyes flash, tracking something behind me. "Oh, thank God. He's leaving."

I turn to catch a brief glimpse of tousled red hair passing the doorway before Carl vanishes down the hall.

Tilly's body visibly relaxes as she steps out from behind me. "I think I'll join the French club out back—they're dancing with a huge crowd in that empty fountain. I can blend in better that way, just in case."

Before I can follow her outdoors, Brandon reaches for my hand. "Wait, Tess, I was hoping we could chat for a second." He leads me to one of the upholstered couches and sits me down in a cloud of dust. His fingers fidget on his lap and I furrow my brow. "All this relationship talk has me thinking about our future."

Oh no. For one wild moment I'm certain he's about to propose. We're eighteen and haven't even graduated high school, and I'm sure he's about to get down on one knee with a ring. But instead, he says, "I think we should break up."

My mind goes blank. I can't make the reality I was expecting match the words coming out of his mouth. "I'm sorry . . . *what*?"

"I don't want to hurt you, but I've been developing feelings for a girl in the jazz ensemble. I saw her when we entered the party. And now I'm thinking it's not fair to you if I'm not fully into this." He waves his hand back and forth between us.

My brain can't compute. *Brandon's* not into this? Brandon, who brings me morning boba and hangs on my every word? Brandon, who snuggles with me in warm socks and gets excited about calculus?

"But . . . but I was going to break up with you," I stammer.

"Oh good." He sighs. "So, that's all settled, then. This was easier than I thought."

Everything at this party is moving too fast. I can't keep up. I had a plan for how my last days of high school would go. I had a plan for that scholarship. I had a plan for how Brandon and I would coast through the summer, casually breaking up before we were forced apart to our separate colleges. Sure, he'd be sad, but I'd let him down gently. How in one day have my plans blown so off course?

"No, totally. This is . . . super easy . . . exactly what we both want." I can't get my bearings through the loud rushing in my ears. This *is* what I want, isn't it? Is it just that I thought I'd be the first to say it? "Yeah . . . absolutely . . . such a relief."

I'm getting left behind all over again. First my mom, and now Brandon. I'm second place, always. And I know it's not fair since I wanted to break up, too, but that doesn't stop the old hurt from cracking open—a deep, raw wound for Brandon to pour salt into.

"Well, I'm going to go find her, then. Wish me luck." He crosses his fingers and shakes them at me before dashing back to the foyer, like he expects me to be excited for him.

Like he isn't leaving me stuck on a dusty couch.

At a party I'm supposed to be hosting.

Alone.

CHAPTER 5

Reed

"Bro, where the hell did Kira go?" I shout at Santiago over the music blasting through the halls as we wind our way through the packed ground floor. If it was crowded when we got here, it's verging on out of control now. Even though I gave her a hard time earlier, I'm still amazed Tessa pulled it off. Or did she? I can see her having the initial idea, but organizing a party like *this*, ordering a keg, that seems beyond her. If she did do it, though . . . what a legend.

"I don't know. I lost track of Kira a while ago. She said there was someone she had to talk to."

"Who?" A pang of jealousy rears its head, but only for a moment. Whatever Kira and I once had is gone now.

"I don't know, man. You know Kira, she does what she wants." Santiago shrugs.

This is true. Santiago and Kira have been two of my closest friends since middle school. I met Santiago at the skate park in sixth grade while we were practicing ollies, a passion that didn't last long for me. I've always been better tinkering with my hands than pulling stunts. Now I remote control BattleBots to perform tricks—much more my speed. Kira came along a year later. She was the only person who responded to the flyers we put up in the cafeteria to start our band, The Undeniables. We've been playing music together ever since.

Which reminds me. "I hope my guitar's okay. I should have dropped it off at home before coming here."

"It's going to be fine." Santiago's hand lands reassuringly on my shoulder, like he has a clue. It was stupid of me to bring it, and we both know it. If anything were to happen to my dad's guitar, I'd never forgive myself. He didn't just play it. He made it. And now it's all I have of him.

As we push through the crowd toward the front entrance, Tessa is descending the stairs from the second floor. She's alone. If I want to try again for a reset between us, this might be my moment. She brushed me off before, but maybe that was because Brandon was around.

I'm about to tell Santiago I'll be right back when Tessa comes to a stop, focused on two people tussling at the base of the stairs. Tilly Sanderson's in a heated argument with some short redheaded guy in slouchy jeans and an IT'S ON LIKE DONKEY KONG T-shirt.

"No. How many times do I have to say it?" Tilly's eyes are red. Has she been crying?

"You're sick and don't know what you're saying. I'm getting

you out of here." The guy tugs on Tilly's arm as Tessa rushes down the remaining stairs to step between them.

I can't quite catch what Tessa says next—it's hard with the group of screaming freshmen in front of me. I nudge Santiago, nodding toward the entrance. "You seeing this?"

"Who's this asshat?"

I keep watching them.

"This doesn't concern you, Tessa." The creep shoves Tessa aside, knocking her into the wall, and begins pulling Tilly toward the door.

"Carl, what part of 'It's over' don't you understand?" Tilly yells, and heads turn.

I start to push my way through the sea of humanity before my mind can catch up.

"I am trying . . . to . . . help you." The guy, Carl, emphasizes each word through gritted teeth, his fingers digging into Tilly's arm. She tries to pull away, but his grip is strong.

"Get off her!" Tessa tries to pry him loose.

Something feral snaps inside me as I wrestle my way to the middle of the foyer and step between Tessa and Carl. "You heard her, asshole. Back off."

Carl spins around as Santiago arrives beside me, and though he's playing it cool, electricity radiates off him like a live wire you'd avoid in a storm.

"I don't think you're wanted here," Santiago states matter-of-factly.

"Go." Tessa scowls at him.

I pull the front door open and wait. I don't break eye contact with Carl, though he glares right back, his fingers flexing.

There's a moment when I'm sure it'll come to blows. It's not usually how I roll with the robotics club, and if you asked me yesterday, I would have laughed at the idea of throwing a punch. But here, in this moment, I'm 100 percent sure I could—and would. Carl seems fairly certain, too. His eyes dart around the circle at all of us like he's a cornered animal. When his gaze lingers on Tilly, she flips him off.

He takes a step toward her, seething, but Santiago places his body in the way. It's subtle but clear. Carl's eyes flash at the challenge. "Whatever. I was trying to do you a favor, bitch." He heads out the front door instead.

"Yeah, keep walking!" Tilly hollers, before bursting into tears.

Tessa pulls her into a hug. "I'm so sorry that happened."

"You okay?" I ask, the insanity of the situation catching up to me. My pulse is skyrocketing. Did Carl and I almost . . . get in a fight?

"I was about to claw him in the face. What a jerk." Tilly steps out of Tessa's arms to wipe the tears from her eyes. "I sure know how to pick 'em."

Santiago and I exchange a glance. What was Tilly ever doing with that clown?

"Well, good riddance," Tessa says, as Carl exits the front gate. "Why was Creepy Carl even here?"

Creepy Carl. Okay. That tracks.

"Look around, Tess. Who isn't here? This isn't a high school thing anymore." Tilly's right. There were a few party crashers from town earlier, but now that it's gotten later, I don't recognize half these people.

"Should we go?" Tessa asks. "You don't look so good."

"In a minute." Tilly fans herself. "The French club wanted to take photos against the wall of mirrors in the ballroom, but I got . . . interrupted."

"Sure, just text when you're ready," Tessa says as Tilly takes off down the hall.

There's a loud commotion from the other side of the foyer as the varsity swim team runs through yelling something about making a human pyramid in the backyard.

"Dude, we should do a human pyramid!" Santiago seems to have snapped back into party mode.

"That's a hard pass," I reply.

"Your loss. Come on, everybody, pyr-a-mid!" Santiago's voice trails toward the back exit, a small crowd racing behind him.

"Careful, there's a whole bunch of poison ivy out there!" Tessa calls after them, shaking her head. "Don't say I didn't warn you all."

Tessa and I are left standing together awkwardly. *Say something, genius.* I shove my hands in my pockets while her eyes scan the room, looking for a rescue.

"So, whose funeral?" I ask at last, cringing that this was the best I could come up with.

"What?"

"The dress." I gesture toward her ensemble: the black lace, the short skirt, the emo vibes.

"Of course you'd make fun of something I worked so hard on."

"It seems a little macabre for a graduation party, that's all."

"Your SAT words don't impress me. And I'll have you know the little black dress never goes out of style."

"Well, what does impress you, Tessa Sinclair?" I hold my breath. *You. You impress me, Reed.* Is this what I expect her to say? *You got into Harvard. You beat me in the battle for valedictorian. You sexy, sexy beast.*

But instead, she just squints. Her gaze travels over my kite-surfing shirt from my cousin's company in Spain, past my dark jeans to land on my Converse.

And . . . my shoe's untied. Great.

"You're being strange." Her head cocks to the side.

"No, I'm not." I stoop to quickly tie my laces.

"Yes, you are. Must everything be an argument?"

"By that logic, wouldn't I be acting strange if I agreed with you?"

"Fair point." She lifts her chin and walks away.

"Wait, did you agree with *me*? Because now *you're* being strange." I follow her farther into the house.

"Leave me alo—" She comes to a screeching halt, jaw on the floor. We're in some kind of fancy parlor, or at least it used to be, where across from us on a tattered couch is Brandon—Tessa's Brandon—only he's full-on making out with Kira.

What the hell?

"*This* is the girl from the jazz ensemble?" Tessa whispers, so low I almost don't catch it.

"Trouble in boyfriend land?" I drawl, pretending it doesn't sting just a little. What do girls see in him?

"We broke up." A hot flush overtakes Tessa's cheeks and runs down her neck.

"Oh?" I feel strangely unsteady on my feet. Is this because I dared her to come here?

We both stare at Brandon and Kira from across the room, almost hypnotized. They still have no idea. I'm weirdly detached, like I'm watching some nature documentary about the mating habits of pygmy marmosets. Her leg is hitched up over his. I can practically hear the little sucking noises.

"He looks like he's rebounding okay," I observe.

"Yeah, with your girlfriend," she bites back.

"She's not my girlfriend. She can kiss whoever she wants. And apparently, she wants your sloppy seconds."

"Don't call him that. Brandon's a very nice guy."

A *nice* guy? That's what Tessa wants? How about a guy willing to tell her the truth? "Looks like he's passionate, too. Check out those moves, clutching her thigh, running his hand through her hair. Is he *biting* her neck? Damn! You know, I never saw him exert that kind of passion with you. Maybe it was you." I shrug playfully.

I know Tessa likes a little challenge. *Come on, prove me wrong.*

"Shut up." She suddenly finds something fascinating on the floor to inspect.

Is she actually hurt? Tessa knows this is how we roll. I never worry about her feelings because we talk to each other like this all the time. But she does seem broken up about it all. "Maybe we should make out over here to make them jealous," I mutter.

"Yeah right," she scoffs, then tilts her head up. "Wait . . . you're serious?"

Our eyes meet for a beat too long. "No."

My gaze drifts back to Kira. At least someone is having fun tonight.

"Oh my God, of course. You're still pining for her." A bark of laughter flies from Tessa's mouth. "Four years and you never could close that deal, could you, Reed?"

"I am pining," I confess, searching her face for any indication she understands. Tessa's biting her lip again, sending a flash of warmth over my skin. I turn away.

"Ha! I knew it! I'm good at reading people."

"No . . . you're not." My hands slide back in my pockets. Of course Tessa doesn't want anything to do with me. We're too stuck in our ways. Did I really think one party would erase years of sniping at each other?

Well, screw it.

Watching Brandon and Kira all hot and heavy cooked my brain—that's all this is. I plead temporary insanity.

Some older guys from town walk past, eying me darkly. The last one purposely knocks into my shoulder as he passes. "You better watch yourself tonight," he threatens, and his friends snicker.

Wait—I know them. They used to work at the factory. The one my stepdad shuttered. They'd protest in front of our home and send death threats to my mom after we got doxxed. I cross the room quickly.

Tessa chases me down. "What was that about?"

"Some guys my stepdad knows," I say vaguely. We're veering dangerously close to territory I want to steer clear of with her. "How about we drown our troubles instead?" I need something to take the edge off.

"Um . . ." She glances over at Brandon.

"Just . . . hang on." I make a small detour to the back study where I stashed my guitar earlier. Thankfully, it's still tucked in its case in the corner, safe for now. I cruise into the kitchen wondering what Tessa likes to drink. Beer? Cocktails? I should have asked. How do I even mix a drink? I'm in over my head. I grab a couple Solo cups of things people are already whipping up. Hopefully, she likes whatever this is.

Tessa's still frowning at Brandon when I return, like he's the black hole of breakups and she can't pull away. I thrust a drink into her hands.

"Where did you get those?" She peers into the cup skeptically.

"It's a party. There's alcohol everywhere."

"What is it, though?"

"Jesus, Tessa, it's a drink of some kind. I don't know. People were mixing them in the kitchen."

"Fine." She takes four giant gulps, almost gagging. "That is vile."

Shit. Maybe I should have tasted them first. "Here, we can trade. I grabbed two different kinds." I switch our drinks, tip my head back, and down the rest of hers. "You're right. That's awful. I can make us something better." I hope, anyway. I take our cups and wander back to the kitchen.

Luckily this time there are cans of beer on the counter, which I grab. When I return, Tilly's hovering over Brandon and Kira. "It's curfew. I've got to go. It's already taken me forever to find my bag. I keep misplacing it." She waves her hand toward the foyer, referencing the earlier debacle, before pulling her water bottle out to take a sip. "Are you coming, Brandon?"

"Can we give Kira a ride home, too?" Brandon asks as he and Kira stand, straightening their clothes.

When I hand Tessa her beer, the rest of them stare open-mouthed between us—the tension palpable.

You're drinking with Walker? Tilly's eyes seem to ask Tessa as she nods in my direction.

Something hardens in Tessa's expression as she watches Brandon tuck in his shirt. "You can go. I'll stay with Reed."

My eyebrows hit the roof.

"Excuse us." Tilly grabs Tessa's arm; I still catch her harsh whisper as she tugs her away. "I thought you wouldn't be caught dead with Reed?"

"Brandon got to have his fun," Tessa mumbles, before their voices are absorbed into the party noise.

I crane my neck, dying to know what they're saying about me, but it's a lost cause. All I know is they hug goodbye, then Tilly calls over her shoulder, "Tessa, make your sister pick you up later. Reed can't drive, he's been drinking." She waves her keys and nods for Brandon and Kira to follow. Brandon throws Tessa a small apologetic smile as he passes, but her expression is unreadable.

I saunter over and clink my can against hers, acknowledging the strange twist of fate. We study each other for a beat, trying to wrap our heads around this odd night.

"Salud." I raise my drink.

"Salud? Seriously? Could you sound more pretentious?"

"Tessa, you do know my family's from Spain, right?"

"What? They are? I had no idea." She looks down awkwardly, then takes another sip of her beer.

I guess she's been paying less attention to me than I've been paying to her. "*Salud* is like saying cheers."

"I know what it means," she says quickly. "I just thought you were trying to be . . ."

"What?"

"I don't know. Suave or something."

I throw my head back, laughing. "I'm sorry, have you met me?"

She looks unsure, like she's really seeing me for the first time. "Well . . . salud, then."

We both tip our cans back. Maybe this night's salvageable after all.

As I scramble to think of something to say, Yannick Krause, the German exchange student, barges into the room banging a spoon against an empty glass bottle.

"Zer iz a beer pong tournament in ze dining room und vee are undefeated." He grabs Jenny Chu's hand and raises it in the air. I forgot they were dating. "Does anyvone dare to challenge our vinning streak?"

Yes. This is what the night needs. A little fun. I smile and nod, a wicked glint in my eye.

No, she mouths at me, shaking her head.

"Oh . . . yes . . ." I continue to nod, my smile blooming.

I'm ready to dare her again when Tessa startles me by grabbing my hand and lifting it in the air. "We do! Prepare to be destroyed!"

I almost spit out my drink. All these years I thought Tessa was a prissy do-gooder, wound up tighter than those braided buns she likes to wear. But here she is tugging me through the crowd, determined to kick Yannick's butt in a drinking game. And I can't help feeling a little thrill that she's more than she appears.

I follow her into a dining room covered in intricately patterned peeling wallpaper, with a sparkling crystal chandelier draped in cobwebs overhead. A large ornate table, once the centerpiece for entertaining the glitterati of the day, currently houses a handful of Ping-Pong balls and red plastic cups at each end, all half-full of beer. Oh, how the mighty have fallen.

Jenny glares at us as she reviews the rules. "We're playing ten cup. Each player shoots once per round. If you sink it, they drink it. Elbows behind the table for your shot. And . . . you get one rerack per game. Got it?"

"Not even close. Can you go over that again?" Tessa asks, a little crack in her confidence.

"Who knows. Who cares." I shrug. "Do we go first?"

"Vee do. Vee are ze reigning champions." Yannick almost seems insulted we asked.

Flipping his long golden hair away from his face, Yannick eyes his mark with the precision of a military sniper. With a snap of the wrist, his ball lands with a splash in the cup nearest me. Jenny follows with a direct hit to our front cup. They fist-bump, already gloating over their undefeated title.

I remove the balls and hand us each a drink. "Salud again, partner."

We down them. I'm already feeling a little unsteady on my feet. But I need to focus because we're up. I make a big show of picking out the best Ping-Pong ball and shaking it around in my palms like I'm throwing dice in Vegas. I blow into my hands, then hold them up to Tessa's lips. "For luck?"

She rolls her eyes.

"No? Okay. But if I miss, that's on you." I wind up like a pitcher on a mound, but accidentally aim too high when I shoot and the ball ricochets off the chandelier before smacking Yannick square in the face. Tessa snort-laughs as Jenny's eyes narrow.

"Krause, sorry, man. I didn't mean to hit you, I swear. I just have shitty aim."

Yannick shrugs off my apology. "Zen you vill go down."

"No one's taking *me* down." Tessa shakes her Ping-Pong ball around like dice, too, to mock me, even locking eyes with me as she gives it a good-luck kiss. "Allow me to school you on how it's done."

My lips twitch in an almost grin as I gesture for her to step forward and do her thing.

Tessa concentrates, lines up her angle, and shoots. With a quick bounce, her ball leapfrogs over the cups on the other side and rolls across the floor.

"Well, look at that." Jenny's tone drips sarcasm. "I guess you two aren't perfect at everything."

"Excuse me?" Tessa's head snaps up.

"Oh, don't act all innocent, Sinclair. I'm sure you've heard by now. I'm surprised you're not home crying in your pillow. We all know your family can't afford to buy their way out of a paper bag."

"What's that supposed to mean?" Tessa rounds on her.

"Jenny, I wouldn't piss off Tessa. She throws a mean punch."

I nod in her direction, but Tessa looks confused—like she's unsure if I'm coming to her defense or ganging up on her, too.

"The punch is what I'm talking about." Jenny sneers. "It looks like you can kiss your scholarship goodbye."

"What?"

"Principal Evans sent me an email tonight." She pulls out her phone as proof. "Ms. Fieldman called him from the hospital to say the scholarship is mine now. I guess slugging her didn't win you high points for moral fiber."

Tessa's body goes rigid. "No. You're lying."

"Do you want to read the email?" Jenny flips her phone around: Exhibit A. "But don't worry, we can still see each other when I'm home from Stanford on break and you're cleaning my house. Isn't that what your mom did? Or was it sewing?"

Something flashes behind Tessa's eyes, and she begins marching around the table, cheeks flushed, hands fisted. "No one gets to say I'm not good enough. That my family's not good enough."

"Whoa, hold up, firecracker." My arm rockets out, holding her in place before she does something she'll regret. Again.

Tessa's breath comes hot and fast. "I already planned on writing Ms. Fieldman a letter of apology tomorrow, begging her forgiveness. So, I wouldn't get too comfortable, Jenny."

"That's a very bad idea." Jenny stalks closer. "That money's mine now, and I don't like it when someone takes what's mine."

"Are you threatening me?" Tessa scoffs. "You're unreal. You don't even need it."

Jenny shrugs, flipping her hair over her shoulder as she walks back to her end of the table.

"Is this because of eighth grade? We were friends, Jenny. I confided in you. Trusted you. You're the one who gave me the ultimatum and said I had to pick between you and Tilly."

A sharp, shocked laugh escapes Jenny's lips. "Tessa, do you really think I care about some fight we got into five years ago? That it's been eating away at me all this time because of feelings?" She grabs a Ping-Pong ball. "No. This is about winning. You had your chance, and now it's my turn. So don't even think about interfering. Because . . ." With a quick flick, she sinks her ball into another of our back-row cups. "I win."

Yannick, fully in the zone, scores another shot beside her. How are they doing that?

"Get 'em, killer." Jenny plants a long and lingering kiss on him in congratulations as Tessa and I watch awkwardly. It's only then that I realize my arm is still snaked tightly around her waist from where I tried to slow her down before.

Tessa seems to realize, too, her eyes snagging on mine, an eyebrow lifted. I pull my arm back to my side.

We return to the game, but it's hard to concentrate. The alcohol is going to my head and Tessa's so pissed she can't focus. Although I'd love to take Jenny and Yannick down, it's a lost cause. We're annihilated at beer pong. The events of the party become increasingly fuzzy after that.

There's Tessa and me dancing downstairs. One of her buns has unfurled as she waves a glow stick in my face, laughing. The lights strobe on and off, highlighting the freckles on her nose.

Then flash: We're in a back room, as a fight breaks out outside. People press themselves against the windows, jockeying for a look. There're screams and gasps when someone's body slams against the side of the house.

Then somehow, we're upstairs hiding in a closet from those guys who hassled me earlier. My heart is beating so fast it feels like it's going to break out of my chest, *Aliens* style, as I strain to hear if they've chased us. I feel the heat of Tessa's skin beside me. Was she throwing up before as I held her hair back, or did I only imagine that part?

It's hard to keep up.

My thoughts skip like stones cast over a pond.

What . . .

. . . is happening . . .

. . . to me?

We stumble out of the closet dizzy and doubled over with cramps. I hug my stomach, bracing against the deep ache inside, the sour taste at the back of my throat.

I've been drunk before, but this . . . this is next level. If only I could find some water. I'm so thirsty. I need to sober up.

Surprisingly, Tessa remains at my side. I want to tell her thanks for sticking it out with me, but it's . . . the vertigo . . . hard to get a breath.

I'm . . .

. . . losing focus.

I drag myself into the second floor bathroom and begin vomiting in the toilet. How could I let this happen? Why did I drink so much?

It pours out of me until I dry heave, body shaking.

I've broken out in a sweat. My shirt is drenched with it.

Shit.

Where's Tessa?

The cool tile feels so good against my cheek. My eyelids flutter.

I can't keep them open.

Find . . . Tessa.

I try to claw my way to the surface, to check on her, but a fog, thick and dark, settles over me like a warm blanket, knocking me out.

And dragging me under.

CHAPTER 6

Tessa

AFTER

My mind rises slowly through the deep, drifting past layers of silt and sand. Hoisted ever upward through the dark and endless fathoms. I don't have the energy to open my eyes but sense it's bright as I near the surface. Blindingly bright.

Don't wake up, I whisper, coax. Not yet.

Stay hidden behind the veil of sleep.

There was something I wanted desperately to hold on to. The shadow of a thought. A moment of choice.

Rise or fall.

Stay or go.

I was grasping it. Dredging in the silt for an answer of some kind. Or perhaps, having already made up my mind, I don't want to face the gravity of the decision.

Hold. Wait. Dream.

Were it not for the occasional splashes of red and blue across the backs of my eyelids, my mind might have opted to sink back to oblivion. Instead, it snaps into focus, my eyes fluttering open.

I'm not in my bed. I'm not sure where I am exactly, only that my hip juts into a hard wooden floor. Above me hangs the slanted roof of an attic ceiling. Lights flicker hypnotically overhead through the early-morning haze.

Red. Blue. Red. Blue.

Strobing on and off, they're like party lights, but not. Then a memory jostles loose, unlocks.

The party.

All at once, visions of last night fly back to me. The mansion. The breakup. Hiding from those guys with Reed. The alcohol. So much alcohol.

Oh my God. Did I pass out here? Did I never make it home? I smack my palm to my forehead, arriving back in my body piece by piece. Stupid Reed and his stupid idea to play a stupid drinking game. And me, foolishly thinking I have something to prove. My father's going to be furious. I push myself up from the floor, patting my pockets for my phone. It's gone. Of course I'd lose my phone. Could this day get any shittier? Now I've no way to call Jillian or Tilly to come get me.

My anxiety is mounting again, and that leads nowhere good. I need to breathe. Focus. I can get myself home. I am capable. I am smart. *Breathe.*

I just need to find someone and borrow their phone, that's all. Though it's oddly quiet. Did everyone go home already? Why in the world did I climb to the rickety attic of this creepy mansion and fall asleep? Reed's nowhere in sight.

He must have ditched me.

Damn him.

I rub the sleep out of my eyes and head for the window.

A thick mist hovers over the ground. Like fog rolling off the ocean, it swirls in eddies around the trees, bushes, front porch. It presses against the windowpanes. It's so dense I can't even make out the front gate.

But the red and blue lights on the street are unmistakable, even if the cars themselves are concealed. The police are here. The party's been busted.

For one wild moment I imagine climbing out the attic window to shimmy down from the upper floors in a daring escape. But then I remember Mika Rogers's sixth-grade birthday party, when I panicked after scrambling to the top of the rock wall and had to be rescued by a burly employee named Mr. Cougar while Mika screamed that I'd ruined her sixth-grade year. Heights and I don't mix.

I could hide until the cops leave, but who knows how long that will take, and my dad is definitely freaking out by now. Since staying forever isn't an option, I creep down the narrow attic stairs. My plan for trying to resurrect the scholarship for outstanding moral fiber evaporates with each step.

Dear Ms. Fieldman, after punching your lights out, I went to a blow-out graduation party, drank myself into a stupor, then got busted by the cops. But please, I swear, I am a very together and dependable person. I was merely corrupted by my evil nemesis, Reed Walker. It was him I meant to be punching. If you knew him, Ms. Fieldman, I swear you'd want to punch him, too.

On the third floor I see my first cop. I press my back against the hallway wall, trying to make myself as small as possible. But when he glances my way, he doesn't seem concerned. When I step onto the landing, two more officers walk past. I expect to be scolded. Arrested, even. Doesn't that happen when parties are busted in the movies? But no one breathes a word to me. When I descend to the second floor, the action really gets going. The police are everywhere, from uniformed beat cops to detectives in suits and ties. There's caution tape. Cones on the floor. A somber vibe.

My brain can't make all the pieces slot into place. There are no students. What happened here? Was there some kind of crime? Maybe it was lucky I fell asleep in the attic after all, away from the action.

"Excuse me," I ask an officer snapping photos of the surroundings. She brushes past, ignoring me.

"Did they ID our Jane Doe?" She joins a group of men gathered on the other side of the room toward the large second-story windows overlooking the lawn below.

"We're working on that now."

It's only then that I notice the small lump on the floor by their feet, covered in a tarp. No, not a lump.

A person.

I know I should leave. I'm not meant to be here. I should walk out and never look back. But I can't. I'm pulled forward. "What's going on here?" I ask, but no one pays me any attention.

In the end, it's the old-fashioned boots jutting out from under the plastic sheet that snatch my breath away—vintage Victorian boots with the laces looped around and tied halfway up. Did someone steal my shoes while I slept?

I glance down, but mine remain on my feet.

A chill creeps over my skin. The mystery of the boots compels me to step closer, dig further. Like bodies held tight to the earth, like metal filings drawn to a magnet, there's a force now beyond curiosity, beyond anything I've ever known. I need to know who that person is.

I stumble forward, through the chaos, determined to get some answers. "Who is she?" I press again, but the officers huddle together, unconcerned. It's infuriating. "Hey, answer me! Who's under there?" I march up to the edge of their circle.

One of the detectives pulls a pair of plastic gloves out of his pocket, working them onto his hands. "Poor kid, likely OD'd. We've sent off labs for a tox screen. And we're running DNA so we can notify the family." He leans down and pulls the top of the tarp back.

My head spins. Black hair braided into messy buns. The lace dress. The house tilts on its axis as my world explodes. Is this some kind of joke? I stagger backward. I can't suck enough air into my lungs.

She . . .

Me . . .

She . . . looks so pale. So lost. Eyes blank and expressionless, staring up at the ceiling until the detective runs his hands over her face to close them.

"Noooooooo!" someone screams. It's me. I'm screaming. I

need to get out of this room. I don't know what kind of cruel game this is. But as I turn to race forward there's a police officer, clipboard in hand, directly in my path, and inexplicably, though I'm standing right in front of him, he barrels toward me. I brace for impact, but it never comes—at least not in the way I expect.

I'm met with the bitter crush of ice, my sense of self dissolving, as the cold seeps into my bones, drowning out my every thought. I'm consumed with his memories . . . *our* memories.

In a locker back at the precinct there's an engagement ring tucked in his coat pocket.

He's been denied a promotion and resents it.

I'm sad to be here, having lost a friend in my twenties to a drug overdose.

Wait, did that happen to me? I can't tell. I'm totally unmoored.

And then it's over. When I whip around, the officer is suddenly behind me. I don't . . . I can't line the pieces up into reality. How?

I stumble forward, barely able to stand. The cold is marrow-deep. My teeth are chattering, my body shaking. It's as if, for a heartbeat, that cop and I occupied the same space, as if he passed straight through me.

But that's impossible.

And yet . . . I *knew* him. I knew him in a deeper way than I've ever known anyone. But it's already fading, leaving me shivering, empty, and alone.

No.

Not alone.

Standing on the other side of the room, in the doorway,

there's one person in all the spiraling chaos who is staring straight at me, who can unmistakably see me.

His eyes drill into mine, with the same edge-of-panic expression plastered over his face.

Reed Walker.

CHAPTER 7

Tessa

Reed is here.

Reed can see me.

It's like a strange lifeline out of this nightmare. I stumble toward him, only realizing when I step in front of him how violently I'm still shaking.

Reed's eyes are wide with shock, his face pale, as he takes in my trembling frame. "Are you all right?"

"Did you see that? Please tell me you s-saw that," I stammer, arms clenched at my sides in a feeble attempt to calm the shakes.

"You mean the guy walking straight through you? Yeah, that was kind of hard to miss."

"I can't stop shi-ver-ing." My teeth chatter.

"Neither can he." He nods behind me. The officer who

walked through me rocks back and forth in a chair, arms hugged tight to his chest. He looks like he's about to be sick.

"When that guy . . . when he came toward me, through me, or . . . I don't even know. It's like for a moment I lost all sense of myself, but I knew things about *him*. Personal things." I'm on the edge of tears, but I can't let Reed see how freaked out I am. "What the hell is going on?"

Reed's brows knit together. "Tessa, I don't think we survived the party."

"No-no-no-no. That's impossible. That can't be true. I'm talking to you right now."

"At first, I didn't want to believe it, either, but it's the only explanation."

"No. I refuse to believe that." I turn to an officer measuring the room. "Excuse me?" I ask, but she ignores me. "Please, I have some questions." Nothing. I get nothing.

"She can't hear you." Reed sighs. "None of them can hear you. I've been trying."

I pivot to face the room. "We were at the party last night. Who wants to interview us?" I shout, but no one even turns a head. This cannot be happening.

"Where did you wake up?" Reed eyes me cautiously.

"What?"

"You woke up here, right? In this house? Where was it?"

I glance over at the body under the tarp. It can't be me under there. I woke up upstairs, not here. "The attic."

"Huh." He chews that over for a minute, then reaches out to take my hand. "Let me show you something." And though

Reed's normally someone I steer clear of, right now he feels like the anchor I need. I hold on to him like my life depends on it.

Reed ushers me down another flight of stairs to the ground floor. It's packed here, too, with even more police ignoring us. A sergeant barks orders over his radio while various officers scour the downstairs parlors for anything left behind. Reed weaves us in and out of the crowd, careful not to come in direct contact with anyone. Several twisting hallways later, we find ourselves under the twenty-foot-high vaulted ceiling of the grand ballroom. I never explored this room last night, though I can see why Tilly wanted to take selfies here. We're surrounded on three sides by stately mirrors stretching from the floor to the crown molding, each with delicate designs of flowers and vines etched into the glass. Overhead is an enormous art deco chandelier, hanging like an upside-down birthday cake, with strings of pearls and tiers of glittering crystals refracting the morning light.

The fog I saw before is pressed up tight against the wall of windows facing the gardens, itching for a way inside. I shiver again.

"This is where I woke up. Notice anything strange?" Reed drops my hand at last.

"Besides that creepy fog?"

"Yeah." He shivers, noting how it hugs the house.

"Besides that? No."

Reed rolls his eyes, annoyed. "Seriously, Tessa. This is not a trick question. Look around."

I step farther into the room. Glance again at the chandelier, the hardwood flooring that's seen better days, the gorgeous mirrors dominating the walls. And then . . . oh.

My blood freezes like liquid nitrogen, ready to shatter me into a thousand pieces. I whip my head around to check all three mirrored walls as a deep and mounting sense of doom threads through my veins.

"I don't have a reflection," I choke out.

He steps beside me, and we gaze together at the empty room reflected back. A room that doesn't contain us. "Correction. *We* don't have a reflection."

We've been erased. Erased from existence. Just like that. "We're dead." As the words slip from my lips, it hits me all at once, the finality of that statement.

Reed merely looks smug, proud he figured it out before me. Like he can't even let this one moment go without it being a competition between us. "My body's in this house, too."

"Where?" I didn't see another tarp and body upstairs.

He grimaces and walks away from me.

"Where, Reed?" I chase him down.

He sighs. "In the bathroom off the room where you were found. I died in a bathroom. Vomiting, apparently."

"Oh my God. Did we die from alcohol poisoning?"

"I don't think it gets more humiliating. My mom is going to be devastated." He sinks down to the floor, against one of the mirrored walls, head in his hands.

Oh no. My dad. Jillian. Tilly. Do they even know? I came here to this stupid party, the one and only high school party I ever attended, and I died. That's it.

I lean over, placing my hands on my knees as I start to hyperventilate.

No graduation. No college years or trip with Tills to Nepal. No long life ahead of me with a career, marriage, kids. No dreams to fulfill. This cannot be my story. "This is all your fault!" I round on him.

"Excuse me?" His head snaps up, his eyes full of icy intensity. "What did you say?"

"That it's your *fault*, Reed." I throw the word at him. "I wouldn't be in this mess if it weren't for you!" I do my best mocking impersonation of his deep voice: "'*Oh, Tessa, let's have a drink, let's play beer pong and get shit-faced and live out all my frat boy fantasies. Come on, I dare you.*'"

"That's fucking priceless." He stands to face me head-on. "I tried to help you last night after your marshmallow of a boyfriend publicly dumped you, and this is how I get thanked? You blame *me*?" He's fifty shades of red now, about to go full nuclear. "You're the one who jumped up and volunteered for that drinking game, remember? Not me."

"You cannot be serious."

He crosses to me, gesturing in my face. "I never would have drunk so much if I hadn't taken pity on you."

I swat his hand away, raising my voice. "Pity on me? I didn't ask for your help or pity. And I recall it was *you* who started the whole night by saying, 'Let's drown our troubles.' Give me a break. You were looking for any excuse. You dared me to come in the first place."

"Whoa, slow down with the revisionist history. You're the

one who threw this party, remember? I was debating even going except I had to see what the great Tessa Sinclair was going to pull off." He practically spits out my name.

"Well, surprise." I wave my hands in the air. "I didn't throw the party. That was all a lie."

His head jerks back. "So, you lied right to my face?"

"Oh, like you didn't know. You gave me a hard time about the DJ and the keg."

He barks out a cruel laugh. "Did I think you'd ordered a keg? No, I wanted to see you squirm. But I still believed you when you said you planned it. I was trying to help. Get people excited. You let me brag to everyone about how you were throwing this killer event."

"How was I to know you were going to tell a million people? I *lied* to get you off my back. I never asked for your help. I didn't want it then, and I don't want it now. I'm leaving." I head for the French doors at the back of the ballroom leading onto the garden terrace.

"What? You can't leave." He races to catch up.

Despite myself, I hesitate. "Why not?"

"Do you really want to walk outside in that?" He points dramatically at the fog swirling against the panes. It does look ominous. "Who knows what happens when you step outside? You don't know if time even works in the same way. You could vanish, never to be seen again. You could get eaten by sandworms."

"Sandworms?"

"Like in *Beetlejuice*."

"Don't you mean *Dune*?" I correct.

"No. *Beetlejuice*, with the sandworms when they go outside."

I throw my hands in the air. "What are you even talking about right now?"

"I'm talking about—" He lets out a hard breath. "Never mind. I just . . . until we know more, I don't think we should leave, that's all."

Is it dangerous to go outside? All this talk of monsters is freaking me out. I start to pace. "So, I'm stuck here. With you." I glare at him. "Of all the people to be trapped in this house with. You know what"—I pause my pacing as the thought occurs to me—"maybe we're in hell. Maybe this is my own personal brand of torture, having to look at your entitled face every day while you mansplain the afterlife to me." I already feel claustrophobic.

"You're no picnic yourself." He sneers. "And in case it needs clarifying, I don't want to be here with you, either. You're a high-strung, uptight, egotistical pain in the ass. And *my* personal brand of hell is being trapped here while you pathetically weep over your douche of an ex. Which I'll probably have to listen to for the next ten thousand years."

"Right, because that's what I'm doing. I'm spending my time weeping over Brandon." My voice breaks on his name, betraying me.

He stares me down, waiting for me to crack, but I won't give him the satisfaction. It's not even Brandon I'm upset about. It's needing to be here with someone kind, someone who understands me. This situation is so upside down I can't even begin to wrap my head around it. I don't think I've ever felt more alone.

"Oh no." He pouts, sticking out his bottom lip. "Are you shedding a tear because life is hard?"

"Newsflash, asshole, *life* is over." We fume at each other until I can't stand looking at his face—all pointed lines, jagged edges, and a harsh scowl—a moment longer.

I glance at the glass ballroom doors again, and the promise of freedom outside. Why am I taking Reed's word for it? Just because *he's* too afraid to leave doesn't mean I have to stay. I'll go home to my dad—even if I am dead, at least I'll be somewhere safe, somewhere I know I'm loved. Even if it's hard, it'll still be far better than having to deal with Reed's self-important, spoiled attitude.

"You know what? Forget it. I'm leaving after all. If you're too scared of sandworms or whatever, then be my guest and hide out here. You can have your pick of dusty bedrooms." I cruise up to the exit, reaching out to grasp the handle of the closest door, but although I can feel the cold metal of the knob, I can't compel it to move. I check, but the bolt is clearly in the unlocked position.

That stops me in my tracks. Why won't it open? I rattle the handle to no avail. It refuses to slide open or closed.

Reed watches me warily as I try the handle of the other door. Then the windows beside them. One. Two. Three. Nothing will budge. I race to other windows along the outer wall. No lock will shift, no window will crack open.

No, no, no, no, no.

How is it I can feel things but not move them? What is this *nightmare*?

"Well, look at that. I guess you're stuck with me after all." He shrugs one shoulder, lips pursed, but there's something behind his eyes that his flippancy is masking. Fear? He must be as freaked out as I am that we seem to be trapped.

I start pacing again. If we really are stuck here, then we need to avoid each other, that's all. That's the only way we're getting through this. I step forward, hands on my hips, and size him up. "We obviously don't want to be here together, so let's not. We divide up the house and forget about each other. You stay on your side; I'll stay on my side, and we can just, I don't know, rest in peace and all that."

"Deal. You can have the second floor."

"Always the gentleman." I cross my arms, shaking my head. "I'm not going anywhere near there, and you know it. I'll take the third floor, and you can have down here."

"Fine." He doesn't even argue, which makes me wonder if I should have chosen the first floor, but it's too late now.

I blow past him toward the main ballroom exit, heading to the foyer and the grand staircase beyond. When I get to the door, I reach out to slam it behind me, forgetting for a moment I can't move things.

"Ha." His voice is closer than I expected, his laugh jeering. I didn't realize he'd followed me over. "Bet you wish you could slam that door in my face so badly right now."

This time the tears well hot and determined in my eyes, threatening to reveal exactly how scared and alone I feel, how much he gets to me. But I blink them back. He will not make me cry . . . he will not make me cry. "You're a shitty person, Reed, and the last guy on earth I'd *ever* choose to be here with."

He flinches and I feel a flash of victory, knowing I can hurt him, too.

I whip around to march down the hall.

"Well, you're a shitty person *and* a shitty ghost," he hollers in my wake.

After dodging police all the way to the third floor, I make my way to the largest bedroom overlooking the back garden. I stagger a few feet forward before falling onto the floor in a heap of self-pity, sobbing into my knees.

How could I have gotten myself into this situation? Why didn't I leave with Tilly? I don't want to be in this sad, isolated, creepy mansion. I want my home and my bed. I want my dad to tuck me in and tell me it's all going to be okay. The tears keep coming as I smack my hands hard against the sides of my legs, thinking about the pain I'm causing the people I love. This can't be how my story ends. A cautionary tale wrapped around a bundle of terrible choices and tied off with a giant bow of remorse.

When night falls, I crawl on top of the sprawling bed, but I never sleep. I drift along tossing and turning in a sea of regrets, wondering at which exact point I should have made a different choice—like those signs you see that say LAST EXIT BEFORE THE BRIDGE. Where was my last off-ramp? And why didn't I take it?

It was probably letting Reed dare me to come here. I should have ignored him like usual, but no, I had to go and prove myself to him. I shake my head, wanting to focus on anything else. I don't want to consider why I care about his opinion. Or what the challenge in his eyes did to me as he held my gaze in Principal Evans's office yesterday. I hate him. Now more than ever. I bet he's not fretting, or tossing, or crying. I bet he's downstairs sleeping like a baby.

No. That's not fair. He was obviously freaked out, too. But clearly not upset enough to search out my company. Though a small voice in the back of my mind reminds me that I'm the one who came up with this plan. I'm the one who said I'd rather avoid him for eternity. If that's what this even is.

Eternity.

Are Reed and I stuck here nagging and snapping at each other *forever*?

I start tossing all over again.

CHAPTER 8

Reed

I'm dead. Gone. Done. Finito.

Here lies Reed Walker.

Literally, here I lie under some cobweb-encrusted chandelier, sprawled out on the ballroom floor of the van der Born mansion. My new home away from home.

After Tessa stormed upstairs, all the fight drained out of me. I collapsed in the middle of the floor and began counting the crystals overhead before the panic consumed me. It's my third pass. There's 1,114.

I've been dead less than twenty-four hours. At least, I think I have. There are no clocks in this shithole. And if this is any taste of the afterlife, it's going to be one boring fucking monotony.

It's almost unfathomable that yesterday evening I was

strumming my guitar, joking with Kira and Santiago about how legendary the party was going to be as we drove up to the estate. Hell, I even played beer pong with Tessa freakin' Sinclair. For a moment there, I actually felt lucky. I thought it was *my night*. This girl who both fascinated and frustrated me all these years was giggling at my jokes, smiling at me rather than scowling.

Not anymore. I'm back to public enemy number one as far as she's concerned.

You're a shitty person, Reed, and the last guy on earth I'd ever choose to be here with.

Well, it's not like I *chose* to be here. Though a part of my brain keeps thinking if I close my eyes, then I can somehow choose to wake up back home, shake off this strange nightmare. But there's a deeper part of me, the side that festers in doubt, that knows my life's always been a shit sandwich so I probably should have seen this coming.

My hopes were always destined to be flushed down the toilet.

Ugh. Don't think about the toilet. I shut my eyes, pressing my palms tightly against them. Why did I let myself go there? Now I can't shake the image of myself lying face down in a pool of vomit in the bathroom upstairs. The most unglamorous way to die, like in the history of ever.

Is my body still there now? I shiver, staring at the cracks in the ceiling, as if my eyes can bore straight through. I'd be right overhead. How can I be both there and *here*? Because I feel like I'm here. I'm dressed as I was. I can feel the hardwood floor pressed against my shoulder blades. Regret and guilt gnaw at my stomach—there's no mistaking that. The ache is palpable; my limbs are heavy with it.

Guilt. Guilt. And more guilt. How could I put my mom through this?

Again.

It's too much. I can't sit here with all my failings anymore. It's goddamned depressing.

I need a distraction. I push up off the floor for the first time in what feels like hours. It's getting late. The sun's set, but that strange fog still hovers around the property. The way it billows against the windows in the fading light sends goose bumps prickling over my skin. How could Tessa want to walk outside in that? I can still see her rattling all the locks, trying to get free of the house. Just to be sure, I cross to the wall of glass facing the garden terrace and try the French doors myself. They won't budge.

Well, if I'm truly stuck here, I may as well find out what that means. I get to be king of this castle, after all, or at least my corner of it.

I make my way under the large, ornate archway leading to the foyer. It's empty, eerily so. It must be later than I thought. Which is odd, because I could have sworn I heard whispered voices moments ago. I peer out the window onto the grounds in case the police are still here, but the place is truly abandoned, except for the girl who hates me upstairs.

There's caution tape strung across the entrance gate outside, but not much else to betray the chaos of earlier.

So, I wander, a specter gliding through sitting rooms left mostly unfurnished, save the occasional couch draped in a white sheet or paint-chipped end table. There's the sprawling kitchen with bottles of alcohol and crushed beer cans abandoned on the countertop, as if people were enjoying their night until news broke of the tragedy unfolding upstairs.

I walk through studies and smoking rooms with their high-backed chairs covered in torn upholstery. There's even a decrepit library rimmed with empty shelves. It's a cathedral of dust and spiderwebs, with slivers of moonlight slipping through broken shutters that rattle in the breeze—a sad collection of discarded relics. And now I'm joining their ranks, soon to be faded and forgotten like all the rest.

After a thorough search of the downstairs, I find two rooms are out of reach as I'm unable to open doors. If a door wasn't left open from the partygoers or cops, I can't get in now. Eventually I land in the dining room, still filled with the echoes of our battle against Jenny and Yannick. A couple of Ping-Pong balls remain flush against the baseboards, the only evidence that we were here, hearts beating, not so long ago.

I slide down against the wall covered in peeling wallpaper, drop my face in my hands, and full-on ugly cry.

What was it all for?

I knock my head against the wall behind me.

Sorry, kid. All those dreams you had, all that work you put in to ace your tests, captain the robotics club, teach yourself Python late into the night, get into Harvard. Guess what? It was for nothing.

You're nothing.

No one.

Not anymore.

My chest heaves through body-wracking sobs as the weight of my new reality takes hold.

With the soft light of morning, I decide I've had enough moping. I've also had enough isolation. How can Tessa stand it? I was sure she'd get spooked last night, with the branches scratching against the windows, or the wind rattling the walls, and come back downstairs. There's safety in numbers.

But no, I guess Tessa's perfectly happy to spend the night in a haunted house—if she's the one haunting it. Still, are we really going to spend eternity cowering in our respective corners? It's absurd.

I head upstairs. The police are back, but there're far fewer of them now: I take care to skate by without walking through anyone like Tessa did. That looked uncomfortable. I race past the second story—there's no way I'm peeking in there—and tiptoe up to the third floor. Tessa's nowhere in sight.

Did she actually leave, somehow? I wander through bedrooms until I hear her swearing under her breath in the back room facing the gardens. I sneak over, peering around the doorframe.

I don't know what I was expecting—probably Tessa huddled on the floor and crying her eyes out like I've been doing—but no. She's focused on a pair of candlesticks like they hold the secrets of the universe. She's also managed to find, by far, the sweetest room in the house. It has a kind of faded 1920s vibe. A stately mirror hangs over a fireplace that's intricately carved with dancing nymphs, while a moth-eaten, midnight-blue coverlet sits atop the retro circular bed. Long drapes laced with sparkling silver thread cascade from the enormous windows, sending tiny flecks of light dancing across the ceiling.

How did she score actual furnishings while I'm sitting on mouse droppings? No wonder she claimed the third floor.

Standing beside the mantel, she wraps her hand around the base of a candlestick. Once gleaming silver, it's now tarnished to a dark gunmetal gray. Tessa grunts as she attempts to lift it. "Why won't you *move*?"

I step to the side before she notices me and hold my hand against my mouth as I double over with laughter. Of course Tessa is trying to ace the afterlife. Does it get more predictable? Can't that girl wallow in despair like the rest of us?

But seeing her work so hard makes something inside me snap into place. That's what I need, a puzzle. If my mind is whirring on a question, like how this whole afterlife thing works, then I can't collapse under the incredible grief and panic bubbling below the surface, threatening to explode like a geyser. Besides, nothing would satisfy me more than seeing the envious look on Tessa's face when I waltz into her room and casually pick up one of those candlesticks. It's all the fuel I need.

I race downstairs and throw myself with renewed energy into affecting my surroundings. I go about it as scientifically as possible, coming at objects fast and slow, adjusting the variables for time of day, angle of approach, speed. Nothing works.

I feel like I have a body, but I can't fully use it. Is this all in my head? Am I experiencing the memory of touch or are these real objects in the real world and I somehow can't access them?

I don't know.

But as the days drift past, one after another, I find I'm no closer to an answer, just defeated. And utterly bored.

Time moves unpredictably. Sometimes an entire afternoon

comes and goes in a blink, while at other moments, I watch shadows creep along the floor in slow motion. By the third night it becomes clear to me that it's not that I'm having trouble sleeping, but that ghosts don't sleep—which means more endless hours with nothing to do. What I wouldn't give to binge something on Netflix.

But even through the boredom, a small, insistent thought keeps needling me.

Where's my dad?

If we die and become ghosts, then that means he must be somewhere, too. Is he trapped in Denver still, like I'm stuck here? Does he blame me for his death? I've certainly blamed myself enough.

This is all your fault, Reed.

Tessa's words bite at my conscience. I know what it's like to have cost someone their life. And I'll accept that guilt when it's deserved. But this . . . right *now* . . . this is not on me.

I clasp my hands over my head. *Please. Please don't let this be on me.* I can't take being responsible for any more pain.

With all these swirling thoughts, I keep ending up in the study, running my hand along my dad's guitar case. If I could only open it and play, maybe that would somehow, I don't know, call him to me. But even after all the trying, I can't pick anything up.

God, it's so frustrating. Where's the book I can study? Where are the flashcards? If this were an exam, I'd be failing, and I. Do. Not. Like. To. Fail. Is Tessa figuring all this out by now? Is she surging ahead? Is she upstairs right at this very moment, walking through walls, hovering in the air, ghosting it up? Because if she is, I have to beat her, stay ahead of the curve.

With a newfound fire in my belly, I get up to confront Tessa, tell her it's ridiculous we aren't speaking, because there's so much we need to talk about. When I pivot toward the door, the air gusts out of me.

She's here.

She thinks she's being sly, but one of her braided buns pokes past the doorframe. Has she been spying on me, too? I kneel back over my guitar, pretending I don't notice, trying to control my smirk, waiting to see what she'll do.

But she remains silent, unmoving.

"I know you're there." I sigh loudly before she can sneak back upstairs. "Some of your hair's sticking out around the corner. You're not as disguised as you think." My voice is croaky from lack of use, but I'd be lying if I said my heart didn't leap at her being here after all these days alone.

She swings around to face me in the doorframe, hands on her hips, trying to recover her self-respect after getting caught.

"What happened to avoiding each other for eternity?" I ask, an eyebrow piqued. She doesn't need to know how much I've thought about her. How I was doing the same thing, spying on her, earlier.

"I have my reasons," she says evasively.

"Which are . . . ?"

She glances away, likely scrambling to come up with some legit excuse to have broken the code she set.

I shrug with a grin. "Clearly, you missed my winning personality. It's okay to admit it."

"You are so cocky. I should turn around and march back upstairs right now."

"Be my guest." Though I indicate the door, my eyes plead otherwise. *Don't leave. Please don't leave. I'm dying down here by myself.*

She must sense my pathetic desperation because her cheeks flush as she walks into the study to look around. She scoffs when she takes in the guitar case I'm hovering over. "You have got to be kidding me. I'm upstairs trying to understand this whole astrophysical mess we're in, and you're down here trying to play guitar. That is so typical. Even in death all you want is to be a rock star."

"Rock god, Tessa. I want to be a rock god." My mouth quirks as I stand up, hands in my pockets. "I was actually about to come find you."

Tessa's lips purse as she considers me, unsure if I'm telling the truth. But I don't get the chance to explain because there's the sound of a car parking out front and faint voices spilling across the lawn.

We stare at each other in shock, then dash to the grand foyer, taking our places side by side at the imposing front windows.

Though the fog has receded almost to the edge of the property, I can still make out additional headlights flashing past, more cars parking. As the gate swings open, Tessa's dad emerges from the mist, crossing the threshold onto the grounds. Someone's on his arm—her sister maybe? They're followed by a couple. From Tessa's gasp, I suspect the woman must be her mom. Then Tilly, Santiago, Kira, and Brandon are here, along with my mom and stepdad.

My heart beats rapidly.

My mom's here. She's here to save me. For a fleeting moment I'm positively sure of it, until my eyes land on the wreath she's clutching and the situation becomes clear.

No.

She's here to mourn me.

A fierce and painful longing rockets through my body as I lay my hands on the glass, willing them to see me. I want to race outside and hug her, but I can't open the fucking door.

"Do you think they're coming inside?" Tessa asks as they make their way across the lawn. It comes out as a whisper, a desperate hope.

We can't hear them through the glass, but it's enough to see them. Did they come from our funeral? They halt at the front steps, staring ahead with wary faces.

When our mothers walk together to lay the wreath on the porch, a guttural cry rips from Tessa's lips. Her arms snake around her stomach. "She finally had a good enough reason to return to town."

Dressed in black, Tilly pulls a letter out of her pocket and weeps as she lays it below the wreath. Tessa begins to bawl beside me, but I can hardly pay attention anymore. My back stiffens as waves of anger roll off my body. My stepdad—blond hair slicked back, Armani suit tailored perfectly to his slim frame—is already bored and distracted. Everything unsaid between us ignites, ready to burn me whole. *He doesn't deserve my mom. And we certainly don't deserve him.*

"Look at him checking his watch, like he can't even give her this moment to grieve her son before needing to get back on some business call." After glancing at the time, the all-important Steven Walker pulls his phone out to discreetly reply to some email while my mom collapses on the stairs, head pressed to the wreath. It's Tessa's father who stoops to comfort her as she sobs.

My fists clench at my sides.

"Where's your fucking humanity?" I scream at my stepfather. No one glances up. My stepdad tucks his phone away, but it's clear he's itching to reach for it again.

"Reed," Tessa says quietly, though I can't focus on anything but my anger—until the gentle press of her hand on my arm brings me back.

Eventually Tessa's dad helps my mom up and they begin to lead the procession back to their cars out front.

"No. Come back." Tessa turns to me, desperate. "Don't let them leave." Like I can do anything about that.

"H-how—" I stammer.

She steps back, a blazing look in her eyes, then races toward the front door. I brace for the thud, but instead the door warps and flickers. Suddenly, Tessa is standing outside on the front porch, her muscles rigid with shock.

She did it. Somehow, she made her way outdoors, conquering a skill I have no idea how to master.

All my fears rise to the surface, a mounting panic.

I'm going to be trapped in this house, isolated and forgotten. Tessa will leave me behind to the whispers and dust.

I place my palms against the windowpane, leaning forward, as if I could melt through the glass and join her.

Briefly, Tessa turns back to me, shocked and triumphant.

"Please," I beg, eyes wide. *Don't go.* I shake my head quickly, imploring her to stay.

But Tessa doesn't listen.

She turns and bolts after her family.

CHAPTER 9

Tessa

Everything in my body went liquid and loose as I raced toward the front door. My focus singular: *Don't let them leave.* It was a driving drumbeat to my every breath, a desire so strong and all-consuming that before I knew it, I was standing on the porch.

I don't hesitate. In a heartbeat I'm down the steps, sprinting along the mossy stone trail toward the front gate, past decorative Grecian sculptures and the gazebo shrouded in creeping wisteria. My family is already gathered on the street.

"Jillian, wait! I'm coming!" I scream as she's bolting the gate closed behind her.

Remnants of the party are scattered along the path as I race past: beer cans tumbled under overgrown rosebushes, cigarettes ground into the dirt. I guess the police didn't need them as evidence, so here they stay. Living proof that night happened. Living proof I'm no longer living.

When I reach the gate, everyone's already secured in their vehicles. *No, please don't leave. Let me look at you a moment longer. Why didn't I look at each of you more? Hold you. Tell you I loved you every day when I had the chance.*

I grasp the wrought iron bars—my new prison—and watch longingly as Reed's parents pull away, then my father. My mom leans over to kiss my sister on the forehead in the back seat before their headlights vanish into the mist. Candles snuffed out, one after the other.

I waiver, uncertainty tugging at my heart. *Do I follow them?* I'm sure I could make it past this barrier if I tried. But what's the point? We no longer belong in the same world. The finality of that thought tears through me, but I know it's true. We can't communicate. What am I going to do? Sit in my room? Wander the halls of school? Spend my days tormented by a life I can't live?

Even if I wanted to leave, I'm not entirely sure how to get home. Tilly, Brandon, and I got so lost the night of the party. What if I left now and couldn't find my way back? As annoying as Reed is, I won't ditch him just because he's stuck inside. Not after I'd hoped for the past week that he wouldn't do the same to me.

Defeated, I trudge back toward the house.

But now that I'm here I don't really feel like returning indoors. I'm tired of the same old scenery. Besides, I need some time to think. And grieve. I already miss my family so much I can hardly draw breath. If that's even what I'm technically doing, breathing. It's hard to tell what's real anymore. It might be the only way my body knows how to relate to the world, so the habit followed me here.

As I round the circuitous path, Reed's silhouetted in the window, shoulders slumped, forehead pressed against the glass. When he sees me, he frantically waves me over.

But I shake my head. I may not be confident enough to take off down the road, but it seems fine to explore the estate grounds. I never got a good look at them the night of the party.

Reed jumps and points at something. The door maybe? What's his deal? Is he that freaked out about staying inside? God, get over it.

"I'm fine," I yell. "See, no sandworms. I'm going to explore a little." I indicate the path snaking around the back of the property.

He says something, but I can't make it out. Honestly, I have no idea what he's up to. I wave him off, then step onto the meandering path as it cuts through a grove of trees. The trail, buttressed by the large stone wall on one side, opens onto an overgrown tiered garden on the other, ending in a hollowed-out, empty fountain. This must be what the French club wanted to dance in. A series of winding stone stairs lead to the rear of the mansion. From this vantage point it's clear several dark gray shingles have dislodged from the siding. Elsewhere, a section of turreted roof has collapsed, a nest of sparrows making their home from the debris.

Even in its state of disrepair, the property is still grand. Possibly most impressive is an extraordinary glass conservatory off the back of the house. One wall is composed entirely of stained-glass windows—a golden sun with amber, coral, and deep-red rays now catching the evening light. Some of the clear glass panels have fallen and shattered over the years, but two long tables once used to support a garden nursery are still intact. Now they're mostly draped in ivy or the occasional overflowing berry bush ripe with purple fruit.

Maybe it's the sunshine or the freedom of having finally made it out of my gilded cage, but I'm happy for the first time since this tragedy began. It's an unexpected feeling, especially with my heart still tender from watching my family drive away. But as I amble through the back gardens, almost entirely reclaimed by nature, I revel in the experience of being able to move around as I please, led by my own free will.

Arms outstretched, I let my palms graze over the wild grasses growing beside the trail, swaying like ocean waves in the light breeze. Sparrows dart to and from their rooftop nest. Pine needles dance on the wind to accompany the birdsong. It's quiet and peaceful.

Until a shadow moves in my peripheral vision.

I still, my heart picking up speed. Is someone out on the road? "Hello?"

No one responds.

A shiver slips over my skin as I make my way down the sloping hill, past the old carriage house toward a small wrought iron service gate built into the stone wall at the back of the property. It's far less detailed than the one heralding the front entrance. I rest my hands along the bars, scanning the surroundings for whatever caught my eye.

The road is empty of life in all directions. There's only a

country lane with occasional wildflowers blooming, set against open farmland and rolling hills. It should feel quaint and charming, but something's off. I can't quite put my finger on it, until I realize the birdsong has halted. It's eerily silent.

As I lean forward, glancing up and down the lane, the hair rises on the back of my neck, like someone's watching me. But there's nothing except an oppressive fog. It obscures all sound while it gathers more densely over the fields, grows darker, stormier. It rolls across the road to swirl in tendrils around my ankles like so many icy fingers, beckoning me to step forward, come out and play.

Whispers find their way to me on the wind—a thousand pleading voices overlapping. I can't make out any single demand, only a collective, pulsing desire for something that I have. Something the voices desperately want.

I should run. Back to the house. Back to safety.

I'm overcome by the wrongness of the moment, the sense that I'm bearing witness to something not meant for me, something dark and dangerous. But fear and curiosity keep me rooted in place, as if my moving will bring unwanted attention. The best thing to do is to let whatever this is blow past. I clutch the gate harder.

The fog has begun to take form now, billowing hypnotically upward into torsos, limbs, heads. Four shadow-people emerge from the mist, the outlines of their bodies holding shape, with only swirling smoke contained within. They're like phantoms, something out of a nightmare, come to hover over the beds of sleeping children, threatening to steal their souls.

They don't appear to see me, but they glide down the road,

their curled, withered toes dragging along behind them. Reed was right that first night about monsters. Is the mist . . . *alive* somehow? I thought we were safe here—dead, but safe. Are we not?

Adrenaline courses through me.

Run, Run. Why didn't I escape when I had the chance?

But I need to be smart. Careful. The creatures drift along, arms outstretched, appearing to head toward town.

Go now. Before they come back this way. I take a cautious step back, but one turns sharply in my direction. Even without a face I know it's staring straight at me. *Shit.* Before I can pull my arm away from the gate, it's upon me, having closed the distance between us in a breath. A shadow-hand darts out and latches on to my wrist, holding me in place. Clawed fingers dig into my skin. I try to tug my arm free, but although the figure's made of vapor, its grip holds true.

"Let me in," it begs in a harsh whisper.

"Let go of me!" I brace my feet against the bottom of the gate to leverage myself loose. But it only holds on tighter.

"Now." The word is a command, though behind it there's pain and a kind of desperate longing. Lights flicker inside the house behind me. Can Reed see me out here?

The longer the creature grasps me, the more it takes on a human form. I try to pull my arm out of its viselike grip, but my energy leaches away as it grows stronger. It's no longer a collection of shadows but a woman, the dark mist coalescing into an elegant black corseted dress with a bustle and evening gloves wrapping up pearly white arms. A feathered hat sits atop her head.

Though her body has taken shape, her face remains half-formed. Scabbed-over sockets stand sentry where her eyes should be, while her cheeks are hollowed out by age and rot. A rattling breath escapes her gaping mouth. "Please," she begs.

My knees start to buckle, my strength draining. *What's happening to me?* "Reed," I try to yell, but it comes out a feeble whisper, stuck in my throat. My mind is still hanging on her "Please," so full of ache and longing. And those eye sockets: I can't stop looking at those haunting empty holes.

"I don't know how to help you," I sob back.

Beyond her, the three other creatures have noticed our tussle. They glide over, arms grasping to pull me to them. They want to drag me out into the fields. They want to use me until there's nothing left. I'm sure of it.

And then a voice rings out from behind her, clear and sharp, breaking our tug-of-war. "Dust to dust, be gone. You are not welcome here." The figure whips around, a sneer on her withered lips, before her body becomes insubstantial again, dissolving into the breeze. As quickly as the four creatures appeared, they vanish, the whispers on the mist dying with them like a wave carried out to sea.

All that remains is an elderly man standing amid the blue cornflowers, thistles, and daisies, dressed in his Sunday best—tweed hat, brown slacks, and a buttoned vest. He studies me from across the road, taking my measure.

I freeze. How can he see me? Where did he come from? He doesn't look that spry, and yet here he stands, having somehow traveled down this lonely country lane by himself in a matter of minutes. I have so many questions.

"How did you—" I begin, but then a familiar deep voice cuts me off.

"You are not going to believe this." Reed charges down the path. What is happening? I thought he was stuck inside. I whip my head back to the road, but the old man is gone. *What? How is he so fast?*

He knew the smoke people were there, and what to say to make them to leave. Something about *dust* and *be gone*. I'm pretty sure he knew I was dead. And yet . . .

"So," Reed huffs, jogging over to me. "I figured it out. I watched how you approached the door, kind of taking it at a run. And it worked." He looks entirely too pleased with himself. Like I beat him for a moment, but he's caught up to me and now we're on even footing again. "This place is bigger than I realized. It took me a while to find you."

"Dammit, Reed! Couldn't you see I was in the middle of something?" My knees finally give out and I collapse onto the dirt.

"Whoa." He takes a step forward then pauses, as if he's unsure what to do with me. "It looked like you were daydreaming. Are you okay?"

"Do I look okay?" I gesture with trembling hands toward the road behind me. "You're telling me you didn't see any of that?"

"Any of what?"

I let out an exasperated sigh. "Oh my God, I'm going to throttle you."

He flinches. "Didn't you see me waving before? I have news. I had to figure out how to come out here to tell you. Look." He holds up his phone.

Great. So he's here to gloat about picking things up now. I

initially hoped he'd searched me out because he knew I was in trouble, but nope, he just found something he'd lost.

"So what? You found your phone. Yay for you. Good luck making any calls." I slowly stand, annoyed, as my strength returns. "Meanwhile I'm out here being haunted by smoke people and trying to talk to some strange old man who could see me."

"What?" For the first time, he glances over my shoulder out to the road. "*Smoke* people?"

"Yes, smoke people, creepy swirling smoke people who came out of that mist. One of them grabbed my arm and demanded I let her inside and I'm kind of freaking out right now." As I say it aloud, I realize how terrified I still am. My hands won't stop shaking.

"Hey. Okay. Okay. Deep breath. Hang on." He walks over to the gate and peeks out nervously. "Do you think they're coming back?" He's worried about his own neck. Figures.

"*Seriously*, Reed?" I shake my head. "You're really shit at comforting people. No, they're all gone now." My arm still stings where her decaying nails dug into my flesh. I start pacing, the adrenaline finally catching up with me. "So, you can see why I really don't care that you found your phone because *I* found some old dude who knew how to make the smoke people go away but I didn't get to ask him about it because you interrupted us and I'm pretty sure he could see me, and I have no idea how, and my energy's all depleted from where some creature tried to siphon off my life force—or my *not-life* force because I'm *dead*, and I just want something to make sense!"

He watches me retrace a path between the carriage house and a large oak, concern etched onto his brow. "I'm sorry that happened to you. I should have said that before. You just . . . took me off guard, that's all. You have every right to be upset. I'd probably have pissed myself."

I let out a small laugh. My emotions are all over the place. I'm not used to getting any sympathy from Reed; under normal circumstances he'd be picking apart my story or suggesting my imagination was getting the better of me. But it seems like he believes me.

"It makes my skin crawl a little," he adds, "because there have been a couple nights downstairs when I swear I heard whispers outside."

I come to a halt. "And you didn't think to tell me this?"

"I told you earlier, I was about to come find you."

"Was that before or after you started messing with your guitar case?"

A blush creeps along his cheekbones. "I wasn't sure if I'd actually heard it, okay? I haven't been able to sleep. I thought my mind was playing tricks on me. And I swear I was about to come tell you, but then there you were downstairs and our families arrived, and I never got the chance. Maybe if you'd come back indoors like I'd asked, I could have mentioned it, but *no*, you ran off on your own."

I bristle but don't want to get into another argument with him. "Well, it's them. The smoke people definitely whisper. They want something. From us or . . . maybe from this place."

He nods slowly. "It doesn't sound like they can get past the gate onto the grounds, so that's reassuring." He takes a few steps toward me, closing the distance. "We'll figure it out. If there's something here they want, then we'll uncover it and decide what to do next. Why don't you start at the beginning and tell me everything that happened?"

I glance at Reed, finding more warmth in his dark eyes than I'd been expecting. I'm not alone in this, and that thought is far more comforting than I realized: Even if he is my nemesis and drives me up the wall, he's in this with me.

"Look, I know we tried avoiding each other, but maybe we're better off teaming up," he says. "I mean, who knows why we're here? We can't have been the first to die in this house. You'd think this place would be flooded with ghosts if everybody stays, but clearly that's not the case. Like . . . why did we remain? And we don't know what that thing was that grabbed you or what it was after. But we're smart, Tessa. You've discovered things, I've discovered things. We could work together, put our differences aside for a bit, and see if we can figure out what's going on here." He fishes for something in his pocket. "Because I just found—"

"Oh my God, there are more important things than your phone." That didn't last long. I'm already frustrated with him, but he reaches out to stop me from marching back to the house.

"Wait. It's not *my* phone."

"So?" I shrug.

"Have you been able to pick anything up in this place?" He holds it aloft.

"Yeah, I get it. Rub it in my face. *I'm so special, look, I can pick things up now.*" I take a deep breath. Maybe that was uncalled for.

"No, that's what I'm trying to tell you. I can't." He looks at me significantly. "But I could pick *this* up."

That gets my attention.

Our eyes hold. Like me, Reed's never shied away from

a challenge. Sometimes I wonder if I've been one of those challenges.

"Okay," I acquiesce. He's right. He's discovered things I haven't. Maybe it doesn't always have to be a competition between us. "We can work together, assuming I can go more than five minutes without wanting to strangle you."

"Eight-minute trial run, then?" he asks, that disarming dimple back.

"Fine." I sigh, offering my hand to shake. "A trial run."

When he grasps my palm, my breath catches and the briefest smile flits across his lips.

As we fall in step together toward the house, I sneak a glance his way. He's focused on the trail, his mouth moving slightly like he's thinking out loud to himself. I'm tempted to laugh, but it's also kind of endearing. I've never so much as wanted to team up on a group project with Reed, but there's no denying he's brilliant.

I suppose if I had to be trapped here with someone, I could do much worse.

CHAPTER 10

Reed

So, it's really not your phone?" she asks.

"Tessa." I look at her scathingly. "Do you honestly think I'd own this ancient device? My mom had a phone like this before I was born." I turn it over. Dark gray with a small antenna, it fits perfectly in my palm in its closed position.

"Well, flip phones are kind of a thing now. They have a whole vintage vibe."

We're seated side by side against one of the mirrored walls of the ballroom. The sky outside is a mixture of dusky rose and burnt orange as the sun dips behind some trees on the horizon, reminding me of the stained-glass window on the greenhouse outside.

"Let me see it." She reaches for the device. "Maybe someone from school left it behind, or one of the cops?"

"I've passed by that entranceway table a bunch of times since we died, and it's always been empty. Then you ran through the door after your family and that phone appeared. You triggered it arriving somehow." What I don't say is how impressed I am that she conquered that crucial skill before me. I can't handle her gloating right now.

She flips the phone open and closed a few times, examining the small screen.

"That's why I was trying to get your attention so badly, to tell you something had changed. When you mastered the skill with the door . . . I don't know . . . it's like you leveled us up."

A smug smile breaks across her face, a flash of victory. She knows I wish it'd been me. "Have you tried turning it on?"

"No, I was waiting for you, in case someone called."

She gawks. "You think someone's going to call?"

"How the hell would I know? But we should be prepared for anything."

"Maybe the creepy smoke things will call." Tessa wiggles her fingers at me. "Reeeeeeed," she rasps, making her voice sound as spooky as possible, "how do you like your new fliiiiiip phooooone?"

I ignore her. "That side button should power it on."

Tessa rolls her eyes. "No need to mansplain. I know how to turn on a phone." She presses the side button, then flips it open. We both lean for a closer look as the small rectangular screen fills with a string of numbers, counting backward.

"Whoa," I breathe.

"Maybe it's a bomb." She looks ready to toss it across the room.

"A bomb?" I scoff. "We're already ghosts, are we supposed to die all over again?"

She shrugs. "Okay, maybe not a bomb, but it does seem like it's a timer for something. Makes you wonder what happens when it gets to zero."

"Someone calls us?" I reach for the phone, pushing the green button. We both tilt our ears to the receiver. Tessa's so close her breath mixes with mine. It's distracting. I make myself focus, but nothing happens—not even when I select the big circular button in the middle. "What a piece of shit."

The numbers on the home screen continue ticking backward. Every discovery we make here leads to more questions.

"There aren't even any apps," I grumble, brushing my hair back from my eyes. I'm so tired. How can ghosts be tired?

Tessa takes the phone and taps around. The only thing it seems able to do is turn on and off. "Great, so we have a useless phone circa the nineties counting down to some death day apocalypse or maybe just to a call from the welcoming committee and still no answers." She sends the phone skittering across the ballroom floor.

I lean my head against the mirrored wall behind me and sigh deeply. "You know, the most absurd part is that when I found that phone, I was sure it was a sign my dad would call. That he'd come for me." A quiet sob slips from my lips, no matter how much I'd rather Tessa not see me like this. I pinch the bridge of my nose. "I mean, he's dead. I'm dead. Why hasn't he come?" I drag my eyes back to hers, feeling utterly lost and helpless. It's embarrassing.

"I don't know if it works that way," Tessa offers, not shying away from my gaze, from the dark places I tuck away from the world. She seems surprisingly willing to look at them. "I'm sure he'd try to reach you if he could."

I wish I could believe that, but he'd have every reason to hate me. It's my fault he's gone. If I hadn't begged to come home early from my friend's house because I was having trouble sleeping, if I hadn't put my comfort over his safety, made him travel through a snowstorm that night, sliding out on black ice, then he'd still be here.

Years of therapy, and that voice is still there in the back of my mind: *You're a terrible person and you deserve what you get.*

Tessa leans her head toward me. "You remember that day in sixth grade in Ms. Baker's class? I'd snuck back after school to grab my sweater and found you sitting beside your mom. You were hugging your backpack with an unopened package of goldfish crackers on your desk."

"Yeah, I remember." My voice wavers, the events of that horrible afternoon racing back to me: my mom weeping because I was having a hard time "moving on," Ms. Baker offering her a tissue, while this pesky girl with freckles and braids gawked at me from the wall of cubbies. "I was sure you were going to tell everyone what a pathetic crybaby I was."

She scooches around so she's facing me. "I want you to know, Reed, I never breathed a word. Not to Tilly or anyone. And not because you glared at me as you crushed your goldfish crackers into dust. Which was kind of a hardcore kid-world threat, to be honest." She flashes me a weak smile. "I could just . . . I don't know, tell how much you were hurting."

"Thanks for that." I wipe my thumb across my eyelids,

catching the small tears pooling in the corners. "I actually had a ticket this summer to visit my dad's side of the family in Spain. My last name used to be Peña before my mom married Steven Walker." I shake my head. "Having to change my name, when I was eleven, the name I'd grown up with until then, it felt like . . . like we were erasing him."

I run my fingers along the woven bracelet my cousin sent me, shoving the pain back into the corner of my heart where I keep it tucked away. "Most of the family lives in Seville, but my cousin Carla and her husband, Rubin, are in Cádiz, about two hours away on the coast. They run this kitesurfing school, Surfear y Volar, Surf and Soar." I indicate the graphic on my maroon shirt. "I was going to learn to kitesurf this summer, spend time with Carla, with my aunts and uncles, get to know them all better."

"Get to know your dad better, too, I imagine," she says gently.

"Exactly." I let out a hard breath. "But now I'm stuck here instead, forever wearing a T-shirt that reminds me of the family I'll never know."

"Well, if it makes you feel better, I died in someone else's wedding dress."

I quirk my head to the side, taking in her ensemble. "That's someone's wedding dress?"

"Yep. I discovered it in a discount bin at my favorite vintage store in Albany, Second Place. I loved the lace and the cap sleeves when I found it. So I raised the hemline, sewed in a bodice, and dyed the fabric black. You know, made it my own. Oh, I made these, too." She waves her hands, showing off her fingerless gloves.

"Wait. You actually made all that?" My mouth drops open. "It's amazing."

"Thanks." She shrugs off the compliment. "It's nice to know someone appreciates it. I was pretty proud of it." She reaches down to untie her boots, kicking them off onto the hardwood ballroom floor. With the sun fully set, the first stars are breaking through the darkening night. "So, it looks like I'll be spending eternity wearing someone else's discarded dreams."

"It could be worse."

She arches an eyebrow at me.

"Like . . . what if you were a team mascot and died the night of the big game, having to spend eternity dressed in your mascot outfit? That's definitely worse."

"Hold up." She laughs, and it reverberates through the hollow room. "I need to go back for a minute. Why would you be dying in your mascot outfit?"

"Any number of reasons."

"Like?"

"You owe money to the mob. Or . . . you interrupted a key play and the team had you offed in the locker room."

"Offed in the locker room? That's all you've got?"

"Oh, like you could do better?" I challenge, but there's laughter behind it. Not many people can snap me out of a funk. I'm surprised to find Tessa might be one of them.

"Duh. Obviously. Lovers' quarrel."

"In your mascot outfit?"

"Yes," she says. "Picture it. Two star-crossed mascots from opposing teams, deeply in love, but it turns sour when she learns about his affair with the concession lady selling those giant foam fingers. Betrayed, she buys two, strangling him the night of the playoffs with her big foam hands. No fingerprints, see?" She taps her head, playing up her smarts. "That's how you pull off the crime of the century."

"Have it all figured out, do you?"

She kicks one foot on top of the other, leaning back on her hands. "I'm just sayin' . . . if I *had* to do it, that's what I'd do."

I take her in, a smile tugging at the corner of my mouth. "Tessa Sinclair, ruthless mascot assassin."

We grin at each other. For one breath.

Two.

And I realize: I like how her eyes crinkle at the edges. And how her smile reveals itself slowly, like an unfolding secret. It makes me want to excavate for more. It's the smile of someone when their guard is down. She's not gloating, or trying to one-up me, or score an extra point.

And how must I seem to her? It's so surreal to be sitting in the dark together, with the moon rising, grinning stupidly at each other in the abandoned van der Born mansion. I shift my eyes away, worried I've been staring too long, and pretend to find something fascinating out the window. "Seriously, though, I can't believe you made that dress. It looks professional."

She seems happy to land on a safer topic after whatever strange moment passed between us. "It helps that I've been sewing since I was seven years old, when my mom got me my first Singer machine for my birthday. I don't know if you'd remember this from middle school, but she came to speak once for one of those career days."

"That's right. Something about wedding dresses. I tuned out most of it. Sorry. Twelve-year-old boy."

She chuckles softly, surprising me with how easy this feels. "I remember being so embarrassed that my parents were thinking of coming at all. Neither of them went to college and everyone else's parents were doctors or bankers or—Wait, didn't your mom come, too?"

"Yeah. Architect."

"Right. And here's my mom who works as a tailor, sewing for a living."

"I remember she was kind of a hit. Didn't she bring fabric and her sewing machine?"

"She did. And don't get me wrong, she's majorly skilled. I feel bad now that it bothered me, but at the time . . ." She trails off, gazing at the giant chandelier now glittering in the moonlight. "Being in this room kind of reminds me of her. She'd occasionally get hired for these massive weddings, in Albany or even in New York City. Usually everything was prepared long in advance, but sometimes there'd be an emergency. The gown would tear, or the bride gained or lost weight and the dress didn't fit. On those days, she'd arrive early, before the ceremony, to work her magic. Sometimes she'd bring my sister Jillian and me with her, and we'd take off our shoes and glide all over the dance floors of these giant ballrooms while she sewed." She wiggles her toes, covered in black socks, and takes a deep breath. "I didn't lose my mom in the same way you lost your dad, but she did abandon us. Or at least, that's how it felt." She peeks over at me, like she's surprised I'm still listening intently. "In eighth grade, when my parents got divorced, she took off with her new husband and family to Phoenix. Jillian and I hardly see her now. And I don't understand how she could do that, how she could pick up and leave like we meant nothing to her."

I knew Tessa lived with her dad, but I didn't know any of this. She holds her cards close.

Tessa finds an interesting pattern to trace along the wooden floor. "I have kind of an embarrassing confession." She doesn't look at me, and my stomach tightens. "All last week I was sure you were going to brave the fog and ditch me. If my own mom didn't think I was worth sticking around for, why would Reed Walker be any different?" I'm shocked she'd confess so much to me.

I lean down until our eyes connect. "Honestly, I was worried you'd leave *me*. I know we haven't always gotten along, but I'd rather not be here by myself. I was bored out of my mind, too."

"For real, the boredom was overwhelming." Her fingers begin tracing the woodgrain pattern again. "Maybe I'm not being fair to my mom, because the thing is, in recent years, she's wanted us to visit more, but . . . I've resisted. My dad gets lonely. I couldn't bear the thought of leaving him behind. Still can't." Her voice cracks at the memory.

"That's why you decided not to travel far for college." I smack my hand to my head.

"One of the reasons. Probably the main reason, but the other was financial."

"Sorry for being an asshole about all that," I say with a grimace. She'd have every reason to hold that against me. But I hope she won't.

"It's okay. I know my dad didn't want me to make sacrifices.

But I worry. Especially now. Who's going to look after him? Who's going to remind him to take his blood pressure medicine, or make sure he eats something besides ramen? He needs me." Now it's her turn to wipe her tears away. "Sorry. I didn't realize this was going to hit me so hard."

"Hey," I say quietly. "We've both been through a lot, but who's to say *this* has to be a miserable experience?" I'm suddenly reminded of sitting beside her in Principal Evans's office. Was that just last week? My dare feels like a lifetime ago. *We're pretty fun. Why don't you come find out?* I did promise her a good time, after all. "What am I known for?" I slide down until I'm sprawled out in a fake model pose, like I'm basking in the sun, head propped on my hand.

"Is this a trick question?"

"Nope."

"Uh . . . you're a cocky, obnoxious know-it-all who takes up too much space." She waves at me spread across the floor.

"True." I nod. "But I'm also fun." I kick off my Converse, standing in my socks. "Do you know what we need?"

"To get a life . . . ?"

"Ha-ha." I offer Tessa my hand. "Come on. Get up."

"What are you doing?" As she places her palm in mine, my fingers twitch at the current crackling up my arm.

"Isn't it obvious? We're skating."

After she stands, I take off at a run across the floor, gliding the final distance in my socks to the other side, arms windmilling for balance. "Uh, this is amazing. What are you waiting for?"

After a moment, Tessa sprints toward me, attempting some kind of ambitious pirouette in her socks, but loses her balance and smacks straight into my chest. She lands with a thump on her butt while I hit the mirrored wall, the wind knocked out of me. Which is probably a sensation my body only thinks I should be having.

"Pretend that was graceful," she chokes. "I didn't mention it before, but sock skating is actually a full-contact sport."

"I always suspected you lived on the edge, Sinclair." I offer her a hand up again. "So, how does this work? Should we just skate around?"

"Well, we could. But I have a better idea." She scans the room. "That crap phone can't do much, but it looks indestructible. It can be our hockey puck."

I glance at it skeptically, lying against the baseboard on the other side of the room. "Are you sure? We might break it."

"Nah. Kick it gently if it makes you feel better and get behind this totally responsible choice." She races over to grab the phone and her shoes. "My boots can mark my goal against this wall; your shoes can mark yours. Whoever scores ten points first wins."

"What's the prize?"

"I'd say eternal respect, but since we're dealing in eternity, how about gloating rights for the night?"

I look at her appraisingly. "Gloating rights for the week and winner gets to ask any question they want, and the loser has to tell the truth."

"Sure. Since I'm going to win, I'll take those odds." She winks at me, and my heart stutters.

"So cocky." I tsk.

"Me?"

"Yes, you. It looks good on you, though." I turn to grab my Converse, feeling strangely elated by her shocked expression.

After my goal's set up against the opposite wall, I join Tessa in the middle of the room. She places the phone between us.

"Rules?" I ask.

"There are no rules in high-contact sockey. Just win. Win at all costs."

"So basically . . . school?"

Tessa's mouth falls open. "That's how you think about *school*?"

"Isn't that the game we've been playing for the past four years?"

"You mean a game everyone's playing, or just us?" she asks, but I take this moment to make my move and kick the phone between her legs. It careens across the floor.

I race to the other end of the ballroom, thrilled to have the goal in my sight. Tessa chases after me, but I've got too much of a lead. Then out of nowhere she slides on her dress the final distance and blocks my shot.

"Damn, girl. I see how this is going to go."

"Catching up to the fact that you're going to lose, are you?" Still on the ground, she swings her leg forward, sending the phone flying to the other end of the ballroom. God, I hope we don't break that thing.

When I pivot after it, she grabs my foot, crashing me to the floor.

"You are ruthless." I should have known Tessa wouldn't go down without a fight. I wriggle out of her grasp.

"I like to win," she says. And it's true. While I'm down, she launches herself in her socks as fast as she can toward the other wall. She thinks she has this in the bag, but I race behind her and wrap my arms around her waist, lifting her off the ground.

"I like to win, too," I taunt.

"Put me down!" Her legs flail, but I hold on tighter.

"You said no rules!" I laugh, carrying her back to the other side. Her breath is hot against my cheek as I score my first goal. "I think I'll play the whole game like this."

"Or . . . how about like *this*?" She wraps her hands over my eyes so I can't see.

I stumble forward but catch myself, keeping us both upright. "Careful. You're going to kill us."

There's a moment when my words sink in, then we both burst out laughing. I set her down on the floor, my shoulders shaking. Maybe there's some truth to the idea that the worse things are the more you need a good laugh. Every time I'm about to regain my composure, I glance over at Tessa, and something sets us off again.

"I cannot look at you right now." Her body's wracked by gasping breaths.

"Oh my God, make it stop." I double over, my eyes watering.

"It's not even that funny," she says.

"I know." I clutch my side. "It's awful. We fucking died."

We lose it again. I haven't laughed this hard in a very long time. Tears are streaming down my cheeks. I can hardly stand up.

Little by little, breath by breath, we slowly recover. Moonlight pools across the dance floor from the wall of windows facing the grounds. We steady and settle, staring at each other as we're washed in the soft champagne glow.

That's when it starts. The scratching noise.

It begins slowly. *Skritch, scratch.* Like a branch rubbing against the siding of the house. But when the front door handle begins to rattle, I know we're not alone. My eyes dart back to Tessa's. She's frozen in place, body tense, listening.

"It's the smoke people trying to get in, isn't it? They want another go at me." Tessa starts scanning the ballroom for somewhere to hide, but there's no cover. "I assumed we were safe inside." Her voice comes out as a squeak, shaky breath mixed with adrenaline.

The scratching sound increases, accompanied by giggles. "I don't think that's the smoke creatures." My eyes narrow. "I think—"

The front door bursts open and what sounds like a group of people tumbles inside. We tiptoe out of the ballroom, edging down the long hallway, then come to a shocked standstill.

"It's our friends," I whisper, surprised.

Brandon and Kira are there holding hands. Tilly's using her cell flashlight to chart a route farther into the house. Santiago's behind her, carrying two six-packs of beer, along with some junior, Kevin something or other, looking unsure how he ended up with a bunch of recent graduates. But it's when Jenny Chu and Yannick Krause cross the threshold, arms loaded with candles, that I know we're in trouble.

Tessa and I exchange worried glances.

"Who's ready for the séance?" Jenny croons.

CHAPTER 11

Tessa

"A séance? You said it was a candlelit vigil." Brandon's voice is edged with betrayal.

"Same thing." Jenny scopes out the entranceway for a place to dump her armful of candles.

"They are not the same and you know it." Tilly rounds on Jenny, hands on her hips. Everyone's plunged momentarily into darkness without her cell flashlight to guide the way.

"Jesus, Tilly, keep that thing pointed up." Kira riffles through her bag for her phone, turning its flashlight on. "It's creepy enough in here."

"Sorry." Tilly flashes her light down the hall toward the ballroom. It sweeps past Reed and me.

I wince from the glare. No one notices.

"Which room are we headed to?" Tilly shivers.

"This is so cool. Does anyone know where they died?" Kevin doesn't need to sound so giddy about it. He's certainly more excited than he was at student government meetings.

"What a morbid fucker," Reed grumbles under his breath. "Who even is that guy?"

"Kevin Abrams. My vice president. He was always a bit of a weird guy," I acknowledge. "He wanted the junior prom theme to be Creepy Clowns."

"Of course he did." Reed shakes his head. The others begin stumbling through the ground-floor rooms, floorboards creaking as they pass. Reed and I follow.

"I heard they died upstairs," Kevin continues. "In a bedroom."

"A bedroom?" Jenny looks like she's won the gossip lottery.

"Ver zey hooking up?" Yannick drops his candles onto a piano in one of the sitting rooms, draped with a white cloth.

"Oh my God." Jenny sets her candles beside his. "Were they secretly dating?"

Heat rises in my cheeks.

"Remember how close they seemed at the party, Yannick? Didn't he have his hand around her waist at one point?"

"What?" Tilly chokes out.

"Zey ver all over each ozer." Yannick seems pleased to have some tea to spill.

Reed's eyes are on me, but I don't dare look at him. "What is he talking about? Yannick was so focused on the game, he barely noticed us."

"Excuse me, but I think I'd have known if my girlfriend was secretly dating someone," Brandon snaps.

"Would you, dingus?" Jenny crosses her arms. "Because then it wouldn't have been a secret."

"He wasn't," Santiago states matter-of-factly.

"How would you know?" Jenny spins to face him.

"Because he was my best friend, and we talked."

Reed shifts his weight uncomfortably beside me. Maybe he's nervous Santiago is going to say more, but instead he hands out his beers. "This room seems as good as any."

Tilly declines a drink, but everyone else takes one and settles in. "Well, Tessa was *my* best friend, and I can tell you that the only reason she stayed at the party was because you embarrassed her so much." She glares at Brandon, pushing the sleeves up on a new oversized hoodie she probably wishes she could hide inside.

At least Brandon looks guilty. "I feel awful about how that went down."

Kira squeezes his hand.

"Yeah, looks like he's been real consumed with guilt," Reed fumes.

I can't tell if he's annoyed with Brandon or jealous of his being here with Kira. He said she wasn't his girlfriend before. Not that I care. Because I don't. He can like whoever he wants.

Yannick pulls a couple blankets out of his backpack and sets them down in the middle of the room. "Und now ve haf somever to zit for zee zéance."

As people gather around the blankets, Santiago leans over to Tilly, scratching his arm. "So it's officially over with you and that ass from the party?"

Smooth, Santiago. Why not just ask her if she's single?

"Who, Carl?" Tilly rolls her eyes. "Oh yeah. God, what a mistake."

Santiago gives one of those noncommittal guy nods, but he seems happy about it. When Tilly notices him mindlessly scratching again, he admits, "Poison ivy. From the night of the party."

Reed tsks. "You warned him. He never listens. I bet the entire swim team is out of commission."

"I've never done this before. How does it work?" Kira plops down on a blanket, pulling Brandon beside her. He rests his hand on her thigh.

Now it's my turn to be annoyed. "He doesn't have to flaunt it," I whisper to Reed. "I mean, I just died."

"He doesn't know you're watching," he replies.

Jenny places the candles in a circle, and everyone takes their seats around them. She's making a real production out of lighting them, enjoying being the center of attention. Finally, she sits and closes her eyes. "Tonight, we are here to contact the spirits of Tessa Sinclair and Reed Walker. If you're out there, Tessa and Reed, we invite you to join our circle when you're ready."

Reed snorts beside me.

Jenny opens her eyes and instructs the room, "Think about something you might want to ask them."

"Oh look, did that candle flicker? I think that candle just flickered." Kevin rocks back and forth, giddy with anticipation.

"I'm getting goose bumps." Kira pushes her sleeves up, showing her arms off to everyone. "Look."

Tilly sniffles and wipes her eyes. "I guess I'd want to know if she's okay. I'd want her to know that I think of her all the time. That I don't know how I'm supposed to continue without her. We had so many plans together." She stifles a sob.

Brandon leans over to give her a hug. "I know." He looks close to tears himself. My heart aches for them both, even if he hurt me. I miss them.

"We were supposed to go to Nepal together after we graduated from college. We've been planning the trip for years. You have no idea how many mood boards we created." Tilly hands her phone around with our Pinterest board "Go Get Lost" open for everyone to scroll through. I catch glimpses of snow-capped peaks, swinging rope bridges, and colorful prayer flags as the phone passes by. "We mapped out our whole itinerary. How we'd fly into Kathmandu, stay in hostels, and trek through the Himalayas. Tessa said we'd train and then try to summit one of the smaller peaks with hired guides. We'd stand on the summit and yell in celebration, reminding ourselves that there's no mountain, no goal too high for us to achieve in life. Except . . . that wasn't true, was it?"

Brandon pats her on the back. "Do your plans anyway."

"Yeah, go anyway," Kira encourages. "Go for her. She'd want you to."

"I would," I whisper, hoping Tilly knows I want her to do all the things we'd dreamt about. I want her to have the best life possible.

"I don't know about a question, but Reed, if you're out there and listening, this is for you." Santiago raises his beer, then pulls out his phone to play a song. It's not what I was expecting at all. It's a guitar solo. But not rock. It sounds classical. There's strumming cut through with intricate fingerpicking. It's beautiful and haunting.

"Vat is zat?" asks Yannick.

"It's Antonio Rey—he's one of the best flamenco guitarists out there. Reed was working on this song." Santiago's still holding his phone aloft, letting the music transform the space, chase the cobwebs into the night. Reed wanders around the outside of the circle to stand behind him, eyes closing for a moment as he listens.

I stare, stunned. That's why he was carting that case around all the time? To practice flamenco music?

"I remember he said how hard it was to do that section in the middle because of all the dexterity required," Kira says in awe. "He was really good, though."

Reed's eyes pop open at that. They quickly land on me across the circle.

I'm not quite sure what to say. I feel like we've both been laid a bit bare tonight. He knows about my travel dreams, something I never talked about with anyone but Tilly, considering how little money my family had. Somehow it seemed silly to imagine glamorous trips overseas when we were always wondering if we could afford to keep the lights on. And Reed certainly had plenty of opportunities over the years to let people know about his music, but beyond his best friends, he seems to have kept that a secret, too.

"So, not a rock god," I say.

"No, not exactly." It's hard to see by the candlelight, but I detect a faint blush blooming across his cheekbones.

"You play classical guitar, then?"

"Well, not to nerd out on you, but classical and flamenco guitars are different instruments. My dad was incredible with both, but I've been learning flamenco guitar. I guess it was just another way to . . ." He trails off.

"Get to know him," I finish, taking a step toward him, past the candles, into the circle.

"Right." He steps forward, too, joining me.

For a moment, the room melts away and it's just us. Maybe it's because we've been through this intense experience together, but I feel seen by him in a way that I'm not sure anyone has ever seen me before. Like he understands how wonderful and painful it is to be surrounded by our friends. He understands what it's like to have our hearts' innermost desires snatched away. He understands the dueling impulses to want to hug everyone here but also scream at them to leave because it's too hard to face their grief and curiosity over our deaths.

"This isn't working," Jenny huffs. "You need to put the phones away. The spirt world doesn't like electronics." I've no idea where she got that rule, but everyone begrudgingly tucks their devices away. "Now join hands." She's bossy but effective; one by one, people grasp hands around the circle. "Again, we call to you, oh spirits. If you're with us, please join our circle now."

"This is so ridiculous," Reed scoffs.

"Is it, though?" I ask, realizing we've somehow managed to find ourselves in the middle of the circle. I wave my hands to indicate we're exactly where they want us to be.

"They're here," Jenny whispers.

"Of course we'd come. We're bored. They didn't call us here." Reed lets out an exasperated breath.

"Oh my God, the goose bumps are back." Kira giggles.

"Give us all the gory details on how you died," says Kevin.

"What is with that guy?" Reed shakes his head.

"He's being super cringe," I confirm.

"It has to be a yes or no question," Jenny scolds.

"Did you die upstairs?" Kevin tries again.

"Ich krieg gleich die Panik. Ze candles flickered twice." Yannick can barely control his excitement.

"That's a yes, right?" Kevin's legs bounce a mile a minute.

"I don't want to do this anymore." Brandon drops Kira and Tilly's hands, breaking the circle.

"Why?" asks Kira.

"I didn't come here to talk about their deaths. I hear about it enough at home."

My arm naturally reaches to comfort him, then I remember I can't. Old habits. Reed bristles beside me.

"What does that mean?" asks Jenny.

"Nothing. Never mind." Brandon stands, stepping out of the pool of light.

"You know something." Jenny leans forward.

"No, not really." Brandon shrugs.

"Oh, you definitely know something." Now she's standing, too. "You're acting super shady right now. Did you see something that night?"

Reed and I lock eyes.

"What? No, nothing like that. I just have an aunt who works

in the county coroner's office. So I've heard a little about the investigation, but I'm not allowed to say anything."

"You can't drop a bomb like that and walk away," Kevin demands.

"What the hell? What are you saying?" asks Santiago.

Reed snaps his fingers, pointing at Brandon. "He's hiding something. You should do that trick where you walk through him and find out."

I felt awful doing that before. I was completely adrift, like I'd lost all sense of who I was. "I wouldn't wish that experience on anyone. Besides, you heard Brandon, he doesn't know anything. No one's telling him top-secret information."

"Are you sure about that? His aunt's been investigating our deaths." Reed's voice has jumped octaves, but I'm the only one who can hear it. Lucky me.

Kira and Tilly stand to check on Brandon, while the others whisper among themselves.

"I know him better than anyone, Reed. He's clearly uncomfortable and wants an excuse to end the séance. That's all."

"I'll do it if you won't." He begins to cross the room, but I grab his arm.

"No. It was a horrifying experience. You saw how shaken that cop was, too. I don't want that to happen to either of you. You're going to cause a lot of harm for no good reason."

"No good reason? If there was ever a good reason, Tessa, this is it." He pulls out of my grasp.

"What is it with you and Brandon?" I snap.

That stops him.

"You've always had it out for him. What did he ever do to

you?" A rush of memories come back to me from years past. It wasn't just me. Reed's had a million little digs for Brandon, too, usually said in my presence, to get under my skin.

"This isn't about . . ." Reed lets out a frustrated groan. "I mean . . . he's not the guy you should have been with, but I don't have anything *against* him."

"What does that mean?"

He bites his bottom lip, like he's trying to hold back an avalanche of secrets.

"Why do you care?" I press, stepping closer, my pulse quickening.

He leans forward, his face inches from mine. Candlelight dances in his eyes. "Why do you think?"

I hold my breath and my ground.

What's he implying? That it should have been *him*? Then why push at my every last nerve if all this time he's wanted to . . . to what . . . ?

My eyes narrow, daring him to tell me the truth.

In return, he arches a single brow, daring me back. *Admit it,* his eyes challenge. *Admit you have feelings, too.*

Neither of us budges.

When he inches forward—so close now—I don't know where to look. His dark eyes? His full lips? Panic. Panic. For a wild moment I'm sure he's about to kiss me, but instead he seethes, "Are you going to walk through him, or should I?"

"Don't," I plead.

But it's too late. He turns and charges toward Brandon. Before I can hold him back, he's taken the plunge. Is this how it looked when Reed witnessed me with that cop before? His body, once solid, takes on the shimmering quality of a desert mirage. There's a moment almost too vast for my mind to behold as Reed and Brandon overlap, occupying the same space, across two separate dimensions. The candles flare up. A window shutter flies back, smacking the siding of the house. Everyone jumps. Then Brandon drops to the floor, retching and shaking.

Kira screams as she and Tilly dive down to help him. Everyone else is up on their feet. It's chaos with them all talking at once, but my eyes are on Reed.

He's balled up in the corner, teeth chattering, shivering uncontrollably. I kneel beside him.

"What's happening?" Tilly whispers behind me, her voice tinged with fear.

"You've spooked our guests," I scold.

Reed shakes his head back and forth, face pained, eyes closed tight.

"What happened? What did you learn?" I lean forward, my unease mounting.

The shutters bang explosively against the siding again, like a thunderclap, startling all of us, before a draft blows the candles out. The room is plunged into darkness.

"Holy fuck." Kevin trips over his feet, crashing into Santiago. "Let's get out of here."

Tilly and Kira hoist Brandon up as Jenny grabs Yannick's hand. They head for the door, stumbling over one another.

Once again, we're left behind, with only moonlight and dust for company.

And questions.

So many questions.

"It wasn't . . . alcohol poisoning." Reed's panting and shivering, barely able to get the words out.

"What?"

"It's being investigated"—he takes another gulp of air—"as homicide."

"How is that possible?"

Reed raises his haunted eyes to mine. "Tessa, someone killed us."

CHAPTER 12

Tessa

Once Reed recovers from the deep chills wracking his body, he's up on his feet, stalking between the broken piano and the windows, like a tiger trapped in a too-small cage.

"Tell me again," I say. "What exactly did you see when you walked through Brandon?"

"I don't know if I'd say I *saw* it. It's more like . . . I knew his thoughts. I was consumed with his memories." He shivers. "You were in there, too."

My eyes snag on his.

He's not the guy you should have been with.

I can't believe in the midst of all of this, I keep thinking of that moment—his almost-confession. "But our deaths . . ." I prompt, getting us back on track.

"Brandon overheard his aunt talking to his mom about the case. She mentioned how the department was investigating our deaths as homicides after the coroner's report came out. Brandon's mom gasped and knocked her coffee on the rug, but they shut up when Brandon walked in. That's all he knows."

"It doesn't make sense. Why would someone kill us?" My mind spins out, trying to remember the night of the party.

"I know. Who could possibly want us dead?"

"Jenny Chu," I offer.

He bursts out laughing.

"Think about it," I continue. "She's third in line for valedictorian. She clears a path and the title's hers."

"You seriously think Jenny Chu killed us over grades? Jenny, who passed out in biology on frog-dissection day? Who faints at blood tests? You think she has the stomach for murder? Besides, she already got into Stanford. She didn't need valedictorian."

"You saw her threaten me at the party over that scholarship!" I cross my arms. "Though it doesn't exactly make sense. Her family has tons of money."

He pauses his pacing. "They *had* money. Didn't you hear about all the trouble her dad got into for tax evasion?" When I shake my head, he continues, "Apparently, he'd been doing it for years and owed so much in back taxes the government was coming after him hard. Like, we're talking 'losing their house' kind of hard."

"Then he clearly wasn't paying Jenny's tuition. She needed that scholarship as much as me, and she seemed pissed I might still get it after apologizing to Ms. Fieldman."

"So . . . let me get this straight. Your *theory* is that because you were gonna butter up some old lady, that freaked Jenny out *so much* she killed you the night of the party?"

I smack my hands together. "*Exactly*. She had a clear motive. Or maybe, I don't know, she had Yannick do it if she was squeamish."

"She needed money, that's true. But Jenny didn't kill us or set Yannick on us. It's absurd."

"Remember when Mr. Kepler's car was covered in paint?"

"Yeah . . ." His eyes narrow.

"Well, Tilly saw Jenny do that in the parking lot during the spirit assembly. And all because he'd refused to accept her late paper, bringing her whole grade point average down—which, by the way, is what put her out of the running for valedictorian with us. I'm telling you; she's unhinged. Plus, we have history."

"Wasn't that back in middle school?" He taps his foot, waiting for me to explain.

"Yes, but it was a huge fight. I begged Jenny to stay and work things out with Tilly and me, but she bailed."

"I don't know. Sometimes I'd catch her watching you in class, and she seemed . . . sad."

"Or, and hear me out here, she was staring at me and *plotting my murder*."

"Okay, Sherlock, but your theory doesn't account for why *I'm* also dead." He shakes his head. "Jenny's off the list of suspects."

"No one's off the list." I gesture wildly.

"Fine."

"Besides"—I round on him—"who else could it be?"

"Fuck if I know. Maybe Brandon did it because he was so pissed you stayed with me."

I roll my eyes. "Nope. Next. Besides, he left the party. It would have to be a person there at the end of the night."

Reed resumes his pacing. "After we started drinking, it's all a blur."

"There were lots of people there we didn't know as it got later. What about those guys who told you to watch yourself? That was sketchy. What was that about?"

He sighs, sinking to the floor. "I mean . . . it seems extreme."

"Let's start with how you know them."

"I don't. Not really. They were angry at my stepdad. He's what's called a corporate raider." He looks at me uncertainly. "I won't bore you with the bullshit details, but, basically, he and his friends line up financial backers, buy struggling companies or factories on the cheap, and then break them apart and sell them off for parts. They sell the equipment, sell the premises, that kind of thing. Essentially, they kill a company to make a buck and screw whoever gets hurt in the process. He bought and then destroyed the power plant, the one making turbines."

"My dad's factory?"

He nods slowly, biting his lip. "Yep. The same one those guys at the party worked at."

"So . . . your family is responsible for my family's situation."

He closes one eye and peeks at me through another. "My stepdad. Yeah."

"And you *knew*?"

His shoulders slump. "I mean . . . I did know. I felt shitty about it, believe me. But what could I do?"

Bile rises in the back of my throat, a burning humiliation. It's bad enough my dad lost his job, but to know that Reed's family was responsible? Or that Reed was taking pity on me? All while he lived in his fancy house on the hill, drove his electric car, didn't have a care in the world about applying to Harvard, or whether the light or heat could stay on. It's embarrassing.

"I'm so sorry, Tessa." He stands to face me.

I wipe away the hot tears that spring to my eyes, feeling guilty for ever being ashamed of my father or how we struggled. There's no shame in hardship. *Challenge builds character*, Dad would say. *Don't wish for an easy life. Wish for a full one.* But I don't know—the only thing I ever seemed to wish for was a successful one. A life where I didn't have to worry about money or being in his situation. I never wanted to be that out of control. I had countless plans to see me through. Get the grades. Run the school. Run the company. I would ace life one way or another.

Only, look at me now.

I can tell I'm spiraling, about to become a ball of mush unable to handle the challenges in front of me.

Like how someone hated me so much they snuffed me out at a graduation party, and I have no idea who.

I need to regroup. "Okay, that's a solid lead," I manage. "Those guys at the party are weirdly connected to us both. Maybe they didn't like my dad, either."

Reed watches me closely, like he's surprised we're not getting into it over what his stepdad did to my family. But he follows my lead and diverts back to discussing our murders. "Since we were together, maybe they had no choice but to off us both?"

I wander over to the window, staring at the dark grounds. Is that what happened? Did those guys kill us because they didn't like our fathers? It's hard to imagine my dad making enemies, though I do remember him coming home from some union meetings where he said things got heated. People get on edge when their livelihood is threatened.

The wind picks up, ice-cold gusts slipping through the seams. Reed joins me as we listen to it rattle the house. Raindrops ping off the roof overhead, drip down the dusty windowpanes. "We should go to the police precinct and try to overhear more of the investigation." Reed shifts his weight beside me. "We could walk through more people, though I've got to tell you, that is no fun."

"What about the smoke creatures?" It's hard to see much outside, but the fog has receded. It doesn't seem like they're there.

He leans his back against the glass. "Do you remember what that old man said?"

"It was like . . . dust to dust, you are not wanted here . . . or we don't want you here . . . or something like that."

"Okay, so we know the magic words." He shrugs a shoulder.

"Maybe they're only magic words for him."

"Well, it's either walk into town and see what we can figure out or be trapped here forever without answers."

I shiver, squinting into the darkness. "I haven't seen or heard them again. Maybe it's all right to leave. We can take off in the morning." What I don't say is that I'm far too creeped out to run into any smoke people at night.

"Okay." He stretches before meeting my eyes for a moment.

He's not the guy you should have been with.

I wonder if he's about to say more, address the tension between us before he charged through Brandon, or my pain over the news that his stepdad put my father out of a job. But instead, he mumbles "Good night," before heading out.

"Um . . . Reed?" I ask, pulling him up short.

He pauses in the doorway. "Yeah?"

"I need some quiet to think, but I also don't want to be alone. Can I stay down here tonight? Like, on the couch or something?"

He nods. "Of course."

I lie down on the threadbare sofa, fully expecting him to wander into another room on the first floor. But he lingers. "I'll just . . . uh . . . chill on the blankets Yannick left."

We settle in as the wind buffets the house, whistling through the window cracks. Though neither of us can sleep, it's nice to rest. I close my eyes, letting my mind wander. These last few days have been a lot to absorb. I've barely had time to process.

After a while I peek at Reed out of the corner of my eye. His hands are tucked behind his head, while he gazes at the ceiling, lost to the spell of his thoughts. Starlight sets his olive complexion aglow. I never really let my gaze linger on him before. But I look now, taking in the long lines of his body, how his slick black hair fans out across the blanket behind him.

How did I miss how drop-dead gorgeous he was until I dropped dead? Was he always this hot? Or maybe people get more attractive as you know them?

I'm so used to him tucking his hair behind his ears, it's nice to catch him in a moment when he's not all buttoned up. This isn't the carefully constructed persona he puts out to the world. It's not the Reed who wins BattleBot competitions, gloats in the back of calculus after solving some tricky integral, or finds ways to drop his Harvard acceptance into every conversation. This is just a boy. A boy who is lost, and maybe a little bit scared. Something warm twists and unfurls inside me the longer I drink him in. He didn't have to stay in this room, but he chose to anyway.

Admit it.

It's not his fault his stepfather's an ass.

Admit you have feelings, too.

After a moment Reed shifts his head toward me, as if the thoughts pinballing around in my brain are so loud he can hear them. I quickly close my eyes.

In the distance, an owl hoots softly. I can almost make out the frogs in the pond near the road, even as raindrops begin falling in earnest, the beginning of a building storm. And all of it to the soundtrack of his breath. Slowing down, shifting. Not asleep—we don't sleep. Just quiet, contemplative.

"Hey, Reed?" I whisper.

His sigh is more content than annoyed. "Yeah?"

"Thanks for staying."

I don't know if I mean in the room tonight, or in this house. There's so little I know for certain.

Except . . . I'm pretty sure I have a ghost-crush on my nemesis.

Shit.

CHAPTER 13

Reed

The next morning, Tessa and I stand side by side, the imposing concrete-and-brick entrance to the police department stretched out before us. The building looks like a fortress: two stories, ringed by fencing, with dark glass automatic doors. They slide open for the occasional beat cop hauling in a cuffed suspect or lawyers from the DA's office toting briefcases and speaking animatedly about plea deals and trial dates.

"Are we sure we want to do this?" she asks. "Do we even want to know?"

I nod. "Yeah. We want to know." It's been eating away at me all night. Who stole my future from me? From *us*? I'm determined to find out.

"Okay. I guess we look for a homicide department or something."

As we reach the automatic doors, I pause, waiting for them to slide open, but of course we don't register. "Here goes nothing," I mumble as we step through the glass.

Inside, the space is just as utilitarian. There's a large wooden reception desk at the entrance with an officer standing behind a plexiglass window, scribbling on a form. Rather than check in, we drift through a locked door into the back offices of the precinct.

Being a ghost has its privileges. I'm finding I no longer need to take doors or walls at a run. I can either choose to smack up against something or imagine all the space between atoms and simply sift past another structure. It's a question of intent. Do I want to have form or not?

The downstairs offices are bustling. Some cops are typing up reports; others appear to be getting briefed in a back room.

"Now what?" Tessa asks me. As if I've ever been here before. As if I have a clue how any of this works.

"I guess we . . . wander around, see if we overhear something?" I turn to head past the desks in the closest aisle in the hopes of picking up on some conversations when a female officer yells behind me, "Hey, Anderson, what's this about you crying like a baby over that YouTube video with the hatching chicks?"

The room erupts in laughter. Anderson begins to respond from my right, "That's not what happ—" when suddenly, the female officer, holding up her phone with the video in question, plows straight through me.

Dammit, not again.

The room becomes ice cold. My brain slants sideways. I can't remember why I'm here, or even who I am. I'm consumed. My entire world is a jumble of memories. She's having a secret affair with her supervisor. There's a lump in her left breast she's having biopsied next week. She wants to save up to buy a house, but it always feels out of reach. Wait, or is that me? I can't always tell what's hers and what's mine. *Make it stop*, I think.

"Make it stop," I hear her whisper. And then it's over, she's past me, and I crumple to the floor as she sinks into a chair, shaking and shivering, on the verge of passing out. Several people rush over to help her, including her supervisor, his brows pulled tight in concern, probably hoping she keeps their secret.

Cool hands wind around my waist, attempting to lift me to my feet, with no luck.

"No, I need a minute." I shake my head, teeth chattering.

"We have to get you out of here. It's too crowded." Tessa begins tugging on my arm, indicating an empty corridor off to the side.

"Wait," I say breathlessly, as I scramble unsteadily to my feet. "It's upstairs. That's one helpful thing I saw. She's a detective. That's where we want to go."

Tessa edges me toward the stairs, her arm wrapped tightly around me, hugging me to her side. It's difficult to walk like this, but I don't care. I like it here beside her too much.

I know she thinks I'm a shitty person; she's said as much. But something feels different with Tessa now. Like we're finally on the same side. It's probably wrong to let my heart hope, but there have been some signs. At least, I don't think she hates me anymore. Like that time we both wound up in detention after she threw a book at my head for asking "too many rude questions" during her presentation on radioactive isotopes. Or the death glare she gave me when everyone laughed because I said her eighth-grade winter formal dress looked like an upside-down pineapple. Which, in all fairness, it did.

So I was a little idiot. We both were. Can't people get a second chance?

"I'm beginning to see why ghosts wander around at night. There are fewer people to run into." Tessa's eyebrows are crinkled in worry.

"And here I thought they liked moaning in the dark and dragging chains around for fun."

"Your snarky humor's back. That's a good sign."

"I'm okay. Honestly," I reassure her with a smile, pleased she finds me funny. "Thanks for the help."

Her hand slips, landing on my hip, and both our eyes track it. She quickly releases me. "Of course."

The awkwardness between us rushes back full force. Everything unsaid last night hangs heavy in the air. Is this what we both want? Or are we merely the only two people around, scared and searching for comfort? She fidgets with her fingerless gloves while I toe the floor with my sneaker, willing myself not to stare at the arms she had wrapped around me moments ago. They're good arms.

And shoulders.

And legs.

And . . . now I'm staring.

Stop being weird.

I drag my gaze away, landing on a bulletin board along the back wall. "Whoa. Are those our pictures?"

There are only a couple people here and there, hovered over

computers or on the phone. It's easy to navigate a route. There are several photos pinned to the board, ours and those of a few other people who must be under active investigation.

"Okay," Tessa says. "Let's spread out. Check out people's desks, peek over their shoulders at computers, see what you can discover."

We take off in separate directions to snoop. It would be far easier if we could pick things up, but we can only look at open files, active computer screens, overhear conversations within earshot. No one is discussing us, and as far as I can see, no one has conveniently left out evidence on their desk for us to peruse.

"Any luck?" I shout across the floor to Tessa, realizing there's no need to be quiet or sneaky. No one has any clue we're here.

"Nope. This guy is writing an email to his mom. And the lady behind him is on the phone about another case."

I head back to the bulletin board. I'd only really checked out the photos before, but there are a few reports tacked to one side. I take a closer look. They're from the coroner's office. "Tessa, I might have something here."

She rushes over.

"It's an autopsy report. This one's for you." I swallow.

The report is dense. It's hard to know what I'm reading at first. "A toxicological analysis and gas chromatograph, whatever that is, were performed and proved negative for cocaine, amphetamines, barbiturates, arsenic, and strychnine."

Tessa's voice is close, near my ear. "There were high blood alcohol levels detected, but they don't think that was the cause of death."

"So, what was it, then?"

"Oh God," she mumbles. "Look at the coroner's notes here. *The larger vessels of the brain were distended with dark-colored blood. The lungs were filled with air from an obstructed condition of the respiratory organs, appearing significantly darker in coloration than natural.*" She shivers. "Some stranger cut into my lungs. My brain."

"*Our* brains," I counter. "A shame, too. They were good brains. Well, mine was, anyway." I smirk at her.

"How can you joke around right now?"

"What else are we going to do? We can't change the situation. All we can do is try to understand it. Except, without finding our files or being able to turn the pages of this report, we could be out of luck."

"I don't know . . . maybe we can still understand it. The autopsy determined my pupils were *considerably dilated*, and down here it says tropane alkaloids were present. See, *Toxic levels of tropane alkaloids, atropine, hyoscine, and hyoscyamine detected.*"

"What is that?"

"Well, I did ace AP Chem. If I had to guess, I'd say it sounds like we were poisoned. Dilated pupils can be a sign of overdose but also of poisoning."

I cross my arms, quirking my head to the side. "Are you, like, a . . . forensics expert all of a sudden?"

"What? My dad watches a lot of *CSI.* Plus, these compounds are toxic at the level they detected in us."

"So, someone drugged us?"

"Well, not with a synthetic substance, no. These are organic compounds. I think we ingested something toxic."

"I didn't eat anything at the party—did you?"

"No. Which means . . ." Tessa points at me. "I was *right* about Jenny. It must have been in our drinks and she had the perfect opportunity with that game."

"Maybe . . . but not the motive." I rub my chin. "It's got to be someone else."

"As I recall, you also got us drinks."

"Right . . ." My eyes narrow. "But I didn't kill us, so what are you implying?"

"But didn't you grab cocktails other people made at one point?"

"I did. But they were making them for themselves, so I don't think they were poisoning them. Maybe somebody roofied us later when we weren't looking."

"Who wanders around with toxic compounds to slip into drinks? The factory guys?"

"Those guys are a bunch of tools. Maybe they'd deck you in a bar fight, but poison? None of it adds up." I knock my head a couple times against the bulletin board. Then I pull back with a start. Someone's scribbled something in black ink up the side margin of the second page. "There's something written on the next page." I step aside so she can peek. "There . . . in the margin."

"It looks like it says *homicide* with a question mark, but underneath it there's something else." She presses her face as far against the wall as it can go, but since we can't move the paper, we're stuck with only the scribbles that are visible. "I can't make out the full word, but it looks like it also ends with *i-c-i-d-e* followed by another question mark."

"Homicide homicide?"

Tessa rolls her eyes. "I don't think they'd write homicide twice."

"Why not? It was a double homicide." I chuckle to myself. "What, too soon?"

She give me her best "I'm not amused" face.

"All right. Focusing." I lean against one of the cubicle desks.

"Pesticide?" she offers. "Did we somehow ingest poison that way?"

"No, that doesn't make any—" I pop up. "Shit. What about suicide?"

Our eyes meet.

"That could be it," she says slowly. "And if they're unsure whether this was a homicide or a suicide, that means they might eventually throw out the case and then whoever did this gets away with it."

"Okay. So, we don't give up. We keep digging. Figure out who it was." I turn back to the report, but it's suddenly harder to read. The bulletin board is limned in shadow. "Did it suddenly get dark in here?"

"Someone must have turned the lights off." She glances around, but everyone's still at their desks behaving normally. There are a couple cops chatting by a water cooler, another on her phone. No one is acting like anything is odd.

A chill prickles up the back of my neck. Or is that the temperature dropping?

"Look at the windows." Tessa nudges my shoulder.

The fog is back. It's billowing against the glass, slowly engulfing the building, a rising tide. Frozen crystals spread along the panes, icy fingers come to claim us at last. My breath catches.

"It's them, right? They're here." My normally deep voice comes out as nervous breath.

A chorus of whispers winds its way up to our floor, full of desperation and unquenchable need.

Tessa's eyes dart around wildly. "They followed us."

CHAPTER 14

Reed

"Come on." Tessa nods her head for me to follow. We edge along the back aisle of cubicles toward the second-floor windows with their sweeping view of the street below. Whatever we do next, we need to see what we're up against.

"I don't think they can see the mist." I wave my hand at the police.

The world is covered in a twilight glow, with the fog so thick it's blotting out the sun. There's a lot of commotion out on the street. While we were inside there was an accident; a minivan hit a cyclist. The driver is sobbing to several police officers who've run out of the precinct, while the bike, a bent cage, is still buckled under the front wheel. The injured cyclist, strapped to a long board with their neck in a brace, is being transferred onto a gurney by two EMTs. A small crowd of shocked onlookers has gathered on the corner.

But I'm not watching them, not really. Scenting death on the wind, the smoke people have come. My mouth drops open, knuckles white from grabbing the ledge in front of me. This sounded so theoretical before. It's another thing entirely to witness bodies, legs, clawed hands forming out of the ether. There must be at least thirty of them coalescing from the fog, moving toward the ambulance as the gurney is loaded inside.

They whisper a lament, a keening, haunting sound as they glide toward the cyclist. Yearning. Rasping. Begging. It's a cacophony of longing. Like nails on a chalkboard, it makes the hair rise on the back of my arms.

They didn't come for us after all.

Just in case, I don't dare make a sudden movement. No need to alert them we're here. "That's the creepiest thing I've ever seen."

Tessa's shiver runs from her shoulders to her toes. "Now you get it."

While an EMT initiates chest compressions, the smoke people rush the ambulance. They pour in through the still-open back door, arms outstretched, breath rattling, pressing against one another in a desperate attempt to force their way inside. An army of grasping hands reach for the dying cyclist in a panic, as if they want nothing more than to pull him under with them.

"Why would they charge him like that?" I feel lightheaded, like I'm going to be sick. I still haven't fully recovered from walking through that cop.

"I remember how it felt before when that creature grabbed

me, like it was draining me of something essential, of whatever life still clung to me here, to make itself strong." Even with the color drained from her face, Tessa's hands are fisted at her side, determined. "We have to do something." She turns to bolt down the stairs, so focused on trying to help that she doesn't notice the sun slowly reemerging from behind the clouds.

"Wait." I grab her hand, nodding at the brightening sky. The smoke people pause what they're doing, whipping their heads behind them. "I guess they don't like sunlight?"

She punches my arm. "Reed, look!"

"Ow." I wince, shooting her an annoyed glance. "I know. They're stopping."

"No." Tessa takes my chin in her hand and tilts my face toward the other end of the street. "There."

Standing on the corner is an old man. His eyes are trained on the ambulance as he mumbles something under his breath, a brown bowler hat clutched in his hands.

"It's him. The man who helped me at the back gate. He's in the same tweed suit as before."

Finishing his commands, the man watches intently as the smoke people begin to vanish one by one into vapor.

I point to the street below. "Whatever he's saying is making them leave and the fog disappear." With the blue skies returning, it's almost as if they were never here.

Satisfied, the old man turns to leave as the ambulance pulls away.

"Hey!" Tessa jumps and waves her arms. "Wait!"

I stiffen beside her. It still might not be safe to call attention to ourselves.

But her movement catches the old man's eye. When he spots us at the window, he smiles and tips his hat.

In that moment I realize we're not alone. He's dead, too. And Tessa's right to make a connection. We're probably far safer knowing him than not.

"Hold on." Tessa gestures for him to pause, and he nods, understanding. She tugs on my hand, dragging me back downstairs, dodging cops along the way, until we can dissolve through the front entrance and make our way to the street corner.

A strange trilling hope rockets through me for the first time in days.

Maybe we can finally get some answers.

Crowds are still gathered in tight groups on the street as we skid to a stop in front of the old man. Though his shoulders are curved by the toll of time, he still carries himself with a kind of gravitas. Deep wrinkles thread the planes of his face, carving out a series of tributaries—a map of his life—each victory or defeat etched in place. White tufts of hair swoop behind his ears, while a pair of wire-rimmed spectacles rest on the end of his nose, now checkered with brown age spots. His eyes, however, are full of youth and crinkle warmly when we arrive.

For the first time, it occurs to me that I'll never grow old. I'll never have gray hair or a face that proudly shows I have lived a hard-won life. Tessa and I were robbed of that. It makes my blood boil thinking of the murderer who stole our futures from us.

"So, you kids are holing up in the old van der Born place. You know, I went to a party there years ago, in that grand ballroom," he says wistfully. "This was before the house got turned over to the historical society. Spectacular mansion back in the day. Shame they haven't done more to fix the old place up again."

"You don't seem that surprised to see us, which makes me think we aren't the only ghosts around." Could that mean my dad is still here?

"I run into a few of us ghosts from time to time. And then of course there's . . . *them*." He nods toward the ambulance, where the smoke people hovered moments before.

"What are they? What did they want with that cyclist?" Tessa asks.

With a small thrill I realize her fingers are still laced with mine. Maybe she's too distracted to notice. I, on the other hand, feel the entirety of my consciousness now drawn to that singular connection between us, her cool skin against mine. It takes everything I have to drag my mind back to the present moment.

"How do you send them away?" I continue peppering him with questions, afraid he'll vanish again, like at the mansion gate, and we'll never get our answers.

"Oh, that's easy. You say something to remind them they're dead. That'll send 'em scurrying. Happy to share all I know. In fact, my place is around the corner. Why don't you come back for a chat? I already feel myself hollowing out from being gone too long."

I'm not entirely sure what that means. Tessa and I exchange glances.

"Lead the way," she says.

The old man takes off down the sidewalk in the direction of the town center, cruising past the police precinct and toward a block of stately homes lining the historic district.

"Name's Hal, by the way," he calls back to us as we round the corner onto a quiet block with fresh-cut lawns, white picket fences, and bushes overflowing with pale blue hydrangeas.

"I'm Tessa, and this is Reed." She races to keep up; he's far spryer than his age suggests.

I'm about to ask more when Hal points to a beautiful two-story home up ahead. Like many of the buildings on this block it's constructed from bricks, complete with white trim, black shutters, and an imposing red door adorned with a golden knocker.

Before we enter, Hal turns to us. "My wife, Bessie, and I moved in with our daughter and grandkids a few years ago. The kids live here still, but I believe they're out at the park, so we should be able to make it upstairs without trouble."

Hal steps through the door and we follow, three flights up a narrow wooden stairway, to a small attic bedroom. The walls are covered in family portraits, some black and white with stoic relatives from long ago, others with Hal and his wife, in faded color, dressed as Santa and Mrs. Claus, surrounded by wiggling grandkids beside a Christmas tree. Hal plops down on the quilted bed and motions for us to make ourselves comfortable.

"Is Bessie still here?" I hope that's not too personal a question. I lean against the wall by the dresser while Tessa takes a seat on a large wooden chest across the room.

"I went first." Hal sighs, removing his hat and setting it

down on the bed beside him. "It's hard being the first to go. You see your partner in pain and feel so helpless. I waited for Bessie, sure she'd join me. I watched as her health deteriorated rapidly from the heartbreak. She ended up passing a couple months later, just as she arrived at the hospital. When the time finally came, she went quick, before I realized what was happening or could be by her side." He breaks down at the thought, burying his face in his hands. "It seems she moved on without me. Or, that is, I think she did."

"I'm so sorry," Tessa whispers.

"Yeah, that's awful." I eye Tessa warily over the top of Hal's head.

Laughter and squeals sound up from the street below, breaking us out of the sad moment. The front door opens and little feet patter inside, dashing through the halls. "So not everyone . . . *stays*, then?" Maybe my dad isn't here after all.

"No. Most don't stay." Hal recovers, wiping his fresh tears aside and smoothing out his jacket. "As far as I can tell, people remain because they can't quite tear themselves away from this plane yet. In my case, I couldn't leave without her. In yours . . ."

"We were murdered," Tessa says. It feels strange to hear it out loud, but there's no point in keeping quiet about it.

"Well, there you go." Hal's eyes are full of sympathy as he looks at us both anew. "When we ran into each other before, I was on my way to Bessie's grave. She's buried out near the van der Born place, a beautiful little cemetery up on the hill. I like to visit from time to time. I expect I'll be out your way again before I decide to move on."

"What do you mean, *move on*?" I try to make myself comfortable on a small stool by the window, but it's far too short to accommodate my legs, which bend at awkward angles.

Tessa tries to contain her smile, eyes darting away.

"You know, move on . . . go through the door." Hal waves his hand dismissively.

"What door?" I ask. "The attic door?"

"The attic door?" Hal softly chuckles. "No, the *door*. The biggie. The one bordered in light with the timer. The one that showed up right after you died."

Tessa shrugs at me.

"We don't have a door like that," I reply.

"Of course you have a door. Everyone gets a door. You got the phone, right, with the countdown clock?"

I pull our phone out of my pocket and flip it open. We haven't spent much time looking at it since our game in the ballroom. The numbers are still ticking backward to who knows what.

"Exactly." Hal snaps his fingers. "That's the one. That's how much time you have before your door disappears."

"What happens if your door disappears?" I ask.

"Trust me, you don't want to stay and find out." Hal must take pity when he catches our panicked expressions, because he sighs and continues, "You become one of them. Eventually. You waste away to nothingness. Those people who form out of the mist, they're just poor souls who stayed after their doors vanished. It's like the life force keeping us here, it's connected somehow to that door. That's why the longer you're away from the site of your death, the emptier and more drained you feel. You must be noticing it by now."

I raise an eyebrow at Tessa. It's true that the longer we've lingered here, the more exhausted I've become. I thought it was from processing so much new information.

"Yeah." Tessa nods, eyes locked on mine. "I do feel it. It's like the moment a roller coaster plummets, and your stomach's left behind." She turns to Hal. "Does this mean we need to get out of here?"

"Nah, you have time. When you start to lose your solid form, that's when you worry." He waves his finger at her.

"It does explain a lot about ghosts and why they don't wander far from the sites of their deaths. But what about people who die in a hospital, or the cyclist in the back of that ambulance earlier? Where would his door be?" I stretch my legs forward, trying to find a comfortable position.

"Well, not everyone stays, like I said. But your door is at the site where you died. So it'd be in the hospital for Bessie, if she had one, or in the case of that ambulance, it would be down on the street below. Occasionally, you do see them on the street."

"How do you know all this?" Tessa hops up to wander around Hal's attic bedroom, eyes flitting over the portraits on the walls, too antsy to sit.

"My mentor told me. Great man. Name of Jebediah Garfield. He was a preacher; he was called all his life to serve. Devoted his time here to that as well."

"Can we meet him?" Tessa pauses, leaning against the bedpost.

Hal takes a moment to reply, lost in his memories. "Sadly, no. Jeb wanted to stay, to help more people. So he chose to remain behind. I think he hoped that somehow his good deeds would save him, but I watched him fade away in spite of it all. *Fades*, I call 'em. That's why that creature grabbed you at your fence. She sensed how full of life you still were. She was desperate for a piece of it. Poor souls. They cling here, searching in vain for a taste of something they can barely even remember anymore."

As Tessa makes her second pass around the attic, she reaches for my hand when she wanders by my perch. My heart stutters out a staccato rhythm against my rib cage. Why is she choosing to hold my hand again now? Not that I'm complaining. I can use a little comfort. Her hand feels so good wrapped around mine. *I like this.* I run my thumb along the back of her knuckles to let her know. *I like this so much.* Then I realize it's not my hand she wants but the phone I'm clutching. I can feel my cheeks go pink. She tugs it loose from my fingers, before flipping it open. "1,903,038 . . . so, if that number's in seconds . . ." She takes a moment to run a calculation. "That's twenty-two days, thirty-seven minutes, and eighteen seconds remaining. Well, less seconds now."

Tessa's eyes rise to mine with a shared understanding of how brief that sounds. Twenty-two days until . . .

I break away from her gaze and whatever embarrassing exchange happened between us. Have I been reading her signals all wrong? Like her wanting to stay downstairs with me last night, or her hand brushing against mine as we walked to the precinct? Am I only seeing what I want to see? "How long did you get?" I ask Hal instead.

"Six months."

"How is that fair?" Tessa throws her arms in the air.

"Who says it's fair? When's the system ever been fair?" Hal shakes his head dismissively.

"Shouldn't *this* system be fair?" she counters, sitting beside him on the bed.

"Meh. Maybe it is." He shrugs. "Who knows why some people get the time they get? Jebediah got fourteen months. It depends. Besides, why should death make more sense than life? Good people die young." He waves his hands at us, exhibit A. "And terrible people live a long time. Life's a great mystery, with everything either fated or up to some divine luck of the lottery, so why should death be any different?"

"It seems wrong," she mumbles.

"Jeb suspected we're given the amount of time to accomplish whatever we need to accomplish here—or learn whatever we need to learn—before we can move on. But take it from me, don't let the fear of what comes next keep you here too long, no matter how much time you're afforded. I only have a few days left myself." He shudders at the thought and glances longingly toward the attic door as little voices can be heard thundering up and down the stairs below. "I'm cutting it close. Mind you, each time you walk through a person or do anything that breaks through the planes between the two worlds, you lose a full day off the clock. It's a deterrent, see? A slap on the wrist to keep you from revealing our world. We're not supposed to interfere with the living. That's what Jeb believed, anyway. He thought we'd only scratched the surface of what was possible to do as ghosts. So, you best be careful out there."

"Have we lost time?" Tessa asks, though I haven't been keeping track enough to know.

"We must have. We just weren't paying attention before."

"Well, it happens. People blow through you now and again.

So watch yourselves and keep an eye on your remaining time," Hal cautions us.

"Why don't you go, if you're cutting it so close?" I ask.

"Reed." Tessa shushes me. "You don't have to tell us, Hal."

Hal merely chuckles, a warm sound that reverberates through his chest. I bet he made a great father and grandfather. "I'm working up to it, but I don't know. I'm afraid to stay *and* afraid to leave. Without Jeb here, I've been lonely and a little lost." His expression darkens as he fiddles with his fingers on his lap. "I guess . . . I worry that Bessie's still here somewhere, and we have to find each other. I scoped out the hospital and found a number of doors, but never discovered if any belonged to her. She was suffering from dementia pretty badly at the end. I've no idea if that can follow a person here, but if so, she might be confused and unable to find her way back. She needs me. I've been searching for her all over town. I check the fades out, too, whenever I see them, in case . . ." He shivers. "In case she's become one of them."

I feel terrible for Hal, having to worry if his wife's lost or trapped or become one of those things in the mist. "You think she could still be here, then?" Though I'm looking at Hal, my mind is spiraling about what this all means for my father. Maybe he did stay, for a while anyway. But even if he did remain, surely he'd be gone by now, all these years later.

All hope of finding him leaches out of me. It isn't until this moment that I realize I've been holding on to the wish that he was out here—that it wasn't too late to be reunited—that somehow, I could still apologize for the tragic night that sealed his fate and mine.

But if he's gone, then who knows if I'll ever get the chance?

"Maybe she's here. Or maybe not. It could all be an excuse. I can't accept that she's gone and I'm not ready to go myself. I don't know how to move on without her." Hal pulls his glasses off and dabs his eyes.

"We're here now. If it helps to have someone stay with you when you go through," Tessa offers.

Hal puts his glasses back on and lets his warm gaze fall on her. "Thanks, kid. You're good souls, both of ya, and you don't deserve the fate you were dealt."

Tessa's eyes brim with tears. "Sorry. You just . . . remind me of my dad."

My heart breaks for her. I'm not the only one with family to miss.

"Now, now, don't worry about me." He pats her back gently. "I'll spend my last days enjoying the grandkids, reliving the happy memories we built together. Maybe I'll travel out your way to visit Bessie's grave again. Just work my way up to saying goodbye to it all."

I nod, and we all drift into a long silence. I hadn't considered that I'd need to say goodbye. I thought this was a forever state. Now, suddenly, I only have twenty-two days to learn who killed us. Twenty-two days to feel ready to leave my mom behind. Leave Santiago and Kira. And if I'm not careful, I could lose some of the already brief time I have. It doesn't feel right. How can I possibly accomplish anything in the amount of time I have remaining here?

Eventually I clear my throat and look at Tessa. "We should probably get going. But . . . uh . . . Hal . . . do you think we could see your door before we go? We haven't found one at our place, and maybe it would help to know what it looks like."

Hal lets out a booming laugh. "It's pretty hard to miss. But I'll show you on the way out. The kids are watching cartoons, so it's a good moment to make your escape." Sure enough, I can hear the theme song from *Paw Patrol* playing faintly below. "I bet my daughter's making dinner while they're glued to the screen. It's unlikely anyone will blow through you. Follow me."

We pass through the attic door one by one, making our way downstairs. Instead of heading to the front entrance, Hal walks us past the kitchen, where his daughter is humming as she chops veggies for dinner. He finally stops outside a closed door.

"It's the home office. I died inside from cardiac arrest." His eyes are distant, lost to the memory. "My daughter doesn't like to come down to this end of the house anymore." Hal sighs, then, resolved at last, steps through.

Tessa follows nervously, with me close behind.

There, unmistakably, on the other side of the room, outlined in light, is a large door with a golden knob. Above it, also etched in light, is a digital clock, the numbers ticking backward one by one. Tessa and I stare, mouths agape. This is not the sort of thing you can miss. This is huge. And glowing. Hal pulls out his own phone and flips it open it to reveal a countdown in perfect sync with the timer above the door.

"Why don't we have one?" Tessa worries. "Did we not die in the correct way?" The perfectionist in her afraid we're somehow doing it wrong. Like our grade is going to get docked.

"It's in there somewhere," Hal reassures us. "It's a big house."

“Whoa,” I gasp. “Look.” I hold up my hand, which has become translucent. “Uh . . . Hal . . . what’s happening here?”

“Don’t panic,” he says.

“Too late.” It’s creeping up my arm now. “You said we should worry when our solid form starts going.” I scan the room for somewhere to run, not knowing where or why, just that I need to do something.

“Hang on, son. It’s okay. I only meant that’s an early indication that it’s time to get back to your place for a recharge,” Hal advises. “You still have time.”

I can’t tear my eyes away from my fingers, which are coming in and out of focus.

“It’s a long walk back to the mansion. We need to get going.” Tessa tries to shake me out of this spell.

Shit. “Right.” I snap to attention.

“Slow down, you two. Let me leave you with one of the best things Jebediah ever taught me. You’re ghosts, remember? You don’t have to abide by the laws of physics in this realm. If you want to go somewhere, as long as you’ve seen it before and can call it up in your mind’s eye, you can vanish and reappear there. Just hold tight to the image of where you want to go. This little trick is going to get you out of a lot of tight pickles. Think of a destination, focus your energy on that image, and . . . poof. You may be spending your days in this netherworld, but no one said it couldn’t be fun.” He winks at us.

“Should we try it?” Tessa asks.

“Let’s aim for the front gate.” I’m eager to return and get recharged. I still can’t see my fingers.

"Okay. The front gate it is." She reaches out to grasp Hal's hands. "It feels so good to know we're not alone."

"No. You're not alone. You kids come back anytime. Happy to help."

I close my eyes and imagine the wrought iron gate in front of the van der Born mansion. Even with *Paw Patrol* blasting in the background, vegetables sizzling in the kitchen, and a firm pat from Hal on my shoulder, I concentrate on the filigreed metal details, the vines winding their way through the iron bars, and the moss-covered path behind. I expect to feel a breeze against my skin, or some sense of movement, but I don't. When I open my eyes to ask Hal how to do it again, I find the dark gate before me and our turreted mansion home up ahead. The only sounds now are wind in the trees and the occasional frog croaking in the pond.

After checking to see all ten fingers have come back, thank God, I whip my head around to find standing beside me, grinning at the magic, the girl who steals my heart a little more each day.

Too bad I only have twenty-two of those left with her.

CHAPTER 15

Tessa

"These rooms still give me the creeps," I say as we edge onto the second-floor landing.

"Why do you think I was happy to stay downstairs when we divided up the house? I didn't want to pass this area ever again."

"Did you see your body? The morning we woke up here?"

"Oh yeah. And it wasn't pretty." Reed grimaces as we pass by the bathroom where he was found. I try very hard not to think about him lying in his own vomit, his body's futile attempt to reject the poison.

"I'm glad they had me covered at first. Well, except for the boots." I shiver, glancing at the empty patch of floor near the windows where my body was discovered. Memories of that first morning flash back to me: cops photographing the area, the red and blue lights outside, the group of detectives huddled around my crumpled frame on the floor.

The caution tape and plastic sheet are gone now. In fact, the only remaining trace of the investigation is a small pile of evidence flags forgotten on a dusty end table.

"Where should we begin the search?" Reed asks.

As I'm turning to suggest we divvy up the second floor to poke around, I spot the telltale glow of our door. We had one all along, we just didn't come up to this floor to investigate until now. It's outlined in light, straddling the wall that separates the front room from the bathroom, linking the dueling sites of our deaths. A large series of numbers is ticking off backward, edged in light above the door frame. I flip open our phone and find the numbers are in perfect sync: 1,900,498.

Reed puts a finger to his temple and closes his eyes. It's a pose I recognize from sitting diagonally from him in calculus. It's his doing-computations-in-my-head pose. I always found it annoying, like he was showing off his "Big Brain" to the room as he worked without a calculator, but now I find myself somewhat endeared by it.

"Twenty-one days, twenty-three hours, fifty-four minutes, and change," he says.

"That's what I get, too," I agree.

We both stare, hypnotized, while the numbers continue to tick down. At least when we were alive, we had no idea when things would end. This is so much worse. Time is literally slipping through our fingers. "Where do you think it goes?" I ask, to distract myself before another minute vanishes forever. "Is it a doorway to heaven?"

"Isn't it supposed to be a stairway?" he muses.

"Okay, Led Zeppelin. I didn't know anyone listened to that song besides my dad."

"You might be surprised by my tastes." He nudges my shoulder, and my heart skips a beat. Then he turns back to study the door. "I mean, honestly, who knows? It could be heaven. Or hell. Or purgatory."

"Is that what you believe?"

He shrugs. "I don't know what to believe. My family's Catholic, but I've never been religious. The whole afterlife idea sounded like nonsense before, yet here we are."

"Here we are," I echo, staring up at the big clock of doom. It's kind of like the stopwatch Tilly and I used when I was trying to perfect my time for the one-hundred-yard dash ahead of last spring's track tryouts. Thinking of that competition gives me an idea. "Maybe it's none of the above. Maybe it's like a series of tests. You confront how you died here, then you move on to some other challenge."

Reed wanders around the room, considering. He needs to move while he thinks. Like me. "Who knows if we even remain ourselves when we walk through? Maybe we disintegrate and become one with the universe or something."

What? No. I want to stay me. "So we're supposed to walk through without knowing? What a system. We have to trust that it's better than staying here?" Why is that idea so terrifying? I'm already breaking out in a sweat.

"The way I see it, we didn't really know what to expect before we died, so it's not really that different. And we already know we don't want to stay here, not if it means being stuck as one of those smoke creatures forever." He glances out the window uneasily.

I stagger to the wall as my legs start to buckle. Why can't we remain close to our friends and families? Why do we have to go at all?

"Tessa, are you okay?"

No. No, I'm not okay. Panic mounts. I don't want to step through a door and disappear into nothing. I don't want to leave my dad behind. Or Jillian. Or Tilly. How do I leave *everyone* I know and love? We have only three weeks remaining. That's no time at all. "I'm not ready." It's all I can choke out. I slide down to the floor, gasping for breath, a fish on dry land. *No. No. No.* Not now. Not in front of Reed.

"Tessa?" he says again, but it sounds faraway this time.

It's hard to hear him over the pounding of my heart. I can't get enough air. Can't even think. My mind is racing too fast to hold on to a single thought. *Better the devil you know.* The idea's there, then it's gone. *If I stay and become one of those things in the mist at least I'm here. Maybe I can still see my family sometimes.* Then like that, those thoughts are vapor, dissolving as fast as they arrived.

"Hey, hey, hey." Reed slides down beside me. "I think you're having a panic attack. It's okay."

I shake my head furiously, clutching at my sides, scared I can't seem to draw a full breath. It most definitely is not okay. Nothing about our situation is okay. It could be so much worse on the other side. I don't know what to trust.

"Hey, look at me. I've got you." He reaches for my hand, steadies me. "Take a breath. In and out. Good. Focus on me.

Slowly . . . in for five . . . shhhh . . . out for five . . . take your time. Breathe with me . . ."

Through the spiral of fear, his voice anchors me to the world. I try to focus on his face, those kind eyes, his forehead cinched in worry, and his words. The whooshing in my ears begins to take form, becomes language that I can understand, and I follow his lead, slowing down my breathing. In and out . . . one breath . . . then another . . .

"There you go." Relief breaks over his face.

I don't know how long we sit like this, only that the afternoon shadows grow long. Eventually I start to feel more like myself.

"Do you want to talk about it?" he asks gently, running his thumb along the back of my hand. The slow, repetitive rhythm is a comfort, like his solid presence.

"I don't know if I can do it," I confess, the words barely a whisper. "I know it sounds crazy, but I don't know if I can go through that door. And then, what if I can't? You're going to leave me, and I'll be stuck here all alone."

"I'm not going anywhere without you. That's a promise. We will walk through that door together. When we're ready. Okay?" He's looking at me so intently—no joke, no smirk. There's nothing casual about it.

"Okay." My hands are shaking. I look down and notice I'm still clutching the phone.

He pries it gingerly from my fingers and pockets it, wrapping his hands around mine. "Together."

"Together." I nod, feeling incredibly grateful that he's here with me.

After a moment, he drops my hands, mouth quirking up in a

smile. I'm becoming better at recognizing Reed's moods. This is how he likes to enter his smart-ass mode. "Or we *could* stay and do the smoke thing. It might not be such a bad gig. We'd get to hang around the fields all day. Take shape one creepy limb at a time. Scare the newbies. Could be kind of fun."

"Stop." Some kind of sniffle-snort-laugh erupts from my nose along with a bubble of snot.

Smooth. Real smooth.

I quickly wipe it away. How unfair is it that snot has followed me to the afterlife?

If he noticed, he doesn't say. "I'm thinking we need better names, though, if we're going to become one of the SPs."

"SPs?"

"Smoke People."

I wrack my brain for a good nickname but come up empty. My thoughts are still scattered.

"Like," he continues, "I'm thinking you could be Smokey the Bear, and I could be . . . Smokin' Hot?"

I almost choke. My cheeks flush, betraying me. "Wait, so I'm named after a firefighting bear in jeans and you're what? A model?"

"Would you prefer I was Smoke 'Em if You Got 'Em? Or Holy Smokes?"

"How are these even nicknames? You seem confused about the concept."

"Or, maybe Up in Smoke? Wait, I've got it." He pivots toward me, fingers cocked. "Smoking Gun."

"What is even happening right now?" I feel lighter and have no idea why. He's such a goof. These antics shouldn't be working, but they are.

"We're doing nicknames for if we stay. Come on, keep up. I'm going to call you Smokey B. I think it has a better ring to it than Smokey the Bear, and—"

I interrupt before he can name himself. "And I'm going to call you Smoke Alarm because you're loud and you won't shut up."

"Smokin' Hot Alarm, you mean."

I roll my eyes, though I can't keep the smile off my face.

"Come on, let's go explore the rest of the house." Reed bumps his knee against mine. "Maybe there's other important stuff we've missed." He hops up, reaching a hand down for me to join him and providing me with just the distraction I need.

I've never appreciated him more.

CHAPTER 16

Reed

We spend our next days scouring the estate, determined to locate any clues that might uncover the circumstances of our deaths. Tessa insists on a methodical approach, from a grid pattern to search the grounds to assigned rooms to inspect. She really has watched a lot of *CSI*.

But, so far, the only things our investigation has unearthed are a lavender bra someone left draped over a statue of Adonis in the garden, a vape pen forgotten on a mantel, and a partially ripped love note crushed into the dirt. When we peek behind the last of the closed doors on the third floor—finally accessible now that we've mastered traveling through barriers—we discover a used condom lying in a corner. Tessa mumbles something incoherent while I make a retching noise, and we both hightail it to her bedroom to recover.

In our short time at the mansion, we've each found the nooks we like to retreat to for a moment of quiet. Tessa has her room, while I've discovered a secret spot on the roof. But suddenly, here we are together on the moth-eaten coverlet of her circular bed. Early evening sunlight catches the silver thread lacing through the curtains, sending a scattering of sparkles across the ceiling. It's like sitting inside a disco ball.

I stretch my legs out and fiddle with the phone. My fingers glide along the slick gray casing as I inspect it for the hundredth time.

"It's kind of weird having you in my room. Like, I keep expecting my dad to poke his head in to check if you're staying for dinner." Her eyes take in the cavernous space. "That is, if my dad and I lived in a creepy, desolate mansion."

I softly chuckle. "Yeah, I know. We never really hung out like this before." It's an unexpected kind of intimacy to sit here beside her. On her bed. The one she's not-sleeping on at night. Her shoulder brushes lightly against mine.

I clear my throat. *Get your head out of the gutter.*

"So, what now?" Defeat creeps into her voice. "Seems like we've hit a dead end."

"I don't know." I flip the phone open and closed again. "All my life I've had projects: Science fair entries, BattleBot competition builds, band practice with Kira and Santiago. I'm no good without direction." That's when the big feelings creep in.

What will the world look like with a Reed-sized hole in it? What's the statute of limitations on forgetting someone?

I push my palms against my eyes, stopping that train of thought fast. *You haven't forgotten your father. People won't forget you.*

"Hey." Tessa shakes me gently. "Earth to Reed. What's going on over there?"

"It's just . . . does it ever become too much sometimes . . . imagining them all moving on without you?" Thinking of my mom sends a guilty jolt through me. *How's she holding up?*

Tessa's hands drop to her lap. "Sometimes," she whispers, then shifts to face me on the bed. "It might help to visit them. I did. With my family."

I jerk back. "What? When?"

"Last night." She says it like it was nothing more than walking to the corner store. "I've been meaning to tell you all day. I just wasn't sure how."

I stare, stunned.

"Once I realized it was as easy as closing your eyes and—" She snaps her fingers. "I guess I decided to . . . confront it, you know? Face my grief. And my father's." Her voice breaks at the memory. "But . . ."

"But what, Tessa? Jesus." I jump off the bed, agitation coursing through my limbs. "What if something happened to you, and I had no idea where you were?" It's embarrassing how much it stings that she'd leave without me. I mean, there's no rule that says we have to tell each other everything, but this seems . . . big. "Why didn't you say anything?" Though I try to mask the accusation in my voice, I know she hears it, how pathetic, lost, and lonely I feel.

"I thought about coming to find you, maybe going together. Honestly. But in the end, it felt like something I had to do alone." She closes her eyes tight, resting against the headboard behind her. "Are you pissed?" She peeks at me.

"I don't—maybe." Crap.

My heart picks up speed.

I need to know my mom's okay. Laws of physics be damned. "I'm going."

"Reed, I don't know if—"

I bring the full force of my concentration to the living room with its sleek gray paint and posh leather couches—finance-douche chic. When I open my eyes, I'm there, among the expensive abstract art my stepdad never gave a shit about but thought would impress people. The only thing the room ever communicated to me was a cold, unwelcoming austerity. Or maybe I was confusing that with the man whose house we'd moved into.

Except the view. That was impressive. Sitting high on a ridgeline with a sea of pines and red oaks laid out before us, and the occasional hawk circling overhead—it was peaceful.

It's peaceful still. All the lights are off. They must be out.

I beeline to the music room, the only place besides my bedroom I ever felt comfortable. It had been more like a corner office, but my mom took it over to showcase my dad's guitar-building paraphernalia in a glass case along with his family portraits. I dissolve through the door and am greeted by the lush red rug, a basket of castanets, and the drum set and mic stand from our Undeniables band days.

The sun is arcing toward the tree line, but its evening rays softly illuminate a picture of my father and grandfather. My dad must not be older than six. They're proudly standing beside the cypress trees they cut down to age the wood. My family's long tradition of working as luthiers, making flamenco guitars, meant working with thirty-year-old cypress for the best sound.

I lean closer. My dad's mischievous smile and mop of black hair look so much like mine as a child, before that childhood was stolen from under me.

I trace my finger over his impish grin. I hope I made him proud in the time I had here.

What kills me is that this summer in Seville, my uncle was going to teach me how to craft a guitar out of wood my father and grandfather had chosen—maybe even the wood in this photo. It was going to be my guitar, but it would have had their fingerprints all over it. It's not until this moment that I realize how much that meant to me. My stomach tightens around the thought. I was going to be able to hold something that wasn't just mine but *ours*. Only now I'll never get to.

Just as I'm wishing I could pluck the strings of the nearest guitar to hear the sound reverberate through the hollow room, my attention snags on a commotion down the hall. I guess my stepdad is here after all. I send myself to his office in a flash, worried he and my mom are fighting. But Steven Walker—with a phone to his ear—sits alone in a dark room, backlit by the sun seeping through closed blinds. He's decked out in a full tuxedo, blond hair disheveled, with his bow tie loose around his neck.

And he's livid.

"Listen to me, you piece of shit. I'm onto you and so are the police. You call and threaten me again and I'll have your fucking balls on a platter."

I can just make out the angry cadence of the voice on the other end of the line.

"Oh, *fuck me*? Well, fuck you! You and that worthless factory." He slams his cell down on the desk.

Whoa. Is he still getting death threats?

I stagger back as the thought slices through me: Could this be the same person who came after Tessa and me at the party? *No, no, no.* Was this always about getting revenge on my stepdad? You sell out people's livelihoods to make a buck, they're going to be pissed. But would they kill over it? I know Tessa and I considered this theory, but I'd never put much stock in it. Until now.

Shit. Is my mom in trouble?

She got some seriously disturbing texts after someone doxxed us. And it's his fault she's even in this position. Dammit. What's he done?

My stepdad yanks open his lower desk drawer on a loud sigh and pulls out a glass and a bottle of scotch. He promised my mom he wasn't drinking anymore.

The liar.

He's supposed to be here for her right now. She just lost her son for Chrissake. Not only is he not taking care of her, wherever she is, he's secretly drinking again. And he's quite possibly put her in serious danger.

What a waste of space.

He tilts the bottle in a hefty pour, then swirls the amber liquid under his nose before taking a long drink. His eyes almost roll back in his head at the taste. Great. How long has this been going on? He's never hurt her, but he's definitely an angry drunk. Shit. Shit. Shit.

I pace in the small office feeling helpless to do anything but worry. I let out a frustrated scream and smack my hand against the bookcase, but it only travels through the wall and back.

My stepdad leans his forehead against the glass and, in a sight I've never witnessed before in my life—not even when he accidently slammed his fingers in the car door on our one trip to Disney World—Steven Walker tears up. His shoulders quietly shake, his breath coming in tiny choking gasps. I assume it's the stress from that ominous phone call, but then he pulls a framed photo toward him on his desk—my senior class portrait. I thought he kept it there for the *appearance* of family, like it was something he was supposed to do, even though he never came to my Little League games or birthday parties or ever made me feel like I was welcome here. But he really does seem upset.

Over me.

He raises his glass to my picture. "You could have gone far, Reed." He knocks another one back. "I was damn proud of you."

So many confusing emotions tumble through me. I walk right up to his desk and lean over him. "First of all, screw you for drinking and lying to my mom about it." I wave my hand toward the bottle and raise my voice, though of course he has no idea I'm here. "And screw you for never being there. For icing me out and making me feel like you wished my mom hadn't come with strings attached." My throat tightens around all the words I never said, only buried deep inside. "And . . . screw you for mourning me and making me feel like you care. You're not supposed to do that. You're *proud*?"

I wanted to hear that from a different man.

A better man.

And yet I don't know what to do with these feelings. I needed him as a father. To be loved, seen. Acknowledged. Now he shows up, after I'm dead, pretending he cares. "Dammit." I smack my hand against the desk. "I can't think you're an asshole when you say shit like that, and I want . . . I need"—I sink down against his desk—"to think you're an asshole."

All the fight leaks out of me like a deflating party balloon until all that's left are the two of us, him on one side of the desk and me on the other. We're straddling some great abyss that's always existed between us, only the chasm is even wider now. There's no getting across this divide—the living and the dead. There's no mending what was broken, as if that's even possible.

Why did I come here?

Steven checks the time on his cell. "Where is she?" he mumbles before downing the rest of his drink, then tucking the bottle in his desk drawer. He heads out of the office, calling for my mother. "Beatrice, we have to go."

Is she here?

I follow him down the hallway, through the living room to the sliding glass door to the porch. He opens it, sighing. "You're not dressed?" He leans unsteadily against the side of the house and begins tying his bowtie.

I travel through the glass door to find my mom sitting silently on the far side of the porch. There's a chill in the air now that the sun has dipped below the ridgeline, but she remains in a T-shirt and sweatpants, goose bumps rising on her arms. She never turns to look at my stepdad, only staring off into the distance. "I told you, I'm not going."

"And I told *you* we have to. We talked about this. This deal could be huge for us. They're expecting us both there."

"People will understand." Her eyes remain on the treetops as their shadows creep ever closer.

"You can't let grief rule your life." There's a bite in his voice now, and I bristle. He should be looking after her. She's not well. Who cares about his event? It can wait. It can all wait.

"Well, you can't *schedule* grief, either, Steven. It doesn't turn on and off. I'm not like you, penciling it in," she snaps, turning to him. "Go if you want. I don't care."

They fume at each other for a long moment. "Fine. I'll make your excuses."

She doesn't say anything else, and he storms off.

I cross and kneel beside her. Her face is blotchy from crying, and her hair is a tangle. I did this to her. Me. She lost her husband and now she's lost her son.

"I'm so sorry, Mom," I whisper as guilt gnaws at my insides.

The doorbell rings, making me jump, but my mom's unfazed. I can hear my stepdad mumble down the hall, "Good luck with her," before the door snaps shut behind him. A moment later my mom's best friend, Dahlia, steps outside onto the porch, a throw blanket in hand. She gently lays it over my mom's shoulders and gives her a tender squeeze before pulling up an adjoining chair to sit beside her.

An immense wave of relief breaks over me—just knowing someone is looking out for her—but it's coupled with a crippling sense of helplessness that that person can't be me.

It should be me.

"I'm sorry," I say again, though it will do little good. "I wish . . ." What? I'd never gone to the party? I'd told her I loved her more? "I never meant . . ." I try again, but seeing her so broken, the guilt becomes too much.

I shudder against the weight of it and send myself back to the mansion as fast as my imagination will take me.

CHAPTER 17

Tessa

In a flash, Reed appears on the bed beside me. I jump. "That didn't take long."

He shakes his head, dropping it into his hands. Is he okay?

He doesn't say anything more. So I give him some space. After a moment, I gently touch his arm. "It's harder to do than you think. That's what I was trying to tell you . . ."

He nods.

"I couldn't even go inside last night," I confess. "I watched my father through the window sobbing as he washed dishes, and I lost it, too. He looked so much older. Haggard. And I realized I couldn't hug him or comfort him. I could only stand there and know I did this to him. I stuck the knife in his back when he was already lost and in pain, barely hanging on after his job vanished." I hug my knees to my chest. "Otherwise, the house looked exactly the same, which surprised me because somehow, I expected things to seem different . . . because . . ." I sniffle. "Because . . ."

"Because *you're* different," he finishes for me, finally meeting my gaze.

"How did it go for you?" I ask.

"It was . . . *a lot*." His eyes go shiny, and I reach out a comforting hand.

He grabs it like a lifeline. "My stepdad's drinking again and not showing up for my mom *at all*—which should surprise no one. I hope she leaves him. She deserves so much better." Then, before I can process what's happening, he leans his head on my shoulder and quietly goes to pieces.

Reed has always seemed so impenetrable, like he enjoys mocking the world from his carefully crafted perch on high. But now I'm wondering if that was all a defense, a cover-up for the things happening at home. His life wasn't as perfect as I thought. He's been hurting. He's hurting still.

I slide my arm around his shoulder and pull him closer. He gives over, trembling against my side. I'm overwhelmed, knowing he feels safe enough to show me the deep dark parts of himself he keeps partitioned off from the world. The great Reed Walker. Just as lost and alone as the rest of us.

"I got you," I murmur into his hair, glad to return the favor after he helped me through my panic attack.

"I know." It's all he gets out while he clings to me.

We sit like this for a while, in the golden evening light. I stare, transfixed, as the shadows of the candlesticks glide slowly along the mantel. Until, at last, Reed breathes against my skin, barely above a whisper, "Thank you."

I hold him closer.

In the quiet that follows, the phone pings.

Reed's body tenses against mine. My fingers dig into his shoulders. We pull apart, eyes wide. "You heard that, right?" I ask.

"Yeah." He reaches into his pocket.

"Did we get a text?" My heart picks up speed over what that might mean.

Instead of the usual countdown timer on the phone screen, there's a tiny, old-school icon of an hourglass.

"What? Where'd the timer go?" I ask.

Using the center button, Reed toggles between two screens, one with the timer still ticking away and the other with the little hourglass symbol. It's a relief to know we can still track our remaining days here: Nineteen and counting.

"An hourglass." Reeds eyes narrow at the small pixelated image. "As in . . . the sands of time? Is it a reminder that our time is almost up? Because we have the timer for that, and we're already freaking out about it, so I don't think we needed the reminder."

"Could it be an app?" I peek closer at the small gray icon. "Did old phones have those?"

"The APPterlife." He snickers, then catches the look I'm giving him. "Sorry. The dad jokes spill out of me when I'm nervous."

"Reed! This is huge." I pull the phone closer to inspect it. "Something must have changed. Why did this suddenly appear?"

"Maybe it appears when you have nineteen days left," he

guesses. "Otherwise . . . I don't know what's changed, except we both had a good cry." I can still feel the searing touch of his fingers pressing into my skin as he clung to me, body shaking in quiet sobs.

Then it hits me—what we were crying about. "We both went home."

Our eyes lock. Could that be it?

"We did. But why would going home make an app appear?" He uses the buttons to highlight the small icon. "I'm clicking it." With a deep breath he selects the hourglass.

We both gasp as today's date and time appear: Thursday, June 29, 7:22 p.m.

His eyes snap to mine. "I wonder . . ." He fiddles with the settings.

Suddenly the world goes pitch-black. "What did you do?" I startle forward. How is the phone controlling the light outside?

"Whoa . . ." He stands up.

Wind howls against the shutters as a crack of thunder rumbles in the distance. Seconds ago, it was a lazy summer evening; now it's a stormy night. "I'm kind of freaking out here, Reed. What is going on?"

"I don't believe it." He hops off the bed. "I randomly set the date and time stamp back to Sunday, June twenty-fifth, and here we are."

"What do you mean, 'Here we are'?"

He flips the phone around and waves it at me. "It's now 11:20 p.m. on Sunday. I think we just went back in time." He lets out a shocked bark of a laugh.

Stunned, I grab the phone out of Reed's hands. The minute

ticks over to 11:21 p.m. I'd think it was a joke, but it's definitely nighttime.

"We're fucking time travelers!" he shouts at the ceiling.

"How is . . . wait . . . do you hear that?" I strain my ears against the wind whistling through the window cracks. There's a faint sound of voices and something else. "Laughter. Someone is outside laughing."

We race out of my bedroom to the windows overlooking the front lawn. I catch some shadows slipping along the mossy path below. I can't remember what happened here four nights ago, but then it hits me.

"The séance," we say together.

"We were in the ballroom. That's why we didn't hear them outside." Reed points down below and sure enough, I can see Santiago step into a patch of moonlight, a six-pack of beer tucked under each arm.

"So does that mean we're skating through the ballroom in our socks right now?" I ask.

His eyes go wide. "I think so. Oh God, is this going to be one of those time paradoxes where if we see ourselves we'll—"

"Die?" I interrupt. "I think we're good there."

"I was going to say, 'go insane.'"

I'm about to respond, but then Tilly steps into view and my heart squeezes so hard I can hardly bear the ache. She looks sad, even from up here. She's standing away from the group and fiddling with the hem of her dress. It's her discomfort tell: fidgeting. Tilly is the bubbliest, most happy-go-lucky person I know. Usually. It was rough last year when her mom went through chemo. But thankfully she's in remission, and Tilly was finally getting back to her old self. To see her sad again is gut-wrenching.

"I'm going out there." Without waiting for Reed to answer, I close my eyes and picture the lawn. When I open them again, I'm standing out front, surrounded by my friends, exactly where I imagined. In a blink, Reed is beside me. We shake our heads at each other. That trick is amazing.

Jenny and Yannick are stealing a kiss in the shadows, even with their arms overloaded with candles. Kevin, my VP from student government, is taking selfies with the mansion behind him. Brandon is by the gate showing the commemorative plaque on the van der Born estate to Kira, who seems genuinely interested.

Only Santiago looks as uneasy as Tilly. "It's strange being back here," he says.

"There's the wreath we laid before." She points to the house. It's still lying on the porch, where our moms placed it after the funeral. The wind has now blown it flush against the siding, Tilly's letter to me swept off into the night somewhere.

"You okay coming here?" Santiago asks.

"I think so." She nods, but the shiver that runs over her skin says otherwise.

Santiago sets his six-packs down, shrugs out of his black hoodie, and hands it to her. "If you're cold . . ." He tugs on his long sleeves. "I have these."

"Oh . . . um . . . thanks," Tilly mumbles as she takes the sweatshirt from his outstretched hands, their smiles lingering. She slyly leans her head to the side to catch the scent as she pulls it on.

It takes me a moment to close my mouth. So that's where her new sweatshirt came from. Reed's eyebrows are raised beside me. He's clocked the exchange, too, and seems just as taken aback.

"If you can't handle being here, Tilly, you don't have to stay." Jenny saunters over. "You've been acting weird all night." Leave it to Jenny to ruin the moment.

"Back off, Jenny, her best friend just died." I can see why Reed likes Santiago. I always wrote him off as a stoner musician with no ambition and never understood why he and Reed were friends. Reed is one of the most ambitious people I know. But now I wonder if I misread Santiago. He's loyal. And fearless. He's a good friend. He'd be so much better for Tilly than the trash she usually dates. And if I've been wrong about Santiago, maybe I've been wrong about . . . a lot of people.

Reed's smiling, proud to see his friend standing up for Tilly.

Jenny sighs. "I know. That's why I'm saying she can leave. We don't want negative energy interfering with tonight's plans."

"It's not just that." Tilly glances down at her hands. She's picking at her nails anxiously. "I mean, it's partly being here again, but it's also . . ." She pauses to take a breath. "I had something weird happen to me earlier tonight. I was jogging along the river road when this car almost barreled into me. The driver was probably texting or something, but the car swerved so close that I had to throw myself into a ditch. I completely scraped up my knee. But the whole way back home I kept thinking about how you never know in life. One moment you're here and the next something can come at you out of nowhere and that's . . . it. I don't understand how Reed and Tessa . . . they were just *here*. I had my arm tucked in hers, on this path, as we walked up to the party. How can someone be and then just *not* be? Especially a force like Tessa. It's like, on one hand, I know she's gone, but then I also can't understand it at all. Like it's all a big joke and they'll show up tomorrow and we can laugh about it."

Everyone else stares at her, silent. But not me.

"Oh, Tilly." I step close, wanting with every fiber of my body to wrap my arms around her. But I can't. "I'm here," I offer instead, just like I was here through her mom's cancer treatments, or her many disastrous relationships that ended in broken hearts. And like Tilly was here for me through my parents' rocky divorce, or when I sobbed on my thirteenth birthday because we couldn't afford a party that year. I step closer, heart in a vise. I want to be here for her always. But I only have nineteen days left. So instead, I vow to show up now, in every way I can. "I promise, Tills."

Tilly doesn't hear me, of course. No one does.

There's a shuffling beside me, and I realize that's not entirely true. Someone hears, and that someone slips his hand into mine. When I glance up at him, at the pain behind his eyes, I know he feels it, too, the pressing ache of wanting things to be different—the bone-deep desire to reach out and hold them, our friends, even oddball Kevin, with his inappropriate morbid jokes.

Everyone takes off for the front door. Yannick and Jenny giggle as they try to pry it open before all falling inside in a tumble.

Tilly flips on her cell flashlight to illuminate their path. Kevin looks giddy, like he's stepped into his favorite horror movie. Brandon and Kira marvel at the wooden compass-rose design on the floor. And then my breath catches because there's us, standing in the hallway in a sliver of moonlight. Reed's in his maroon kitesurfing shirt beside me in my black lace dress, dark hair spilling out of my buns from all our sockey antics in the ballroom. We can no longer see ourselves in mirrors, but here I am suddenly reflected back. I was expecting a ghost, some echo of my former self, but instead there's merely a girl, hair mussed, cheeks rosy, eyes inquisitive. Tilly's phone flashlight glides over us as she searches the room. No one sees us. And it doesn't appear that the Reed and Tessa from four days ago can see the Reed and me now. Everyone here is caught in that other time. We follow our four-days-ago selves as they wander after the others into the front parlor with its broken piano and plaster-cracked walls.

"This is the weirdest déjà vu experience I've ever had in my life." Reed shakes his head, stunned.

It really is a kind of out-of-body experience, watching something that previously happened, occur all over again, word for word, days later. Yannick throws down his blankets, Jenny makes a production out of lighting her candles, clearly enjoying her role as spirit medium. Tilly shares about our Nepal travel dreams and Santiago plays his song for Reed. It's even more beautiful to hear again. I can't believe Reed is skilled enough to play like that. But the most fascinating thing of all is not watching the séance, which I was busy watching before. It's watching Reed. Not the Reed next to me, but the Reed from four days ago.

Whenever I'm lost staring at our friends, he seems to be staring at me. Heat flushes my skin. I feel intensely aware of the boy standing beside me. Is he watching me now as I watch him, watching me? It's enough to make my brain hurt. He shifts from one foot to the other, as if he knows what's captured my attention and he's not sure how he feels about it.

Does he really stare at me that much? To check I glance up, but he's taking in the room, scowling as Kevin asks about our deaths.

Now I feel stupid. Maybe I'm misreading everything.

But then our four-days-ago selves are facing off, ignoring the séance happening around us, to argue about Brandon. Reed's insisting I walk through him, and the way he steps closer to me . . . the tension feels undeniable.

"You look like you want to kill me," I mumble, unsure how else to address the fact that the versions of us across the room seem about to throttle each other.

"Something like that." His eyes follow the action as intently as mine.

"It's funny . . . when you leaned toward me, it's like you were almost going to . . ." I don't finish the thought, doubt creeping back in. *Almost going to kiss me*, I think at him instead.

As the Reed across the room leans toward the other Tessa inside the séance circle, the Reed in front of me leans forward, too. "Like I was almost going to . . . what?" His eyes sparkle, daring me to finish the sentence.

My gaze flicks to his lips, betraying me.

From somewhere far away, the other Reed seethes, "Are you going to walk through him, or should I?" I don't turn to follow that conversation. I'm lost to the boy in front of me, distracted by the way his brows pull together in concentration, two sharp black lines, adding a kind of punctuation to his face, as if when he looks at you, he means it. There are four very light freckles spilling across his nose, which I somehow never noticed before. And his lashes—long, dark, and feathered—hover over a pair of eyes that burn into mine while he tries to ferret out my secrets. Reed is revealing himself to me piece by piece, and it's far more than I ever realized was there.

Just as I'm studying him, he's studying me. And if there is one thing Reed and I know how to do, it's study.

He ducks his head down, nose skimming mine, until he breathes against my mouth. "Almost . . ." he prompts.

His lips—so very close—are an excruciating promise.

I can no longer tell if he wants me to complete my thought, or if he's referring to the *almost*ness of this moment. All our *could be*s are balancing on a knife's edge. We don't have to subscribe to the prior versions of ourselves here, or fall into old patterns. This could be something different. Something more. I want it to be *more.*

"Almost . . ." I repeat, whisper-quiet, as my lips brush, featherlight, against his.

He lets out a low sound in the back of his throat. His mouth is *almost* on mine. My heart is *almost* his. *Almost. Almost*, I chant. An incantation. A prayer. I don't know if I've ever wanted anything more.

My lips part in invitation. When he sighs against my mouth, my breath catches.

Please kiss me. Kiss me. My entire body is screaming. I'm a tuning fork newly struck, every part of me vibrating. *I want your lips all over me. What are you waiting for?*

Before I can second-guess myself, I step forward and grab two fistfuls of his shirt, pulling my body taut against his. I can feel him smile against my mouth as I press myself to him. My hands knot in his T-shirt, skimming the skin of his stomach. He knows he has me wound up tight. His fingers flutter gently over my arms, tracing a path down to my wrists and back. It's everything I can do not to surrender entirely, but somehow in this moment, I can feel the competition building between us. I will not be the first to give in. The distance between our lips is a fraction of an inch—a gap that somehow manages to feel both minuscule and canyon-wide.

Somewhere, far away, in some other universe, the other Reed has fallen to the floor along with Brandon. Everyone else has jumped to their feet. I can hear them tumbling over one another as the shutters knock against the siding and the candles blow out.

Maybe it's the thrill of everyone racing out of the room, or of being back in time. The rules keep bending and shifting here, and our relationship shifts right along with them. Or maybe it's the permission that comes with being plunged into darkness, but whatever was holding our careful composure in place snaps.

His lips are on mine, hot and urgent. My hands weave through his gorgeous hair, which I've wanted to run my fingers through countless times but always stopped myself. No more.

As our friends run down the garden path and out to the front gate, and the other Reed and Tessa brainstorm suspects, the Reed in front of me slips his fingers down my spine. We stumble out of the room and into the foyer. A light rain pings off the windows as the wind picks up speed. We're traveling blind, bumping into tables, laughing against each other's mouths. Too hungry for this moment to pause. Reed chucks his shirt onto the floor as his feet back against the stairwell and we fall onto the steps.

I run my hands along his chest, marveling at his skin soft and cool under my touch. He reaches for my hip, fingers dipping under the hem of my dress as he hitches my leg over his.

I gasp.

He freezes. "Is this . . . all right?" he whispers.

"Are you kidding?" I laugh, taking his face in my hands. "I can't believe I'm saying this, and to *you* of all people, but yes. This is more than okay. It's perfect." I kiss him slowly, savoring the moment, unsure how we got here exactly but not wanting it to end. The rain is really falling now, pelting the roof, running down the windowpanes.

"God, I always knew we'd be great together if we ever got the chance," he mumbles against my skin, trailing kisses down my neck.

"You did?" I catch his hand and lace my fingers through his.

"Tessa, you must have guessed." He stops and leans his forehead against mine. "I've had the biggest crush on you since the sixth grade. All those years watching you and Brandon, I just . . ."

I sit up. "What?" He can't mean that. "You hated me."

"No." He smiles. "If I was an idiot, it's only because I didn't know how to tell you, and I was jealous as hell that Brandon got to know you in all the ways I wanted to."

"But . . . you've had girlfriends."

"Yeah, on and off. But they weren't . . ." His cheeks flush in a rising pink tide. "They weren't you." He glances to the side, as if afraid he's said too much.

I stare at him, open-mouthed, but no sound comes out. I feel like a cavernous hole in the earth has swallowed me up. All the shaky foundations I built my understanding of the last years on, suddenly gone. Reed was my *nemesis*, gunning for valedictorian against me, spending his every waking moment trying to best me, embarrass me, annoy me. Not . . . *win* me.

He sits forward. "Did I freak you out?"

"No, it's just . . ." I bring my eyes up to his, searching. All our past interactions are slotting into place in my mind with this whole new context. "I really thought you couldn't stand me."

He shakes his head, warm eyes alight. "Don't get me wrong, you're hardheaded, stubborn, and completely infuriating sometimes. But the thing is, I like that about you. I guess I'm a big weirdo." He shoots a sly grin my way.

"You are a big weirdo. Way weirder and more fun than I thought." I wrote him off too soon before. I lost all this time I could have had with him. "I'm sorry I didn't see it sooner, that I didn't really see *you* sooner. I think we could have—"

"Been great together," he finishes for me.

"So great," I confirm. We're beaming at each other now. "Maybe we still can be." I shrug. Then, to prove my point, I pull his mouth back to mine. Back where it belongs.

We kiss endlessly. On the staircase. Through a rainstorm. Suspended in time.

Brandon never kissed me the way Reed is kissing me now—like he's drowning and I'm his only salvation.

We pour ourselves into the moment.

I love all the new ways I get to know him—the low, happy sounds he makes in the back of his throat, or how he runs his lips along my jaw, whispering about the times he wished we'd done this before. I even love how we crack ourselves up over the dorky, awkward ways we bump into and maneuver around each other.

I can't help wondering, how far does this go? How far do I *want* it to go? Because right now I feel ready to tear my clothes off and say, *Yes, you and me together like this forever, please and thank you.*

Only we don't get forever. We only get these few perfect moments.

My heart squeezes at the notion. Then Reed nips at my mouth, swallowing my tiny gasp in return, and my thoughts fracture all over again.

My lips are swollen as the storm ebbs and the first streaks of morning light stream through the windows.

"We should go back in time more often." I laugh, slowly coming to my senses, realizing the other Reed and Tessa will be heading out to the police precinct in not too long.

"Yeah, can you imagine if we—" Reed pops up beside me and pulls the phone out of his pocket. "Oh my God, I can't believe we didn't think of it." He's on his feet.

"Think of what?" I ask.

He thrusts the phone at me. "Tessa, we need to set the clock back and find out how we died."

CHAPTER 18

Reed

We travel back to June sixteenth, swapping the early-morning light of our kissing session for the darkened foyer the night of party. Somewhere in the distance the swim team chants as they build their human pyramid. A group of freshmen teeter through the front door in heels they look unused to wearing, giggling as they take selfies in the entranceway. People have strung up battery-operated lights along the hallways, all pulsing to a deep bass vibrating the windows.

"Okay, we need to focus," Tessa states. "It's eleven thirty p.m. That means Tilly's leaving soon and we're about to play beer pong."

"You're sure the poison came from something we drank?"

"I think we ingested it, and we didn't eat."

I nod. "I haven't had a chance to tell you something

important because the whole time-travel thing happened. But . . . I'm pretty sure I know who did it."

"What?" She gawks.

My pulse picks up. "When I went home, I overheard a threatening call between one of those factory guys and my stepdad. I think they killed us to intimidate our fathers somehow."

Her eyes widen. "Did they mention my dad?"

"I don't—not in the part I overheard."

She bites her lip, her concentration habit. "That's definitely a lead. But I've watched enough crime shows to know we can't make assumptions. We need to follow the drinks. That means watching Jenny set up beer pong. She had the perfect opportunity to slip us something then."

Not this again. "Tessa, it's not—"

"Jenny needed the scholarship money. The motive is there, so . . . let's be *sure*."

It's her pleading eyes that break me. "You win." I cave. "Let's watch ourselves get destroyed at beer pong."

Even after Jenny opens fresh beers to fill the Solo cups at each end of the dining table, Tessa's still suspicious, arguing she could have placed the caps on top to make them appear untampered with. It's not until Jenny swigs from one of the bottles that Tessa concedes she hasn't poisoned them. Still, she insists we watch the entire game, in case they sneak something in when we're not looking.

They don't.

"I told you this was a dead end. Jenny's annoying, but she's no murderer."

Tessa scans the room for additional clues, though I suspect she knows I'm right.

I tap my foot with fake impatience. "Was there something you wanted to say?"

"Fine," she mumbles. "She's off the suspect list."

"I'm sorry . . . what was that?" I lean in, smiling smugly.

"Oh, you heard me, Walker." She gives me a light shove.

"So, now what?"

Tessa squeezes her eyes closed, straining to recall the events of the night. "Before beer pong you got us drinks from the kitchen, right? From things other people were making?"

I nod and she takes off down the hall, like some amped-up Sherlock Holmes.

"We're wasting time. I already know who did it!" I race after her. "Besides, why would someone poison a drink they were making for themselves?"

We weave through the party madness, past rooms shrouded in moonlight where the drama club is attempting Light as a Feather, Stiff as a Board and rooms packed with bodies dancing to rhythmic beats. I even spy Olive Dingle making out with Jasmine Byers through an open doorway. I hope things don't get awkward in Model UN for them later.

At last, we arrive at the kitchen with its large hearth and majestic stone tiles. It was probably entertainment central back in the day. I can almost see the servants, hair pulled back in tight buns, arranging trays of hors d'oeuvres for some fancy van der

Born soiree. A long table straddles the center of the room, now chock-full of every conceivable brand of alcohol and mixers, looking like it might buckle any second under the weight.

The kitchen is so crowded it's hard to avoid running into people. I'm dodging every direction, when suddenly a sophomore I don't know marches straight toward us. Panicked, I try to tug Tessa aside, but it's too late. The girl plows through her.

I'm expecting Tessa to collapse from the ice-cold disorienting impact of passing through someone. But she appears remarkably unfazed.

"What was that?" Tessa whips her head around as the girl races outside to throw up.

"You didn't feel anything?" I ask, confused. Her teeth aren't chattering. She doesn't seem nauseous.

"No. Nothing."

"Huh." A seed of a theory takes form. I spot a couple walking in from outside and charge through them.

There's no overwhelming onslaught of memories. No bone-deep chill from making contact with the living.

Tessa gasps while I beam at my experiment. "Yeah. Nothing."

"Why aren't we feeling anything here?" She wanders over.

"I don't know, but I have a theory. Maybe we haven't traveled back in time."

Tessa raises an eyebrow.

"I mean, time travel might be the wrong way to think about this. It could be more like adjusting the clock back to an instant replay of the night of the party. These people, they're not really here. They're more like an echo of everything that happened that night. Like, you and I, we haven't changed times, we can't affect the world around us or alter anything, we're merely . . . watching the show."

She nods, taking in the room. "That sort of makes sense."

"When you can't have Netflix." I shrug as the replay swirls around us.

"If your theory's correct, then it's like we're the real ones and they're the ghosts." Tessa waves at our classmates.

"Touché."

"And regardless, it sounds like we don't have to worry about avoiding people, which is a relief. So, lets figure this out. When did you get us drinks?"

"A few minutes before Tilly, Brandon, and Kira left." A strand of hair has fallen across my face from all my excitement nerding out over time-travel theories. I tuck it behind my ear.

"Then we set the clock back again to that moment but stay here this time and watch you come in," Tessa suggests.

I pull out the phone and set the time back about twenty-five minutes. In a blink there's a new crowd of people around us, most of them chanting "Brett, Brett, Brett!" as Brett Whitaker—no doubt the guy behind the LONG LIVE BEER AND BROS sign from senior prank day—shotguns a Budweiser. The crowd cheers as he finishes, crushes the can in his hand, and chucks it across the room. "Now, who wants a Whitaker Special?" People whoop and shout as he pours a disgusting concoction of Budweiser, Mountain Dew, Red Bull, and peach schnapps into a number of empty cups.

"Wow. I didn't know what went in that thing." I gag as the Reed from the night of the party waltzes into the room.

When Brett spies the other Reed, he stumbles forward, pulling him into a one-armed hug. "Reed, you've got to try one of these. It's my signature drink, bro, you won't be disappointed."

"Uh . . . sure." Then-Reed takes the offered cup, peering inside skeptically.

"I can't believe you gave me that drink." Tessa scowls at me.

"I had no idea how to mix a cocktail and I wanted to impress you," I admit.

"You should try one of mine, too. I used the good stuff, top shelf." Caden Pierce, our quarterback, pours drinks at the end of the table, near a tight-knit cluster of people deep in conversation. He waves toward a handful of cups ready to go.

Brett chucks a lime at him, which Caden ducks, laughing.

"Thanks, man." Reed nods appreciatively.

Brett drunkenly thrusts one of Caden's cups into then-Reed's other hand. "You can compare. Mine are better, though, bro."

Hip cocked, Tessa turns to me. "How were you friends with those guys?"

"I was friends with everyone, Tessa. No one at school could resist my charms."

She arches a brow.

"*Almost* no one," I counter, then redirect us. "Okay, those drinks were disgusting, but were they *poisoned*? Look around, lots of people are drinking them. Why would only we have died from ours?"

"It's a good question." She purses her lips as she scans the crowd. "Wait . . . holy shit. Check out the cups. One of yours is a different color." Tessa smacks me on the arm. "That wasn't Caden's drink Brett handed you."

I rub my shoulder where she nailed me, then startle when I see who she's pointing at. His back had been to us, but now that he's turned around it's clearly one of the factory guys who hassled us before.

I fucking knew it! "I told you it was them," I say to Tessa.

Some of the guy's friends enter through the rear door. "Yo, Dave, another keg arrived, get your ass out back."

Dave exits the kitchen behind them. If his Solo cup was handed to me, he doesn't seem to care about it now. Which, I'll admit, is a little weird.

I'm torn between following our old selves to see how the drinks affect us or taking off after the factory workers. This feels like a lead. "I think we should follow Dave and his friends," I say, and Tessa nods. We make our way down the back steps, past the swim team's pyramid antics and the French club dancing in the empty fountain, toward the rear of the estate.

"Do you think Dave's drink was poisoned?" I slow my pace a bit as Tessa jogs beside me, trying to keep up with my long strides.

"Why would he poison that drink? It's a pretty elaborate scheme to leave a poisoned cocktail out on the off chance the kid whose stepdad dismantled your company stumbles upon it."

"You're right. That makes no sense. I mean, Dave's no genius, but I'd like to think he could do better than that. They must come after us later." We catch up to Dave's crew in a rear garden gathered around a keg. "Let's wait and watch. If they're plotting something, we'll overhear it."

So, we hang around as Dave and his buddies Leo and Rob

get shit-faced. We learn about T-Bone, Rob's cousin from Schenectady who's going to hook them up with weed. And then there's the saga of Dave's girlfriend Becca who dumped his sorry ass over text.

Tessa's starting to get antsy, since so far we're coming up empty. She suggests we split up so she can go back inside to observe our former selves, while I keep an eye on the factory guys. I agree and remain behind, determined to catch Dave and his friends in the act.

At one point a fight breaks out with some other guys from town, possibly because one of them is dating Becca now. It's hard to keep up. Still, at no point does anyone discuss getting even with our fathers, or plot to secretly poison us.

When the guys head indoors a couple hours later, one nursing a black eye from the fight over Becca, I follow them. Though I'm feeling less sure they're our culprits.

As I arrive at the entranceway, I find Tessa. "Any luck?" I ask.

"No. You?"

"No." I shake my head.

She taps my arm and nods toward the stairs. On the second-floor landing it's us, the original us, from the night of the party. A couple hours in and we're a hot mess. The old me has tripped on the stairs and we're both in hysterics.

"I have no memory of this at all," I say.

"Me, neither. After beer pong, everything's a blur. Though . . ." She grimaces, watching as the other Tessa struggles on the landing to help then-Reed stand back up, before falling down herself. "We've been like this for a while."

When Dave spots drunk Reed, he yells up to him, “Hey, we got a message for your old man. Why don’t you come down and hear it.”

The other Reed lifts his head, but his eyes struggle to focus on who’s speaking.

Rob steps onto the bottom stair, palms twitching, as if he’s ready to launch into another fight. The Tessa from the party tugs on my shirt in a panic and we scramble up the stairs.

“Yeah, keep running,” Rob shouts, but they don’t follow.

Tessa turns to me. “Were we just drunk, or did we seem more out of it than that?”

“It’s strange. It’s almost like I couldn’t tell who was talking to me.” I shift my weight, my agitation mounting. How could we miss something so critical? Are we already poisoned?

“Didn’t we hide in a closet for a while upstairs?” Tessa strains on her tiptoes but it’s unclear where we’ve run off to.

“I vaguely remember that.”

“So, who do we follow now? Do we go after ourselves or stay with Dave and his friends?”

“The factory guys obviously don’t like my stepdad, or me, but they didn’t chase us upstairs.”

She nods.

“And they made no mention of wanting to spike our drinks when we were outside.” Our deaths are just as big a mystery as before. I can tell Tessa’s starting to feel defeated, too.

“It’s seeming less and less likely it’s them.” She sighs.

“Maybe we go upstairs and watch some of the party we don’t remember?” I suggest with a shrug.

We trudge up to the second floor.

"Do you think it was premeditated, whoever killed us?" she asks.

"I mean, what's the alternative? A crime of passion?"

Tessa tilts her head, wondering which seems more likely. "I guess in one instance someone came here with poison, a motive, and the intent to off us, and in the other, they decided in the moment and found whatever they needed here."

I scan our surroundings. "But what kinds of poison are even here?"

Tessa pauses, hands on her hips, as we reach the landing. "How would I know? Do I look like I know the first thing about poison?"

"Uh . . . you knew about dilated pupils being a symptom *and* the whole toxic alkaloid thing. It's more than me." I snap my fingers, pointing at her, as if a lightbulb went off in my head. "Maybe it was you."

"Yep. It was me all along. You've cracked the case. Dun dun dun." She smacks me on the shoulder while I smirk beside her, then we both glance around, realizing that we've lost track of our former selves. "Where did we run off to?"

We poke our heads into the back bedrooms, stepping over the piles of plaster that have chipped off the walls.

"Wait, what about asbestos?" I ask. "It's an old house."

"Asbestos isn't organic." She leads us into the dusty corner room. "It also doesn't kill you immediately."

There's no sign of us, only a chipped vanity and a window covered in creeping vines. Which does give me an idea. "This place *is* crawling with greenery, though." I can just make out the swim team's chants as they build their pyramid out back. How long have they been at that? "What about poison ivy, is that poisonous enough to kill?"

"No idea." She shrugs. "Too bad we can't google it."

A closet door flies open, startling us. The other Reed and Tessa come hurtling out, falling to the floor and gasping. Or laughing. I can't tell. We do not look good.

We're pale and sweaty. The me from the party is moaning. While the other Tessa crawls out of the bedroom on her hands and knees and grabs some girl's dress as she passes to beg for water. "I'm so thirsty." The girl brushes her off.

Meanwhile, the old Reed has pulled himself into the second-floor bathroom to throw up.

Tessa covers her eyes with her fingers, save a small hole to peep through. I wonder if she feels like I do, wanting to leave but unable to tear myself away. "Oh God. I think this is it," she says. "Look where you are. You're in that bathroom where you died. I don't know what we missed, but this seems beyond being drunk."

I look at my former self. I'm clawing at my throat, my breaths strained and rasping. Even though I know it's already happened, a sickening fear churns deep in my gut, an overwhelming desire to run.

Get out while you can.

The other Tessa has pulled herself up only to stagger forward and fall to the floor. People step around her. Someone snickers. Most people are distracted.

I feel helpless watching us struggle.

"Why is no one helping?" Tessa looks around in a panic, though there's nothing we can do. We can observe our past, not change it.

"We probably just seem wasted." I shrug but feel the color leaching from my face. There's no casual way to watch yourself die.

"Something is clearly wrong with us, though. If only someone understood."

"We should go." I grab her wrist. "If we watch, we'll never be able to unsee it."

"Okay." She follows me, then comes to a halt. "No. Wait—"

I look at her questioningly.

Tessa's feet remain firmly planted, her eyes unfocused. "We're missing something. It's right at the edge of my mind." She stares into the distance. "If only . . . someone . . . understood . . ."

She's biting her lip again as the gears churn behind her eyes.

Except it's hard to focus as the former Tessa begs for more water behind us. At least I think that's what she's saying. Her speech is so slurred at this point it's difficult to tell. The Reed in the bathroom now seems completely unconscious.

"We need to go," I say again. "Let's think about this downstairs, where we don't have to watch." I start to walk away but Tessa's hand shoots out, fingers digging into my arm. "Reed," she gasps. "Look."

I turn for one last peek. The poisoned Tessa has yanked herself up onto some guy's jeans. When I catch his annoyed expression, my heart skids to a stop. An electric current of recognition charges through me.

"He's still here." Tessa's voice comes out as a shaky breath.

It's Creepy Carl. The college guy who dated Tilly. His red hair is tousled, but he doesn't seem too shaken. He studies Tessa as she clings to his pants.

"Oh shit," I say. "I thought that guy left."

Carl kicks until she loses her grip and falls to the floor. No one notices.

"Why isn't he calling 911?" I ask.

Poisoned Tessa crawls toward the large front windows and curls up in a ball as her muscles spasm.

"Carl studies plant pathology," Tessa whispers beside me.

My eyes flare wide.

With a quick glance to make sure no one is near, Carl turns and races down the stairs.

"That pasty fucker," I say as we watch him go. "Looks like we found our main suspect."

CHAPTER 19

Tessa

Third time's a charm," I say as we set the clock back once again. This time we do it in the entranceway, making our best guess at when Tilly and Carl got in their fight. We arrive a few minutes early, which is good because I need to sit on the steps for a minute to process what we witnessed.

We didn't stay to watch ourselves take our final breaths, but I'd seen enough. It's one thing to know you're dead. It's another thing entirely to watch it happen. A shiver sweeps down my spine, followed by a growing ball of fury in the pit of my stomach over Carl kicking me loose from his leg.

"I can't believe we didn't suspect the guy called Creepy Carl. We are absolute shit detectives." Reed slumps onto the step beside me.

The scientist in me hesitates. "We can't say it's definitively him. We need proof."

"Oh, come on, his behavior was so sus. Did you see the way his eyes kept shifting, like he wanted to watch but didn't want to be seen with us? Was he mad we told him to leave earlier? I mean, what the actual fuck? Is that any reason to murder someone?"

"I thought he left the party. We saw him go." I gesture toward the front door.

"Clearly he did not."

Right on cue, Tilly races into the foyer with Carl on her heels. Reed and I hop up for a better look.

"What are you doing here?" she asks under her breath as some students from the chess club wander by.

Carl pulls Tilly's hobo bag out from behind his back and thrusts it at her. "You're sick. Let me get you out of here."

"Why do you have my stuff, Carl?" She narrows her eyes, slinging the bag over her shoulder. "And how did you know I'm feeling crappy?"

He shrugs. "I saw you leaning against the wall looking like you might pass out."

"Well, I'm not going anywhere with you." She turns, a little wobbly on her feet.

"Why not? You think you're too good for me?" He grabs her wrist. "Let me take care of you." I feel so helpless watching him put his pervy hands on her. Was he calling and texting her, and I didn't know? Why didn't she tell me?

"Carl, this needs to stop. We broke up months ago. I don't want to be with *anyone* right now." She pulls out of his grasp. "Stay away from me." Some heads turn at her raised voice.

Carl's arm shoots against the wall, blocking her path. "You want this, you know you do. Come over and I'll remind you how much you used to like me."

"No. How many times do I have to say it?" Tilly shoves past him, her eyes filling with angry tears.

"You're sick and don't know what you're saying. I'm getting you out of here." He tugs her arm, pulling her up short.

It's in this moment the other Tessa races downstairs to step between them. "What's going on?"

"This doesn't concern you, Tessa." Carl shoves the other me aside and starts dragging Tilly toward the door.

"Carl, what part of 'It's over' don't you understand?" Tilly shouts. More people have gathered, including Reed and Santiago, who push their way through the crowd. I hadn't noticed before, but Reed's eyes burn with stone-cold fury.

"I am trying . . . to . . . help you." Carl bites out every word.

"Get off her!" Then-Tessa tugs his arms.

"You heard her, asshole. Back off." Reed from the party glares at Carl as he steps between us.

Santiago steps forward, too, arms crossed, looking just as menacing. "I don't think you're wanted here." I'd forgotten how much the two of them had shown up for Tilly in that moment.

"Go." Waves of anger roll off the old me.

The other Reed pulls the door open and waits, facing off with Carl in the entranceway. It's such an intense standoff that at any second, I half expect a tumbleweed to blow past or one of them to suggest drawing pistols at dawn.

When Tilly flips Carl off, the look he gives her is so full of longing and hatred, the hairs rise on my arms. Santiago subtly positions his body between them. From this angle I can see his hand slide protectively in front of Tilly, resting gently on her arm, though he doesn't turn around.

Carl tracks it, too, eyes flashing, but scenting defeat, he pivots down the porch steps. "Whatever. I was trying to do you a favor, bitch."

"Yeah, keep walking!" Tilly shouts as he skulks down the garden path.

"And that's our cue." I nod for Reed to follow.

When Carl reaches the gate, he turns around. Whatever he sees makes him howl, spit flying. I glance behind me to find us all lit in the doorframe. But there's a moment I didn't notice before. Santiago's reached for Tilly's shaking hands, their eyes locked as he whispers something reassuring to her. It's a moment of kindness. But Carl doesn't see it that way.

"Slut," he hisses, stomping out the gate.

We always assumed he'd left the party, but he lingers, kicking some gravel on the road, sending the pieces skittering into the rock wall surrounding the estate. He swears and paces twenty feet away from the entrance. I catch occasional phrases like "two-faced liar" and "screwing someone behind my back." A few people gathered on the street side-eye him. Carl pulls out his phone. At first, I assume he's calling someone to pick him up, but then I recognize the pissed-off voice coming through the speaker.

"I mean it, Carl, leave me alone."

"You told me you weren't interested in anyone, you lying slut."

"I'm blocking your number." Tilly hangs up.

"FUUUUUUUUUCK!" He violently throws his phone on the ground.

Some partiers eye him carefully as they get out of their car. "You okay, bro?" one asks.

"Bitch just made me break my phone."

They shoot him a weird look and hurry past.

"Nobody talks to me like that." He retrieves his cell from the pavement—the screen now cracked—before marching back to the party, muttering to himself. "I was going to help nurse you back to health, but now . . . you sneak around behind my back." He shakes his head. "You're gonna regret not coming home with me."

Reed and I share a worried glance and take off after him.

"Why is he so fixated on taking her home?" I ask.

"It's weird, right?"

My blood runs cold. "Do you think he did something to her, before he came after us?" Oh God, did he poison Tilly first? Roofie her? Did he get to her earlier in the night?

"We know if he did come after her first, she survived it."

Waves of anger roll off Carl as he marches toward the house. Everyone he passes keeps their distance.

My mind struggles to understand the scope of what he's done. "Maybe he didn't want to kill her. Maybe he only wanted to harm her, so he could sweep in and be the hero. 'Take her home.' 'Nurse her back to health,' he said. What if this was all part of some sick plot to win her back?"

Reed's eyes go wide. "Didn't he say something at one point about doing her a favor? Only it didn't work."

"Or it worked, but not enough." Shit. How have I missed all

these signs? I was so focused on Reed and myself, I didn't see all the terrible trouble Tills was in. What kind of friend does that make me? "She told me she felt queasy earlier in the night. I thought she was upset over running into him, but maybe it was something more. Though, how did he slip it to her?" I come to a halt, smacking my hand against my forehead. "Her water. She's never without her water bottle."

"So, he roofied her water or something, but maybe he got the dose wrong, or she didn't drink it all."

It's already taken me forever to find my bag. "Tilly told me she'd lost track of her bag at the party. He'd have had a chance then."

We race after Carl, who's now paused on the porch like he's considering whether to reenter. Maybe he's nervous about getting into a fight with Santiago and Reed, but for whatever reason he avoids the front door. Instead, takes off around the house. But when Carl swings past the greenhouse with its partially caved-in windows and overgrown vegetation, he backtracks, peering inside. In the low light, it's hard to see what's caught his eye.

Carl fumbles with his phone but can't get it to power on, so he returns it to his back pocket. "Hey," he shouts at a group of sophomore girls. "I think I dropped my phone in here earlier. Can I use one of your cell flashlights for a minute?" A petite brunette I recognize from the yearbook committee hands hers over. Carl sweeps the light past the greenhouse ruins, pausing for a long time on a berry bush.

"Did you find it?" she asks.

"Nah. But . . . thanks." He makes sure the girls are out of sight before stepping through one of the broken windows, then picks a handful of plump berries off the closest bush and pockets them. Out of his boot he draws a Swiss Army knife, flipping the blade open. I grab Reed's arm, wondering if Carl is about to go on some kind of stabbing rampage, but instead he pulls the berry bush up from the soil and shaves some of the root off into his hand. He pockets the shavings, along with the knife. "We tried this the harmless way, but screw that." He gingerly steps past the busted glass, heading to the house.

"Do you know what that plant is?" Reed asks as we jog after Carl.

"No. But I'd bet it has toxic levels of tropane alkaloids, like the autopsy report said."

We follow Carl into the kitchen where he proceeds to make some kind of artisanal cocktail. First, he steeps the roots in vodka. Then he muddles the berries in a Solo cup. It figures the guy would have some bougie recipe even when he's plotting murder. At last, he pulls the roots out and mixes the mashed berries with the vodka.

"Why the roots?" Reed asks.

"They probably contain heavier doses of the toxins."

"How did Tilly end up with him?"

"He came into her mom's store one afternoon while Tilly was working. He told her he'd keep coming back until she went out with him. And he did. He showed up around ten times, always bringing a bouquet. Eventually she buckled."

Reed lets out a low whistle over Carl's commitment, and I feel like I need to explain Tilly's choices.

"Tilly thought he looked like a young Prince Harry. She was charmed by his smarts and smile and found his persistence endearing. But I don't know." I cross my arms and study Carl as he works at the center table, around all the alcohol and mixers. "I never saw the appeal. I always thought it was creepy for a college guy to be so insistent on a high school relationship. They dated for maybe three weeks, but he was so clingy that she ended it. Now she says she doesn't trust her own judgment with guys."

Carl strains the drink into another cup, then wanders around the kitchen looking for a place to discard the roots and berries. As he's doing that, a crowd enters and people begin chanting "Brett, Brett, Brett!" as Brett Whitaker shotguns his beer.

In the chaos, Dave arrives and leans with his back to Carl's poisoned cup. But Carl doesn't notice. He's too busy shoving his berries down the sink, hiding the evidence.

"So, it never was Dave's drink," I say as the whole situation starts to make sense.

"I thought that was a weird drink for the factory guys," says Reed.

"Who wants a Whittaker special?" Brett hands out his disgusting concoctions. People clamber for them faster than he can pour.

"Carl tried to make Tilly sick, make her crawl back to him for help and comfort, but when that didn't work, he tried to kill her." Reed gestures toward the table.

"But then . . . look who walks in."

The other Reed, from the night of the party, saunters inside. Carl tries to return to his poisoned cocktail, but the crowd's so thick and unruly he can't push through.

Brett thrusts his drink, and what he thinks is Caden's drink, into Reed's hands.

Carl stares in shock as Reed departs. If he stops Reed, he'll have to acknowledge what he's done, but if he doesn't, he's responsible for Reed's death. Carl cracks the door open and watches as I down some of his poisoned drink, make a face, then hand it off to Reed, who guzzles the rest. Carl shuts the door, eyes darting around the kitchen.

No one has any clue what's gone down. Brett's shaken up a beer can, so it explodes on the crowd when he pops the tab open. People laugh and run in all directions. Carl stumbles in a daze toward the back exit, and we follow. At first, I think he's going to pick more berries, but he slides down against the siding and sits there, staring straight ahead. His fingers tap rapidly along his leg, the only indication he feels anything at all.

On our way back inside, Reed turns to me. "So, case closed. Creepy Carl did it, in the kitchen with the berries."

I glare at him just as the other Reed struts in to get more drinks. "Carl made it, but you're the one who basically *Hunger Game*d us."

"Should I understand that reference?"

"*You* are the reason why we're dead. You grabbed a poisoned drink and gave it to me." Anger suddenly pulses through my limbs, heats my cheeks.

"Tessa, come on, that's not fair." His face has gone bone-white. "That drink was shoved into my hands."

"That's all you have to say?" I tap my foot. "And not . . . I don't know . . . *I'm sorry*?"

He rubs his neck. "Look, for what it's worth . . . I *am* sorry." His face is pained, like the admission cost him. "But at least we have answers now. Carl obviously intended to kill Tilly."

"Tilly doesn't drink, which Carl probably didn't know since

they only dated briefly. But even if she did, there's no way in hell she'd ever accept a drink from him. So no, we didn't die to save her, we just died. We were killed by accident. We are the sad, unintended byproducts of some psycho's stalker revenge."

I storm out of the kitchen and back to the foyer. I can't stand having Carl outside the door while his poison spreads through our systems.

"Look, I get it. This all sucks." Reed races to catch up. "I mean . . . I had no idea what was being handed to me, but I really am sorry, Tessa. You have to believe me." There's a grimace in his voice, like none of this is easy for him. "But doesn't it help a little knowing that Tilly's okay?"

I pause and he almost smacks into me. Something's itching at the back of my mind. "Is she, though?" I turn to face him as pieces of a puzzle shift in my brain, slowly taking shape. "Remember the night of the séance when people were gathered on the lawn, how Tilly said she'd been out jogging by the river earlier that day when someone almost ran her off the road? What if that wasn't some accident with a distracted driver? What if he's still coming for her?"

Reed freezes as a wave of realization breaks over him.

"Maybe we're not here to solve a murder." I lock eyes with him as the gravity of our situation takes hold. "Maybe we're here to prevent one."

CHAPTER 20

Reed

"Here goes nothing." I select the hourglass icon. We're ready to leave this party and its haunting memories behind.

"Do you remember when we started?" Tessa leans over my shoulder to examine the small screen.

"Yeah. 7:22 p.m. on June twenty-ninth." I enter the date and time and the phone flashes RETURNING TO PRESENT in large block letters three times.

Suddenly the party chaos gives way to a soft morning light spilling in through the front windows. We're alone in the foyer once again, bathed in a warm summertime glow.

"What just happened?" Tessa's eyes are wide as she scans our now quiet surroundings. "We definitely left in the evening."

"You saw that message flash across the screen, right? It said it was returning us to the present, but look . . ." I hand her the phone. "It's now 5:26 a.m. on June thirtieth. I think we just . . . *broke* time." The sky outside is laced in pinks and oranges, a perfect sunrise. We step through the door and onto the porch, greeted by birdsong and a promising morning.

"Okay. That's weird. But I have a hypothesis."

I arch an eyebrow at her. "Care to share with the class?"

"Well, you gave me the idea, actually, when you said earlier that you didn't think we were time traveling, but instead watching an instant replay of something that happened in the house."

I wait. Where's she going with this?

"What if time continues to move forward? What if the present that we were trying to return to, 7:22 p.m. on Thursday, is no longer the *actual* present?"

"Interesting." I nod, leaning against one of the rickety banisters on the porch. "So we were spit out now because, *what* . . . we're not allowed to arrive in a time we didn't experience? We skip over the hours we missed."

"Which means—" Tessa begins.

"You can't game the system," I finish for her. "You can't hide out in the past and get more time on the clock."

"Exactly. Which for a hot minute there sounded like a fantastic idea, but if time passes during the replay, it passes here, too."

I playfully shove her shoulder. "Damn, you're smart."

Tessa shrugs with a *yeah, I thought that was obvious* look, but I catch her private smile. "5:26 a.m. on the thirtieth. That's . . ." She runs a quick calculation in her head, "ten hours and four minutes from when we left. Doesn't that cover how long we've been gone? We went to the séance, stayed overnight on the stairs . . ." She blushes a little at that, her eyes drifting to mine. My mouth turns up at the corner, remembering her lips, her hitching breath, our confessions in the dark.

Focus, Reed, focus.

She clears her throat, continuing, "Then we went to the party where we set the clock back a couple times to do more digging. Ten hours and four minutes sounds about right." She tosses me the phone.

"But why be able to do this at all? Why allow us to visit the past?" I stare at the device in my hand, so much power in such small packaging.

"Well, not everyone's been murdered." Tessa shrugs. "But that doesn't mean people escape life without some past trauma or baggage to deal with. Maybe letting people see their memories helps with the process of letting go, helps them leave it all behind."

I lean my head against the post, considering her words. "And what, by going home and confronting our lives, we showed we were willing to put in the work? To face some hard truths? So the hourglass icon appeared with the option to dig into our past?"

Tessa raises her hands then drops them back to her sides. "Your guess is as good as mine."

"Do you think it's helping *us* with the process of letting go?" I remember Tessa's panic attack by the door. *I'm not ready*, she'd said. I'm not sure how she feels now, but I know I'm still not ready. How do I let go, or move on, with my dad's death on my conscience? And now I'm responsible for Tessa's death, too. Because if there's one thing I learned from our trip back to the night of the party, it's that neither of us would be in this situation if I hadn't walked out with that drink of Carl's. That makes two people who'd still be alive today if it weren't for me: Tessa and my father. I'm an absolute menace.

There's no *moving on* from something like that.

When Tessa's eyes seek mine, there's an intensity burning behind them. "We have a killer to stop first."

To be sure our theory is correct, we head upstairs to check that the timer above the door matches the phone. It does.

"Only eighteen days left." I try to hold the wave of worry back, though it feels treacherous, like a rip current ready to drag us out to sea if we let it. Maybe I don't know how to move on from my past, from my litany of mistakes, but that doesn't mean I can't still do some good.

Tessa squeezes my hand. "Then we better use every one of those days to help Tilly. Because Carl's still out there, and I've no doubt in my mind he's coming for her next."

Tessa and I plant ourselves on a bench outside Aunt Betty's, Tilly's mom's store, where Tilly apparently works over the summer hawking locally made jewelry and soaps. Our stakeout to catch Carl has been underway for hours. We don't know where he lives, but if he's stalking Tilly, we're determined to catch him in the act.

What happens when we find him, we haven't worked out yet.

So far, Carl hasn't come in, or even driven by. He's not around when Tilly grabs lunch with some friends from the French club. We spy her through the café window, chatting, sipping iced coffee, and trying to pretend her world isn't imploding. Tessa tenses beside me.

"That would have been me before." Her fingers trace along the windowpane as she watches the girls inside. "Now, someone else gets to fill her shoes as best friend. Maybe not these girls in this moment, but someday."

I hadn't given a lot of thought to Santiago and Kira moving on without me, but in this moment, with time marching on in front of us, it's a punch to the gut for sure.

"What hurts even more is that they don't know Tills like I do. They don't notice how she's drowning. She's putting on a good front, but see how her eyes drift outside, lost and lonely, or the heaviness that hangs over her as she tries to make conversation. I wish I could hug her, talk to her. But I can't even reassure her that I'm okay."

I rest my hand on Tessa's shoulder to let her know I understand, that I also feel the loss, but she shuffles out of my reach, saying something about casing the neighborhood for Carl. I let her go. I need a moment by myself, too. When she returns, I pretend I don't notice how her eyes are red and puffy.

The afternoon progresses with no luck. We don't find any trace of Carl during Tilly's evening jog along the river path. By the time night falls, our hours following her feel like they were for nothing. Maybe we have this all wrong. Maybe Carl isn't coming after her. Maybe he panicked over what he's done and has gone to ground instead.

"I'm starting to get that weird hollowed-out feeling again." I sit beside Tessa on the lawn, gazing up at the inviting warm windows of Tilly's childhood home. Occasionally we catch glimpses of Tilly and her family at the dinner table or puttering and cleaning up. "Remember how Hal said you can't be gone too long before you need a supernatural recharge back at the site of your death?"

"Yeah. I feel it, too. That swooping, empty feeling." Tessa runs her hand over her stomach. "I hate to leave Tills for even a moment, but we should probably head back. We can return in the morning."

Just then, Tilly steps out the front door, tossing a goodbye to her mom as she walks toward her car.

She only makes it a few steps down the driveway when her phone rings. She fishes it out of her purse with an odd expression. "Who is this?" she demands. "Answer me."

Silence.

"Carl, is that you?"

The hairs rise on the back of my neck as I shoot a panicked glance at Tessa.

"I blocked your number. Did you get a burner phone?" Tilly's eyes roam the dark, empty street nervously.

Tessa and I are on our feet. "Is he nearby?" My heart races. He could be lurking anywhere.

Tessa's eyes hunt the neighborhood shadows like mine. We hover beside Tilly as she makes her way to her car.

I can't hear what Carl is saying, but whatever it is has Tilly upset. "I don't know what you think you saw, but he's just a friend. We both lost someone close to us, and he was consoling me. You need to respect my boundaries and leave me alone, Carl. I'm not going to say it again. If you call or text me one more time, I'm . . . I'm going to the police." She hangs up, hands shaking.

Tilly's key fob rattles in her fingers as she unlocks her car.

"We need to find him if he's nearby," says Tessa. "This is our chance." She races down the block, looking behind bushes, garbage cans, anywhere a psycho creep might lurk.

I inspect the side of Tilly's house, in case Carl's lurking in the shadows. With a last nervous glance, Tilly gets in and starts the engine, taking off down her driveway. That's when Carl steps out from behind a tree across the street, heading for a yellow car parked under some long branches.

"He's right there!" Tessa runs down the street toward me, as if I haven't noticed. "Stop him."

Stop him how? My mind casts around for any advantage we might have. What can I use? I can't pick anything up. I can't speak to him. I'm a shit ghost. In a panic, I do the only thing I can think of: I charge across the street and walk straight through him.

I'm drowning in a river of ice as waves of Carl's disturbed memories cascade over me. Carl as a young boy using a magnifying glass to burn ants. Carl pressuring Tilly to kiss him in the back seat of his car, or secretly recording a video as she leaves school for the day. He's swerving toward her by the river, laughing as she scrambles out of the way. His thoughts are consumed by sick fantasies of hurting her. And even more disorienting is how Tessa and I are in there, too, in that flood of memories. Me, with my pupils blown wide, gasping and gagging on my own blood as I dragged myself into the bathroom. Tessa, pulling her hair, begging for water, as she curled up on the floor. It's too much; I need to escape. *Get me out of here.*

Then it's suddenly over. I'm through, shivering on the

asphalt, teeth chattering, my mind trying to pick up the pieces, remember who I am separate from him. I try desperately to bring my awareness to the present; there was something I needed to do, something important, but I'm too overwhelmed by those images of my own death to remember. I roll my head to the side.

Carl's shaking beside me, clutching his stomach. He's fallen to the ground, but clambers back up. "What the—?" he mumbles, pulling his key out of his pocket.

That's right. That's what I needed to do. Stop him. But I can't. Not anymore.

"Tessa," I gasp, when she runs over, looking concerned. "Don't let him get in that car."

As Carl staggers toward his vehicle, Tessa's jaw is set, her mind made up. She steps forward and plunges through him, too. That strange illusion happens again, a ripple effect, like a stone cast in a still lake. Reality vibrates around them, time almost coming to the briefest standstill. Then it's over and Tessa's through. She's coughing, bent double, looking like she's going to be sick.

Carl convulses on his side, face pinched tight. He groans. When his eyes open, and he glances down the block, Tilly is long gone. "I can't . . . *shit*." He pulls himself up partway and crawls the final distance to his car. Hand trembling, he manages to open the door and hoist himself inside.

I stumble over to Tessa and help her up as Carl takes off down the street.

"Did you see which way Tilly went?" Tessa asks.

"She went right." I clutch Tessa to my side. We watch tensely as Carl pulls up to the stop sign, waits, and eventually turns left.

Tessa lets out a deep sigh. "That was insane."

At least we stopped him, for now. But what kind of plan is this? "Are you okay?" I check her over.

"Yes, are you?"

I nod, then lean my forehead against hers. We breathe together for a long moment, slowly coming back to ourselves.

"Of all the times that's happened, that was by far the worst. I didn't like being inside him at all." Tessa shivers beside me. "He's dangerous. I don't think he's ever going to stop."

"I know. He's obsessed. He gets off on the violence. It was one thing to know he watched us as we lay dying, but another thing to feel what he *felt* as he watched. He enjoyed seeing us die. He was thrilled."

"He's *evil*, Reed. This is far worse than we thought."

I take her hands in mine. There's no easy way to say this. "I saw in his mind all his plans for hurting her."

A cry of pain, guttural and deep, tears out of Tessa. She leans over, hands on her knees as she struggles to regain her breath. "You know when she said that thing about going to the police?"

"She should have taken out a restraining order days ago."

"Well, he wasn't thinking about restraining orders. I saw his thoughts, his plans. He's sure Tilly is onto him—that she was threatening to go to the police about our deaths, to turn him in."

The air gusts out of me. "But I don't think Tilly suspects him of our murders."

"He doesn't *know* that. He's full of all kinds of paranoid delusions. Tilly can place him at the scene of the crime. She knows what he's studying."

"Shit." I press my palms against my eyes. "This is not good.

Before he was obsessed with her, but now she's a threat. Her comment about the police changed everything."

Tessa staggers forward, lightheaded. "This is all my fault. I should have been a better friend, noticed she was dealing with all this, left the party when she first mentioned he was there. She was obviously upset to have seen him. And she'd been getting all these texts from someone. I bet those were from Carl and not silly drama with her cousins like I thought. How could I have been so clueless? And now, she could be killed because I wasn't paying attention. I'm a terrible friend." Tessa drops her face into her hands.

"Hey, hey, listen." I reach for her shoulders, turning her toward me. "You were a good friend to Tilly. And we're not going to let anything happen to her, you understand? He's not laying a finger on her."

She searches my eyes for the promise behind them. "I want to believe you, more than anything. But I don't know if I can," she admits. "We lost time, right? Like Hal said we would?"

I pull our phone out of my pocket to flip open. "Two days' punishment for making contact with the living, like he warned us."

"Dammit. Only sixteen days left now."

"With one phone and one door, it seems it doesn't matter which of us walks through someone. We both lose time."

"This is no plan, Reed. Look at my hand, it's coming in and out of focus." Tessa holds her fingers up, unsettling and translucent, as she begins to pace. We've been away from the mansion since early this morning, and having Carl blast through us can't have helped. "We can't save Tilly if every time we try, we incapacitate ourselves and lose more time. We're going to run out of chances. But Carl won't. He'll still be coming for her after we're gone. So don't make promises that he won't hurt her again because you don't know that."

My brows knit together as my own body flickers translucently. It's creepy as hell.

Tessa shivers. "Santiago can place him at the party, too." Her eyes snare on mine. "Carl's fixated on Tilly now, but that doesn't mean he wouldn't come after Santiago later. Not if he viewed Santiago as another threat."

"Shit." My stomach drops.

"In his memories, Carl was watching Santiago comfort Tilly at her mom's store. He was consumed with jealousy over being replaced, positive Tilly was sleeping around."

I drag my hand through my hair. The people we love need us and I've no idea how to help them. It's infuriating. I could kick something, but I can't even do that, so I howl instead, my temper rising. Our friends are in so much trouble.

What are we missing? Why would we be here to stop Carl, if we've no means of stopping him?

Because either we deter him now . . . or we find a way to pause the timer until we can figure things out.

I don't like a puzzle I can't solve.

I make up my mind then and there. "We need a way around this fucking clock."

CHAPTER 21

Tessa

We spend the night in one of the downstairs parlors, where dark maroon wallpaper laced with gold leaves has peeled off the walls to lie in shreds along the floor. Mouse droppings group in the corners beneath a creaky unlit chandelier.

You know, home sweet home.

It took a while to feel whole again, to lose that eerie feeling that's part exhaustion, part numbness from straying away from our door for too long.

I curl up beside Reed on the threadbare sofa as all the sensations slowly return: our breath; his arm draped reassuringly over my shoulder; the feeling of being solid, of existing here, in whatever way that means now. We don't talk much; my mind is too full, a jumble of images of Carl, his disturbing memories and plans, and how helpless I feel to stop him.

As dawn blooms, chasing away the shadows, Reed shifts to face me. He searches my eyes. I had assumed he was thinking about last night, too, and all that happened on Tilly's street, and maybe he was. But that doesn't feel like what he's thinking now. His gaze dips to my lips and lingers there. We haven't kissed since our night on the stairs. We haven't even talked about it.

"Should we head out to Tilly's place now?" he asks.

"It's barely sunrise—she's probably still sleeping. I'm afraid if we go too early, we may run out of steam before we're really needed."

"That's what I thought, too. So . . . how should we spend our time?" That damn dimple of his is back. If only he knew the power that dimple holds over me.

"How would you like to spend our time?" I try to sound casual.

"I have some ideas."

A soft laugh escapes my lips. "I bet you do."

He sweeps some stray hair away from my face, his thumb lingering. My hands, with minds of their own, lace behind his neck, pulling him toward me. We lean back against the couch as he brings his mouth to mine. The kiss is gentle at first. It begins as a promise, our lips brushing past each other with questions asked and answered.

Is this okay? Yes. *Would you like to do this forever?* Yes. *Do you like me like this?* Oh yes.

It deepens, a promise kept. This time we're less urgent than our night on the stairs, when we clung to each other through the storm. Maybe we're surer of each other. Maybe we're finding our rhythm. Maybe all the feelings behind it are deeper. Whatever the reason, it's unequivocally better.

Because this time, it feels like home.

When we startle back to reality, I slip the phone from my pocket (long live dresses with pockets) to check the date and time. July 1, 8:15 a.m. I turn it around for Reed to see. "Tilly doesn't leave until around nine forty for her mom's shop."

Reed switches the display over to the countdown timer. "Fifteen days and change left."

I stand, straightening my dress, and pull my hair down to rebraid my buns. "Today we find a workaround, some way to stop Carl besides walking through him. Even if Tilly doesn't know it, she's depending on us, and we can't let her down." It feels wrong to be away from her for this long when I know she's in trouble.

"Agreed. Today we formulate our plan. We're good at solving problems. At least, for me, when it comes to BattleBots and calculus. How hard can cracking the afterlife be?" Reed pushes off the couch to join me, watching as my fingers work through my long dark strands, weaving them together. "You never wear your hair down. I like it." He slips me a smile.

Will we ever talk about whatever this is between us? Are we deciding not to put labels on it? Is he my boyfriend now? Is that even possible as a ghost? I almost laugh, imagining what

Tilly would think. She'd say I was out of my mind. *Yeah, you know entitled, arrogant Reed Walker? He's kind of my dead boyfriend now, my ghost with benefits.*

"Too bad I like it like this." I shrug playfully as I secure my buns back in place.

Reed's grin disappears as he glances behind me out the window. "Is that Hal?"

"What?" I spin around. Sure enough, crossing through the gate and making his way along the winding, mossy path toward the house is Hal—brown tweed suit, bowler hat, and all.

We race to the foyer, dissolving through the door to meet him on the porch.

"Hey, Hal!" Reed hollers. "Welcome to casa shithole. Don't let the fancy exterior fool you. Do you want to come in?"

"Hey, kids." He vanishes from his spot by the gazebo and reappears down the path in front of us. "Nice to see you two again." He's as polite as ever, but a heaviness hangs over him.

"Are you all right?" I ask.

"Well . . . um . . . I know this is perhaps an unexpected request . . . It's just . . . since Jeb's gone . . ." He removes his bowler hat, clutching it in his hands. "See, my time is almost up. All day yesterday I tried to muster the strength to cross alone, but I couldn't bring myself to do it. I don't want to turn into a fade like Jeb, but when I stare at that gaping hole, this fear overtakes me and—" He pinches the bridge of his nose, hand shaking. "This morning, I visited Bessie's grave one last time to see if that would give me the strength to make the crossing, and then I thought of you two nearby, and well . . ." he chokes out between sobs.

"Of course." Reed jumps in without hesitation. "We'll go with you."

Relief washes over Hal's features before he grimaces slightly. "You might have to push me through." He must catch my shocked expression because he quickly follows up with, "If it comes to that, you have my complete permission. On my own, I freeze. And panic."

I guess I know a thing or two about that.

I glance at Reed, torn. I want to help Hal, of course, but the idea of shoving anyone through their door is a bit horrifying, and more than that, I'm getting antsy to check on Tilly. This morning's make-out session already slowed us down, and I need to know that she made it home safely last night. "Could we come by a little later today instead?" I ask Hal.

"The clock's a-tickin'." He shrugs helplessly. "I only have an hour left."

Reed puts a hand on my shoulder. "Tilly doesn't leave for work for another hour and a half. And Hal needs us."

I know going with him is the right thing to do, so although every instinct in me screams otherwise, I force myself to say, "We're here for you, Hal. Let me check on my friend quickly to know she's all right, and I'll meet you there."

"Thank you." Relief washes over his face. "Shall I wait for you out front?"

I nod.

"Then off we go." With a deep breath, he vanishes.

Reed turns to me. "I'll come with you first."

"Okay," I agree. "To Tilly's place."

I imagine Tilly's house with the magnolia tree in full bloom on her lawn. In a blink, I'm there, with Reed standing beside me. Soft petals rain down around us.

I sigh a huge sigh of relief. Her dad's Sanderson Construction van is still in the driveway, along with Tilly's Honda. Looks like she made it home just fine after all. Thank God.

"Feel better?" Reed nudges my shoulder.

"Definitely." I was worried all night. It's a massive weight off my chest to know she made it back okay.

"Good, because there's a sweet old man who is probably hyperventilating outside his home right now staring at that timer of his."

My eyes drift up to Tilly's room.

"Tessa." Reed sighs, following my gaze to her bedroom window. "He can't follow her twenty-four seven. And her family is here. Carl likes to work in the shadows. He's not coming for her while her parents are home." He reaches out his hand, cupping my face. "You ready?"

"We help Hal and then we come right back here."

"Yes. We'll come straight back," he promises, then before I know it, he vanishes, the trace of his touch still lingering on my cheek.

I take a deep breath and within moments I've joined them at Hal's red front door with the golden knocker. The stately trees along the block rustle lightly in a gentle breeze.

"Thanks again for coming." Hal seems relieved we didn't take too long. "Now, in case you were wondering, no one's home. My daughter's at work and the twins are in day care. It's a bit of a whirlwind inside, but then again, I've always loved a messy, lived-in house."

We pass through the front door to find Lego pieces scattered across the floor, a ride-on dump truck tipped over, and cereal bowls on the counter, their contents full of mush from the milk left behind. "Lizzie has a lot going on," Hal says, as if the place needs excusing. I lived with a single parent. I know how much there is to do because, while my dad tried to pick up what scraps of employment he could, I was usually the one doing the chores. A deep ache courses through me at the memory. I hope he's okay without me. I hope the dishes aren't piling up too much and his blood pressure medicine doesn't lie forgotten in the bathroom cabinet without my constant nagging reminders to take his pills.

"You remember the way?" Hal gestures for us to follow him down the hall and through the office door. If the rest of the house is chaos, this is a small corner of order, save the dust building up on the neglected shelves and desk. It's as if, after Hal's passing, his daughter came in once to clean it and never set foot inside again. I can't say I blame her. Can the living sense the strange portal lurking down the hall? Perhaps she stays away from the memories here, but also the ominous sense that something mysterious and supernatural resides behind these walls.

Hal's doorway to the beyond is still outlined in light, but as the countdown clock nears its final moments, a deep hum buzzes in the background. It's a note barely detectible by the human ear. I feel it more than hear it—the entire room resonating with possibility and purpose.

"Well, no getting around the elephant in the room." Hal eyes the gateway.

Reed hasn't been able to take his eyes off it since we entered.

I wonder if he hears that strange buzzing noise, too. At last, he turns to Hal, as if prompted by that hypnotic sound. "So, do you want us to give you a little nudge, or maybe walk beside you?"

Hal shifts his weight, considering. But if we push him through now, or he plows forward in a moment of courage, we may never get the answers we need to save Tilly.

"Wait!" I blurt out.

Both their heads snap in my direction.

"We could use your help," I start, afraid we'll lose our chance to ask him about gaming the system. Surely Hal's figured things out that we haven't. "The guy who killed us, he's going to strike again, and we have to stop him. But we're running out of time. Unless there's some way to mess with this clock." I wave at the countdown ticker above the door. "If we could somehow pause it or add more time, then we might have a fighting chance to deal with Carl before he hurts anyone else."

"If I had that kind of advice, I wouldn't be standing here now." Hal looks pained not to have more to offer. "I'm sorry, kid, I want to help you, really. I just don't know how."

"But Jeb, your friend, he was here a long time," I persist. "He must have figured something out. Like, if time can come off the door in punishment, then maybe doing the correct things can add it back on. Did Jeb ever mention anything like that? Or maybe he discovered some way to interact with the living besides just . . . passing through them." My anxiety's spiraling. These guys had months here—Jeb had over a year. What were they doing with all their time?

"I wish I had better answers for you both, I really do. But Jeb, God rest him, he faded away like anyone else who remained.

Even the best of us aren't immune to the consequences of overstaying our welcome."

"No. I refuse to believe that. There's some way to get the A grade here, and we need to figure it out. Like the phone trick to replay memories. There must be other secrets to unlock. I mean, what's the point of staying behind if we can't change anything? If we can't help the people we need to help? Isn't that like, the whole point of ghosts?" My breath starts coming fast and shallow.

"Tessa." Reed edges closer, reaching for me like he's trying to soothe a skittish cat.

I whack his hand away. "Don't patronize me, Reed."

He jerks back.

"Is that . . . the *point* of ghosts?" Hal steps closer, having watched me lose my cool. "You want to change things here, and I understand that impulse, but maybe it's really about this place changing *you*. Being here, it's hard, but it's also a gift. It clears the head, helps you see things in a whole new light. Maybe *that's* the point. We get this rare thirty-thousand-foot view of our lives, to understand our choices better, to grow. I used to be so quick to make up my mind about everyone. I thought Jeb was selfish for choosing to fade away, for making me watch him slowly disappear. I assumed Bessie never loved me if she could move on without me. But now I don't think either of those things are true. People are motivated in deeper and more nuanced ways than we give them credit for. Jeb was an honorable man, and I don't think he could leave when he saw others suffering, not if he thought he could help. And Bessie, maybe she never stayed. She was always smarter than me. She's probably on the other side of this door right now, shaking her head and wondering why I'm taking so long." Hal glances longingly at a black-and-white vacation photo of him and his wife on the bookcase, leis wrapped around their necks as she pecks him on the cheek. He pulls his glasses away to wipe his tears. "When you take your time to really look, you'll see everyone's doing the best they can." Hal fixes me with his stare and nods to Reed.

My cheeks heat. I know I can be snappy and quick to judge people, too. Feeling scared and unsure has always made me lash out. But we're all trying our best in the face of terrifying change. My eyes mist over.

"Hey now, if anyone can figure it out, you can." Hal gives me an encouraging pat as I work to slow down my breathing. "You're dealing with a painful situation and a lot you feel responsible for. Maybe I should have spent my time here better than I did, so I'd have more advice to offer." His shoulders sag. "I tried to take it all in, to enjoy my girl and the grandkids, to do my best to say goodbye to it all." He chokes on those last words. "All I know is the days here are gone before you know it. And things can shift in an instant with one wrong move, especially at the end when your time is so scarce. So help your friend if you can. Maybe that *is* the point of being here, to help the living somehow. What do I know? But whatever you do, don't cut it as close as me. When the time comes, don't risk getting stuck here. Be brave."

I close my eyes and let Hal's advice wash over me. God, I've been such an ass. I can't believe I hesitated over coming here, now that I see firsthand what he's facing, and how much harder this would be to do alone. "You are brave, Hal. You always send those smoke creatures scurrying. You saved me at the back gate." I slip my hand into his. "I'm worried about my friend, but that doesn't mean I can't be here for you, too. Both of us." I slip Reed an apologetic smile for smacking him earlier. "How can we help?"

"Yeah, whatever you need." Though Reed is talking to Hal, his gaze shifts to me, as if the offer is for us both. He holds my eyes with the weight of that promise and a million butterflies take flight in my stomach.

Hal's sigh breaks me out of the moment. With his hand still clasped firmly in mine, he turns to face the door, face the mystery of whatever comes next. He inches a step closer, holding on to me like a lifeline, with Reed walking beside him on the other side.

The door flickers, beckons. With each of our slow steps forward, the incessant timer threatens the gateway preparing to close. It's our future, too, I realize, as I face down what's coming. In two short weeks, I'll be confronting the same fate, but I can't let myself dwell on that now. All my effort, all my energy needs to go to keeping Tilly safe.

I peek at Reed as we edge forward another step. He's staring at the door, too, his lips pursed in a slight frown, an uneasy expression behind his eyes. My heart swells. We've known each other, really known each other, for such a short amount of time, and yet it doesn't feel that way at all. There's something that feels inevitable, almost lucky, about landing together in this dumpster fire of a situation. I can't imagine being here with anyone else. Sure, he can still annoy me sometimes, but the good far outweighs the bad.

Eventually, only feet from the gateway, Hal pauses, giving

my palm a squeeze before releasing me. He offers Reed his hand to shake. "You hold on to this one, you hear? She's a spitfire with a heart of gold."

"Yes, sir."

Hal pats Reed on the shoulder. "Good boy. And you . . ." He turns to me. "You remind me so much of my girl, Lizzie. She has a fine head on her shoulders, too, and a big heart. You listen to me now: I may scare off the fades from time to time, but bravery isn't always rushing off to fight the dragon. Sometimes, it's picking yourself up after crippling loss. That's always been the hardest kind of bravery for me to find. But I see now it has to be me, my choice, from here." He girds himself with a deep breath. "We need to face the unknown on our own terms. After all, we come into this world alone and we leave it alone." Hal glances at the door again, facing the ultimate unknown, his expression impossible to read.

"Aren't we supposed to be the ones helping *you* here? You seem like you're handling all this really well." The words spill out, my throat tight, voice quivering. I don't want Hal to go. Why does it feel like losing my dad all over again?

He lifts my face up, his gray eyebrows a tangle over deep, kind eyes. "Chin up, kiddo. Your time will come, and you'll meet it with grace. I know it." He ruffles my hair, shaking one of my buns loose, but I don't care. "And if you think your presence here isn't helping, well, you'd be wrong about that. I didn't know if I could do it, but sometimes other people help you find the strength you need." He nods his head toward Reed, and I'm not quite sure, but I almost catch a wink, just for me.

Then Hal's eyes glaze over, lost momentarily to a distant

memory, a small private smile hovering on his lips. "I used to read *Peter Pan* to my daughter growing up, and then to my grandkids. I've been thinking about that book a lot lately, how when Peter is frightened and fears all is lost, he picks himself up and says, '*To die will be an awfully big adventure.*' It seems my next adventure is here. So, onward, eh? To new stories and distant shores."

And with that, Hal turns back to the door and marches straight up to the edge. It vibrates, alters, no longer outlined in light but dissolving into a vast shimmering chasm. Or at least that's what it looks like from here—like an astronaut taking their first step outside the shuttle, on the precipice of the infinite, full of emptiness but also promise.

"I'm coming for you, Bessie. You hold on, now. I'm coming." And with those final words, Hal nervously adjusts his suit and steps through. The light outlining the door is back, suddenly shrinking in on itself until it's gone.

Hal is gone.

The room is no longer full of magic, full of his larger-than-life presence. It's just a small back office in a big empty house, with a family who desperately misses him.

It's not until I turn to Reed and see the tears rolling down his cheeks that I realize I'm crying, too.

CHAPTER 22

Tessa

By the time we pull ourselves together to check on Tilly, it's five minutes after ten a.m. We head straight for Aunt Betty's to find her at work.

"Why are the lights off?" I ask. "She's usually here by now." A chill prickles over my skin. All the other stores along the block are opening, from Lawson's Deli to Hyperion Realty. It doesn't make sense. I peer through the window, then remember I can step through. Reed follows.

The back door is locked. There's no sign of her morning iced coffee or the crocheted bag she takes everywhere.

No. No. No. Did something happen while we were at Hal's?

It's unlike Tilly or her mom to leave the store closed, especially without a note on the door. "Something's wrong."

"I admit, it doesn't look good." Reed wanders behind the counter, looking for any sign of her. "Should we try her place?"

"Yes." I don't check if he's ready. I call up the image of Tilly's front lawn and send myself there.

Tilly's car is now the only one in the driveway. Thank God. She's still here. She probably overslept and is running behind.

Reed arrives on the grassy lawn beside me. "Tilly hasn't left yet?"

"Not yet. Though it's not like her to be late." My fingers drum against my thigh as I wonder why it's taking her so long.

"Should we go inside and check on her?"

I want to. Desperately. I know I'll feel so much better if I can just see her face. But I waffle. "I don't know. The bathroom light is on upstairs, which means she probably overslept and is finishing her shower or getting dressed. Maybe we give her a couple minutes."

Reed looks mildly horrified. "I never really thought about it before, but you could be a super pervy creeper as a ghost."

"I guess we've been using our powers all wrong." I sit under the shade of the magnolia tree, with a good view of Tilly's bedroom window, in case she walks by. I already feel better knowing she's close. And at least out on the lawn we'll catch Carl if he drives by again.

Reed plops down beside me. "What percentage of ghosts do you think use their time here to spy on people getting dressed, or watch them have sex? I'm guessing fifty percent."

"What? You seriously think fifty percent of people in the afterlife are busy being pervs around town?"

"Uh . . . yeah. You don't? Honestly, the number is probably

higher. I'm reevaluating. I'm going with seventy-five or eighty percent now."

"No way. Ten percent. If that. People are mourning their old lives or busy investigating the reasons why they died. There's plenty for them to do besides . . ." I wave my hand at the house.

"You have far too much faith in humanity."

"Clearly, we know which category you'd be in if you didn't have my steady moral presence to guide you." I knock my knee against his.

"Hey, I'm out here with you, remember? And besides, I don't need to creep around like that, I have a hot ghost girlfriend."

My eyes dart over to his, warm and honey brown. "Is that what I am?" I ask as casually as possible, my heart racing.

"A ghost? Yes. Hot? Definitely. And, my girlfriend? I mean . . . yes? Or . . . would you like to be? I wasn't sure if you needed more time to get over Brandon."

"Brandon?" I actually snort-laugh, which is not my sexiest moment, but I try to quickly recover. "That relationship feels like a lifetime ago. Literally. Besides, I was preparing to break up with him at the party, but he got there first. He's a good guy, though, despite how it ended, so none of your snarky comments." I narrow my eyes at him.

He pretends to zip his lips closed.

"But no, just so it's out there, I'm not hung up on Brandon. I like you, Reed."

His smile is infectious. "Honestly, maybe the whole boyfriend-girlfriend label is wrong. Whatever this is between us, it feels like more than that . . ." He trails off, suddenly curious about the patch of grass in front of him.

"I know." I stop his fidgeting by lacing my fingers through his. "Sometimes it feels like we're here together for a reason. You know?"

His eyes rise slowly to mine.

I'm unsure how to put what I'm feeling into words. It's a thought that's been bubbling under the surface for a while. "What if it wasn't an accident we died here together? Maybe, somehow, I'm supposed to be here . . . with you."

Reed gives my hand a squeeze, but before he can say anything more, the Sanderson Construction van screeches into the driveway and Tilly's father gets out. He's agitated, stumbling on a crack in the cement and dropping his phone. "Wait. Hang on!" He bends to pick it up. "Say that last part again."

I exchange a worried glance with Reed. Something feels very off.

Mr. Sanderson struggles to find his housekey on his overloaded key chain. "They moved her to recovery? But did you get a chance to speak with the surgeon about her injuries yet?"

Reed and I leap to our feet. Is it . . . could it be . . . ? But her car is here. The terror I feel is so palpable I'm afraid I'll collapse under the weight of it.

When Tilly's dad pushes past the front door, we follow him.

"Tell me what you need," he says breathlessly, taking the stairs to Tilly's bedroom at a run. Inside he's a human tornado, careening into lamps, slamming dresser drawers as he tosses her pajamas, socks, and an old T-shirt into a bag. He runs into Tilly's bathroom to grab a toothbrush, then returns and halts in the middle of her bedroom, glancing around anxiously—like his mind is spinning to catch up with his adrenaline-fueled body. "I think I have it all. I'm heading your way now."

There's a muffled voice upset on the other end. "Dammit, Alicia, the store can stay closed for a day." He leans over, hand on his knee, to catch his breath. "Fine. I'll swing by with the bag, then head over to meet the shipment. I'm . . . just glad she's alive." A heavy sob reverberates through his chest. I've never seen an adult cry like that, except for my dad at the kitchen sink when I went home or Reed's mom as she clutched the wreath on our porch. He's no longer Tilly's father, builder of houses, teller of great stories; he's a little boy, alone and afraid. "What's the room again?" His voice quivers. "Two oh four. Okay. I'll be there as soon as I can." Then he takes the stairs two at a time and races outside to his van.

Once we've transported ourselves to the lawn and Mr. Sanderson is pulling away, I tilt my head back and scream in frustration. My body vibrates with waves of hatred for Carl. "How could we be so stupid? We went to help Hal when we should have stayed here with Tilly." I lash out at Reed. "You said she'd be fine. You said Hal needed us, and that Carl can't follow her twenty-four-seven. We underestimated him, Reed. I never should have listened to you."

He rounds on me. "I don't have any special information that you don't have. Okay? I'm trying to make the correct decisions moment to moment like you. And it was the right thing to help Hal. Maybe it was a mistake for us both to go. Maybe we should have split up, but you're not perfect, either, Tessa. When we got here, I said we should go inside to check on Tilly and you said to give her a minute, so everyone's calling balls and strikes here and we're both doing the best we can."

I glare at him, so angry I don't care who gets caught in the crosshairs. "That's supposed to make me feel better?"

Brandon would be wrapping his arms around me now. But not Reed. He stands firm. "Feel how you want to feel, it's just the truth. Besides, we don't know what happened yet."

"Oh, come on. We know enough. He's come for her in some way and now she's in the hospital, in *surgery*. Her dad said she's lucky to be alive! We're failing, Reed." I sink onto the grass, the weight of our mistakes ready to drag me into a dark hole I'm not sure I can climb out of.

"Look." He kneels beside me and blows out a frustrated breath. "We can't stop him if we don't know what he's up to. And getting pissed at each other isn't helping. So, we go to the hospital, learn what happened, and make a plan from there."

I nod at last, blinking tears from my eyes. "Let's find her at the hospital." Tilly doesn't have time for me to be lost in my feelings. She needs me and we're failing.

I'm failing.

Tessa Marie Sinclair, who aces tests and won student body president. Yet I'm unable to do this one thing: make sure my best friend is safe.

Even as I close my eyes to picture the hospital, I can't stop thinking about it. I'm supposed to be the person everyone looks to as an example. I am not my father and his long line of work and money troubles. I'm not my mother and her disastrous marriage.

Failing is something I cannot let myself do.

And yet, in the darkest corner of my heart, I fear I'm an imposter, a fraud, and that's exactly what I will do.

Fail. Fail. Fail. Fail. Fail.

Right when Tilly needs me the most.

I never liked hospitals. I don't know how Jillian does it every day. But we have no choice. We race through the hallways in search of room 204, past overworked nurses, intake stations, and orderlies pushing carts piled high with meal trays, Jell-O cups wiggling.

When we round the corner, I skid to a standstill. A man in a hospital gown stands in the middle of the hall. He suddenly turns and dissolves through a wall up ahead. Of course there would be other ghosts here, but the sight of him is still a shock. Reed catches my eye. He's seen it, too, but he nods for me to continue.

When we arrive at room 204, I'm surprised to find Tilly already here, asleep. She must have been moved out of recovery. Her mom sits beside her, holding her hand. Her father's probably still headed this way.

Seeing Tilly with an IV in her arm, her body bruised and shoulder in a sling, it's too much to take in. My feet give out from under me as I buckle to the floor.

My fault. It's my fault for not helping her sooner, for not figuring this out.

Reed puts a steadying hand on my arm. "Let's clear out of the doorway." He still sounds ticked off about our argument on the lawn, but he ushers me to the opposite corner of the room anyway. It's a good thing, too, because Tilly's dad rushes in, the overnight bag slung over his shoulder. He drops it to the floor and with two long strides he's beside her bed, brushing some hair back from her face.

"She just arrived from recovery," Alicia, Tilly's mom, says. "She's still out from the painkillers."

"Any word from the surgeon?"

"Yes, he came by after we hung up. He said her collarbone fractured in two places and was severe enough to require metal pins. They had to pull glass out of her skin." She grabs a tissue from her purse and dabs her eyes before continuing. "She'll need to use a sling for six to eight weeks, but should be better in time for freshman orientation. They're keeping her overnight, but then she can come home."

Reggie, Tilly's dad, shakes his head. "I don't understand why she took your car instead of hers or why she left so early. If she was heading into the shop, why go the long way around? You said the accident was near the bridge, right?"

"The police said she took the corner too fast and rolled. The car was teetering on the edge of the bridge, Reg. A couple jogging by pulled her out of a broken window before it went over. I can't even imagine if she'd gone into the river in that state."

Reggie sinks down onto his knees, hands folded on the edge of her bed. "Thank you, Jesus. Thank you for keeping my baby safe." His shoulders shake.

Tilly's mom grasps his hands as they cry together.

It feels like we're intruding on their private moment. I nod for Reed to follow and slip through the wall into the hallway.

My heart aches so much for Tilly, it's hard to focus. But I know she needs me to solve this. "What do you think really happened?"

"It's hard to know for sure, but if she saw Carl step into the street last night as she drove away, she might have thought it was smart to use a different car. It'd be harder to track her."

"That makes sense." I pace in the close confines of the hall, trying to re-create the situation in my mind. "So she drives off early, avoiding him, or avoiding her usual routine, and then what? He's driving after her or something, and she ends up flooring it to get away and hits a tight corner and flips?"

"Could be."

"God, I wish we could talk to her." I slump against the wall, defeated.

Reed rubs his temples over a deep sigh.

"Wait." I snap forward. "She's going to wake up and then she can explain everything. They can get the police involved and finally stop this madness."

"And get him on what charges?" Reed flings a hand in the air. "No one knows about us. As for Tilly, she can prove he called her a few times. Or tell them she saw him when she was driving. I don't think that's enough. I'm not sure a restraining order would stop him, either. When I passed through him . . ." He shudders. "He was determined. He was thrilled by the chase. That fucker likes her scared. I don't think he's going to stop unless we stop him, Tessa."

"But how?" I pull the phone out and flip it open, the numbers always ticking down, time slipping through our fingers. I snap it shut with a groan. There's a rough goodbye as Tilly's father heads out to take care of their store, walking past the nurse's station. Her parents have no idea what's going on. "She never told her mom and dad about him. All I can think to do is to stay close to her. We're the only ones who know what's happening."

"Maybe . . ." Reed rocks on his feet. "We've been so focused on her, right? But what if we stay closer to him instead? We find out where he lives. Learn his patterns. When does he follow her? Where does he hide?"

I nod. "Okay. That's a start. We follow Carl. Then we look for a weakness, for some kind of advantage, and we exploit it."

But first, we return to Tilly's hospital room. I need to know she'll be okay in this vulnerable state. I wish I could hug her mom, too. Alicia's always been so kind to me. She used to drop groceries off at our place when my family struggled to make ends meet, saying she got too much at Costco and needed to hand off the extras. I hate seeing her in pain, especially after all she's been through with her health this past year. I hate that she has no idea how much danger her daughter's in.

We spend the day with them. Tilly rouses at one point, but besides drinking some water and hugging her mom, she doesn't say much before she's out again. Nurses come and go throughout the day to check her vitals, adjust her bandages.

I'm so sorry, Tills.

I hope somehow the thought can reach her, that she might feel my presence here and know I'm close, know I'd do anything for her.

Little by little the tension bubbling between Reed and me dissipates. Maybe he takes pity on me for having to see my friend in this state. But whatever the reason, he moves closer as the day progresses, until at last, our pinkies overlap as we lean against the window.

The sky grows dark outside as we keep vigil. Eventually, an announcement rings out that visiting hours will be over in fifteen minutes. Though it doesn't affect us, we should probably head home anyway. I'm starting to get that hollow, washed-out feeling.

Out of nowhere, Reed grabs my arm, his fingernails digging into my skin.

"Ow. What are you—?" I turn to look at him, but the color has leached from his face.

His hand is still clutching me tightly, his eyes fixed on the entrance. "It's him," he whispers.

I follow his gaze to the doorway and almost jump out of my skin to find Carl. How dare he show up here? He's holding a bouquet of purple flowers as if he belongs in her life, as if he has the right to intrude on her privacy.

"Sorry, I don't mean to interrupt." He runs a hand through his messy red hair. "I wanted to bring these for Tilly. One of the nurses lent me the vase." He gives a bashful shrug. *Oh, silly me, forgetting the vase.*

"That's so sweet. How do you know Tilly?" Alicia stands to greet him.

"I'm just a friend. Carl." He offers his hand to shake.

I step forward, preparing to launch myself through him if he tries to hurt either of them.

"I heard about the accident and wanted to make sure she's okay."

"That's very kind of you. I didn't realize news had spread.

Come on in. We can make some room on this table for your flowers. They're beautiful, and so unusual with the berries, what are they?"

"No idea. There was something about them. They reminded me of Tilly." His smile is slow and cruel, but Alicia doesn't catch it as she busily arranges the bouquet.

"Those are from our greenhouse. That's the plant he poisoned us with," I say.

"You know what that means?" Reed turns to me. "That means he was at our place this afternoon."

Here we've been wondering where to find him, and he's been out lurking on our grounds. I don't want him anywhere near us, or those plants, or Tilly.

With a quick knock on the door a nurse pokes her head inside. "I'm sorry, but visiting hours are over." She nods at Carl. When Alicia begins to gather her things the nurse adds, "She's a minor, so you're welcome to stay the night if you like, Mrs. Sanderson."

"Thank you," Alicia says, relieved, glancing at Tilly's battered frame on the bed.

"I'll grab you a blanket." And with that she heads down the hall. After a few final pleasantries, Carl excuses himself as well. As much as I hate to tear myself away, I know we need to follow him. At least we know Tilly's mom will watch over her tonight. I take off after Carl as he heads for the stairwell.

Reed falls into step beside me. "I'll track him through the lobby, but in case I lose him, you pick up the trail in the parking lot."

I nod once, imagine the sprawling lot out front, and send

myself there to wait. A few straggling visitors walk to their cars, but so far, no Carl. Then I remember the mustard-yellow Kia he drove the other night. I search the aisles until I spot it under the soft glow of a streetlamp, toward the back of the lot.

When I turn, Carl is walking toward me, with no Reed in sight. What do I do?

He gets in the car and starts the engine. Maneuvering toward the exit, he takes a right on Elm.

Still no Reed.

I want to go back and find him, but I'm afraid I'll lose my chance at this. Having no idea where Carl's headed, I do the only thing I can think of. I project myself to the corner of Elm and Montgomery and wait. He should be headed this way, and then I'll be able to see his next move. Within a few moments his headlights approach. Neglecting the stop sign, he swings right on Montgomery. I try my trick again, imagining the intersection of Montgomery and Franklin. In a breath, I'm standing under the awning of a drugstore, now closed for the night. I wait again.

My eyes search the horizon for his car, but he never rolls up. Shit. What did I miss? I send myself back about half the distance, but he's not there, either. Did he pull into a garage? After about ten minutes I reappear in the hospital parking lot, only to find Reed stumbling through the aisles.

"Whoa. Are you okay?" I jog over to him.

"I was following him," he gasps. "But it was crowded, and then this EMT blasted through me, and Carl got away."

"You have to be more careful. That's another day off the door. And for what?" I reach my hand out to steady him.

"Don't you think I know that?"

He leans his weight on my shoulder, his teeth still chattering. "Please tell me you had better luck."

I recount the events of the last ten minutes.

"Tessa, that's great. That means he stopped somewhere on Montgomery between those two intersections. There are lots of houses there, some apartments, too. Now we have a pretty good guess at where he lives." He playfully checks me out. "Look at that. My girlfriend is a badass ghost detective."

I can't help my smile. This feels like the first lucky break we've had in a while. "Come on, let's get you home." I tuck my arm under his.

I'm not sure the exact moment it happened, when *home* ceased to mean the house I grew up in and instead became the van der Born estate. But the mansion does feel like a home of sorts now. It's hard to know if that has more to do with the house itself or the boy beside me.

CHAPTER 23

Reed

When we return to the mansion Tessa heads to her bedroom for some quiet to think, and I collapse on a library chair, staring at the empty shelves and imagining what they'd look like teeming with books. Little by little, my energy, my sense of self, returns. It's like going from a sketch book page full of outlines and suggested forms to one shaded in. For a while something essential is missing, until at last, it's not.

Sometime in the middle of the night, I walk to the window, feeling antsy. It's a beautiful night. Not a cloud in the sky. It's the perfect moment to share my secret rooftop hangout with Tessa, the place I retreat to in the dark hours by myself. I pull up the image of her third-floor bedroom and cast myself there. She barely flinches when I plop down on the bed. We're getting strangely accustomed to this weird method of travel. "How are you feeling?"

"Improving, but not quite there yet." She rolls up to sit beside me.

"Yeah, me too. That EMT took it out of me, especially since we'd been away for so long." I lean against the headboard, taking in the nymph-carved mantel and the starlight pooling across the bed. "You definitely scored the best room in the house."

"I know." She smiles. "I love it."

"I've been having a little existential crisis downstairs, how about you?"

"Look at you, bringing out the big words. But yeah, kind of the same. I was worrying about Tilly, though it helps to know her mom's with her tonight. But thinking of her reminded me of all our plans. Like, we'll never go to Nepal now. That sucks. And we didn't graduate together. I really wanted my dad to see that."

"Right? There were these life experiences I always thought I'd have."

"Exactly. There's so much I still wanted to do. I never even . . ." Her eyes dart away nervously.

"You never . . . what?" I ask, tilting my head toward her.

"Never mind. It's ridiculous."

"I'm sure it's not." Now my curiosity's piqued. Did she always want to bungee jump or star in the school play or something?

"I just thought . . ." She covers her face with her hands. "Oh God, why am I feeling embarrassed to say this out loud?"

"Hey." I gently pry her fingers away. "Don't hide." I cup Tessa's hands in mine. "It's just me."

She takes a shaky breath. "It's only . . . I thought I'd add losing my virginity to that list." Her words tumble out in a rush.

Wow . . . okay . . . definitely wasn't expecting that.

I nod slowly, my heart stuttering. "So you and Brandon never . . . ?"

"No. It wasn't that kind of relationship. We tried a couple times, but I don't know, we seemed to work better with cuddling. I am a top-tier cuddler. What about you?"

"Do I like to cuddle? I don't know. I haven't really had many chances." I'm still stuck on the Brandon news. I just assumed they'd hooked up after all those years.

She side-eyes me. "You know what I'm asking. Have you ever . . . ? I mean, you don't have to tell me if you—"

"It's fine, Tessa. Yes, I'm a virgin." There. I said it. It's out of my mouth—this thing that feels like it's been hanging heavy in the air between us—how much I like her, how little time we have.

Her eyebrows shoot sky-high.

"I've done *other* things . . ." I feel like I need to amend, given the way she's looking at me. "But sex, no. My relationships never really lasted that long. I think I'm kind of a lot to handle." I shift uncomfortably. "Or, I don't know . . . maybe I never found the right person."

She holds my gaze.

There's so much asked and answered in the quiet moment that passes between us.

What if we never get to experience this part of life? There's nothing like knowing you have only fourteen days on earth to really crystalize the question.

Should we sleep together?

I guess that's something ghosts can do. If we go through the door and become one with the universe or whatever, this might be our last chance.

"Well, we could. If you want . . ." She bites her lip uncertainly and my heart picks up speed. "Do you . . . want that?"

It's not every day you get an offer like that. Heat rises in my cheeks, and let's be honest, other places. "I do." Now it's my turn to glance away. "More than you know."

"Hey." She places a gentle finger under my chin, turning me to her. "It's just me."

A tendril of hair has spilled from one of her buns. I brush it back, palm lingering on her cheek. "I think about our night on the stairs all the time."

Her eyes widen, even as her fingers trace slowly up my arm. I still at her touch.

"Me too," she whispers.

Tessa's confession unlocks something in me, and I realize how much I want this. Want her. And not just physically, though wow, that's there.

I want to know *all* of her, what she dreams about, what makes her laugh, the passions that drive her and the tender places she tucks away from the world.

My hands drift to her waist and her breath catches. I lift an eyebrow questioningly as I pull her flush against my side. She leans in, lips hovering close, her every breath a promise.

When we kiss, it's somehow both tender and searing. Her tongue lightly skims mine, an invitation.

I moan, hungry, greedy, giddy.

Tessa's hands tug down the collar of my T-shirt as she nuzzles my neck, planting her lips softly behind my ear.

"God, Tessa." I imagine her fingers tracing over my heated skin, when suddenly there's a cool rush of air.

My shirt has vanished.

Tessa gasps, pulling away.

"Whoa." I startle. "I thought about taking my shirt off and then it was gone."

"Yes, please," she says, awash in starlight. Her fingers run across my bare chest. "I like this game."

"Um . . . this is the best game I've *ever* played." I laugh. "I'm going to imagine away your gloves." I put my fingers to my temples and concentrate. *Be a gentleman. Just the gloves. Dear God, don't think about anything else. Not yet.*

When her gaze meets mine, she waves her hands, fingerless gloves still intact.

"Okay. I really did try to do it." I smirk.

"Well, that seems fair. That's one point for the afterlife. Can you imagine the chaos if ghosts could remove each other's clothes at will? This restores my faith in the universe."

"Looks like we don't get any supernatural help." My fingers dance over her palms, an idea sparking. "There are *other* ways," I challenge with a mischievous grin.

Slowly, I pull her gloves off, one by one, the dare back behind my eyes.

But this time Tessa returns it. "You did promise me a good time if I came to the party."

"I did. And I plan to make good on that promise."

"Right now?"

"This very second." My hands slide up her sides and run across her back. Her breath hitches as I find the zipper at the base of her neck. I draw it down slowly, notch by notch, our eyes locked. "Is this okay?"

"Yes," she says breathlessly.

I shift her dress aside and kiss her bare shoulder. I'm the luckiest guy not-alive. "And . . . this?" My lips forge a trail to her collarbone.

"Yes." Tessa leans back, pulling me with her, my weight pressing her to the bed. "Yes, to all of it," she breathes.

I couldn't agree more.

Yes to her and me.

To *us.*

To how much better we are together.

Just . . .

Yes.

After the most mind-blowing night of my life, I remember why I came upstairs in the first place and invite Tessa to join me on the roof, in my secret spot beside the northernmost turret.

Soon, she appears beside me, three stories up, king and queen of our domain.

"Wow." She exhales shakily. "This is some hangout."

"Tuck in, girl." I lean back against the gray shingles, arms behind my head. "And watch the celestial show."

Being so far away from the light pollution of the city means we can even see the Milky Way spilling across the horizon. It's just us, the frogs I've come to think of as our pets, and sprawling land. The world is awash in twilight hues, subtle silvers, and deep shadowy blues. As my eyes adjust, I can spot the hay bales tucked along the rolling fields, the scattered trees lining the lone road into town, and the stone wall surrounding the property. Even the statue of Adonis is visible in the back garden, the lavender bra still draped around his neck from the night of the party.

Tessa snuggles against me.

"You really are a top-tier cuddler." I pull her closer, feeling her warmth.

"It's one of my superpowers." She laughs and it lights up the dark night. "I can't believe you talked me into this. You know, when I woke up in the attic that first morning, for a moment I considered climbing down, but then I remembered I'm afraid of heights." She holds me tighter.

Shit. Was this a huge mistake? "Are you okay now?" I angle my head toward her.

"Weirdly, yes. I think the fact that I can't die takes the sting out of it. I don't know if you remember sixth grade and the whole rock-wall fiasco."

"Oh." I laugh. That day is burned into my memory, too. "I remember the rock-wall incident. Mika was screaming that you ruined her party because you got stuck up there and how she wasn't going to give you a goodie bag because of it."

"It's not funny," she protests, but she's laughing, too. "It was humiliating, but honestly, what a stingy bitch. I don't think she ever forgave me. That girl can hold a grudge."

"I thought you were pretty fierce."

"Are you kidding? I climbed to the top and froze in a panic."

"Did you see me climb up there?" Did she ever notice me in those days?

"You didn't take a turn?"

"Hell no. I was terrified. But I was scared of a lot back then—scared to move across the country, or to have my mom remarry. I wasn't ready to let go of the family we had. I was suffocating, missing my father—" My voice cracks, and I take a steadying breath. "Suddenly I was expected to start this whole new life without him in an unfamiliar place. It was a lot." There's so much I still need to tell Tessa about my dad, but naming my part in his death makes it realer somehow. What happens when she discovers who I really am?

"Reed." She reaches for my hand.

"But you," I whisper, letting our fingers slowly dance over one another. "You never let your fear stop you from trying something. You throw your full self into everything. You're the bravest, smartest, most incredible person I've ever met."

"I'm scared all the time," she confesses. "I have anxiety and panic attacks. I was terrified I'd never get out of this town. That if I didn't keep striving, pushing, winning, I'd be sucked into a life I didn't want, spinning in circles instead of following my dreams."

"And what were those dreams?" Even after all the ways I've gotten to know her tonight, I'm still hungry for more.

"It feels silly to share, since they're obviously not happening."

She's so quiet, the wind almost whips her voice off into the night. Almost.

"I want to know." I tuck a strand of hair behind her ear and kiss her gently. "Tell me and we'll imagine it together, the life you would have had."

"All right, but no kissing, or you'll distract me."

"Ha. Fine." I roll onto my back again. "I'm being very well-behaved and staring at the stars."

She lets out a soft chuckle. "Okay. How do I begin?"

While she thinks, I gaze at the night sky aglitter in starlight, feeling the hard shingles under me, the pull of the earth. It's a world that's both here and not here, touchable yet inaccessible, a tantalizing present that can't be opened. We can play in this world, but it's no longer meant for us. Not anymore. There was a path in front of me, a future I'd been dreaming of that's all but vanished now. But maybe, for this one moment, we can breathe it into existence, together, even if it's only in our minds.

"So, you know how I was into vintage fashion and how I loved to sew."

"Yes." I play along, keeping my gaze fixed on the stars.

"Part of it was financial—I couldn't afford a wardrobe otherwise—but a bigger part was my commitment to upcycling. I could see a space in the market for a company I wanted to launch, one that could have made a huge environmental impact on the fast-fashion industry."

"Really?" my head snaps to her, intrigued. I had no idea Tessa wanted to launch her own start-up.

"Uh-uh. Look up." She points above. "I don't think I can do this if you're staring at me."

"Okay. Focusing." I very pointedly look away, a smile hovering on my lips.

"So there are lots of fast fashion companies that churn out clothes every season, and sometimes they overbuy. When those items don't sell, that's called dead stock. I wanted to purchase that clothing cheap before it ended up in a landfill. Then I'd repurpose it, either through design or by studying chemistry to break the fabric down into other products. I guess my company would've been fueled by science, creativity, and my marketing genius. I really think I could have pulled it off, too."

A bittersweet longing courses through me for all we could have done, for the lives we'll never lead. "Tessa, if anyone could have pulled that off, it's you. I actually didn't know we had the environmentalism thing in common."

"We do?" She turns to me, skin kissed by moonlight. She's never been more beautiful. "Weren't you planning to go into finance like your stepfather? I always assumed that's where you were headed, being groomed to take over his company one day."

I can't think of anything I'd want to do less. I make a fake retching noise.

She gives me a poke. "Okay then, mystery boy. Spill."

"Nah." I laugh. "Not before you look away." I point to the sky.

"Fine." She looks up. "Tell me, what was the great Reed Walker going to do with his life?"

I take a deep breath. Why am I so nervous? I want her to know me better. So . . . let her. "Well, you know I got into Harvard."

She snorts. "I believe you mentioned it a few times."

"God, I was pretty obnoxious about that, wasn't I?"

"Your word, not mine."

Heat spreads up my neck. "All right, well, one more mention."

She waits patiently. Thank God, she's giving me space, keeping her eyes on the sky.

"I was thrilled to be accepted because for ages I'd wanted to study computer science and robotics at their School of Engineering and Applied Sciences. See there's this professor there, Dr. Gupta, who I really wanted to work with. His research is around harnessing technology to combat some of the world's greatest climate challenges. Right now, there's this incredible carbon capture technology in development that can filter CO_2 out of the air. And robotics will be in the middle of all of it. I'm not saying this solves climate change, but the possibilities to do some real good are immense."

"Reed, you are full of surprises. You are so not the guy I thought you were."

"How so?" I turn to her at last.

"We both wanted to save the world." She sighs.

"We wanted to do our part, anyway."

"And now we're lucky if we can save one girl."

"Not just any girl," I remind her.

"No. An amazing girl. Still, it's . . . sad."

We're silent for a long time after that. Out of the corner

of my eye, I catch the vanishing tail of a shooting star. "You know, if we had to give it all up, then at least let it be for a good reason." My mind drifts to Tilly lying in her hospital bed, to Carl dropping off those flowers. "I wish there were some way to communicate with the living. I can't tell you how many times I've wanted to leave a note of warning behind. *Burn those flowers. Whatever you do, don't take a drink from Carl.*"

"It's funny, but there was this strange moment when I walked through him." Tessa sits up, drawing her knees to her chest. "I was so overwhelmed by his awful memories, and I remember thinking *I can't stand it anymore*, and then, I swear I heard him mumble something similar after, but I was shaking on the ground at that point, and it was hard to process."

I jolt forward. "I'm pretty sure he said, *I can't*—and then he was shaking, too. Why didn't you mention this before?"

"It came back to me now, when you were talking about communicating with them."

"Because, Tessa, something similar happened to me, too, back at the precinct. I remember being overwhelmed and thinking *Make it stop* and then that woman, that cop, I'm pretty sure she repeated it . . . or something like it. I dismissed it at the time, but now, you have me wondering."

"Whoa. I think she did. This . . ." She shakes her head. "This is huge."

"This could be the game-changer we've been searching for. What if it's a two-way communication channel and we haven't realized its potential before?"

Her legs start bouncing with excitement. "Maybe it's not just us getting flooded with their memories—maybe we can do our own flooding in return and send our thoughts and ideas back to them."

"And . . . if we can communicate with him, that means we can mess with him." I grab her hand, the wheels spinning in my mind, a plan forming. "We've been going about this all wrong. We're ghosts, right?"

"Right . . ." she says slowly, unsure where I'm going with this.

"So . . . let's get haunting."

CHAPTER 24

Tessa

We check on Tilly a few times over the next couple of days—she's now home from the hospital with her parents hovering constantly, adjusting her pillows and bringing painkillers. She's safe, albeit shaken up. So, we spend our time practicing scaring each other. We brainstorm a list of warnings, phrases, threats, things we can say to terrorize Carl. Reed talks me through the plot of every horror film he's watched in the last five years. I'm now an expert on *The Shining*, *It*, *Hereditary*, and the entire *Scream* franchise, which he says is more funny than scary but can still give us ideas.

We'll start the hunt for Carl this afternoon, using every tool at our disposal to terrify him. Through our supernatural powers of persuasion, we'll show him that it's far scarier to come after Tilly, or to prey on anyone for that matter, than to give up. We will spend our remaining days making his life a waking nightmare.

But as Reed and I sit across from our door and its giant countdown clock, taking a breather after our scare attempts, a little voice in the back of my mind whispers, *What if it doesn't work? Or Carl doesn't care?* With each attempt we lose a day off the door, and with only eleven of them left, we could blow through our remaining chances.

I need a fail-safe.

Some way to know that if all our attempts go bust, I'm not leaving Tilly to fend for herself. If we can't stop Carl, the amount of danger she'll be in when we're gone is staggering. I vow right then not to leave until I know she's going to be all right.

What about Reed?

My feelings for him have grown deep and complicated, with our lives, deaths, and fates so tethered. Why were we only given this one door? Are we meant to continue on together? What happens if one of us departs before the other?

Reed promised he'd wait for me, that we'd leave at the same time, but I don't know if I can promise the same. I might not be able to go when he wants.

I glance out the large second-story windows; the mist is back, rolling up the siding, pressing against the seams, itching for a way inside. Somewhere out there, the smoke creatures must be gathering again. At least I know we're safe indoors. They can't seem to get onto our property unless we invite them inside. What did that woman at the back gate say to me? "Let me in," she'd begged. "Please."

I startle forward as an idea strikes me. If I can't stop Carl as a ghost, what about stopping him as a fade?

I have no idea if I can help Tilly as a smoke creature, but they seem to have powers I don't. Maybe that's the obvious answer in front of me, my final Hail Mary, and I won't know until I'm one of them. If there's even a possibility of stopping Carl in that form, I'll make the sacrifice. I'll do that for her.

But Reed can't know. He'll try to talk me out of it. I glance over at him. His eyes are closed, deep in thought, but he opens them slowly and flashes me a genuine, unguarded smile.

He promised Hal he'd hold on to me. I desperately want to hold on to him, too, to stay with him and face whatever comes next together. It's almost impossible to admit, but in the secret reaches of my heart, I think I'm falling in love with him. The thought pulls my breath up short, almost knocking me flat. I shove the feeling back down.

Because if the time comes, and we can't solve this any other way, I need to do whatever it takes to save Tilly. And I can't ask Reed to do the same. I can't be selfish in my feelings for him. I can't hold him back, even if it hurts.

I have to let him go.

"It's now or never." Reed rubs his hands together, a wicked glint in his eye. We've practiced and planned as much as we can. It's time to do some haunting.

"Is it weird to say that I'm excited?" I feel powerful, like we have the upper hand for once.

"I feel good about this, too. It can work. But we need to push ahead, even when we're reeling from stepping through him. If we drip it out slowly, one scare today, one tomorrow, he won't take it seriously. So we overwhelm him with an onslaught of terror. Agreed?"

"Yes." I nod. "But first we check on Tilly one more time. Make sure she's all right."

We send ourselves back to the magnolia tree on Tilly's lawn. It's around 3:30 p.m. Now that they've got her settled at home, Tilly's mom has taken over her shifts at the shop and her dad is off with his construction company.

"You head inside and I'll make sure Carl's not lurking nearby again." Reed takes off down the driveway, peeking behind cars and trash cans, while I walk through Tilly's front door.

There's the faint hum of the dishwasher running in the kitchen and upstairs Tilly is playing Sasha Sloan's "Dancing with Your Ghost," which feels oddly appropriate. Before I check on her, I inspect the house.

Carl, thankfully, is nowhere to be found.

I save Tilly's bedroom for last. It's still hard to see her injured. I find her leaning against some pillows on her sky-blue comforter, sitting under the Black Girl Magic poster she drew in art class, her desk stacked high with journalism books. Her arm's in a sling, and she's recovering from a black eye and road rash from where they dragged her out of the car before it tumbled into the river. I shudder, imagining how her story might have gone if she hadn't been rescued in time.

Her phone is beside her on the bed, but what she's looking at is our yearbook, spread open to a photo of us. It was a fundraising event for the senior class last fall, a masquerade ball. I was selling tickets when yearbook photographer, Megan Blackwell, gathered us together to snap this picture. Tilly and I are each wearing elaborate masks. She's in a gorgeous bubblegum-pink ballgown, because if it's colored like candy, she wants to wear it, and I'm in a slinky red lace dress that flares at my ankles.

I remember how excited I was when I found that fabric. We both have big smiles on our faces, but what I love most about the photo is how our heads are tilted together with our hands raised in triumph. As student body president, I'm proud of the money we raised, but Tilly . . . I don't know . . . she just seems happy to be there with me. Her fingers trace over the picture as a tear runs down her cheek.

"I love you, Tills." I kneel beside her. "I know you can't hear me, but I want to tell you anyway, you were . . . *are* . . . the best friend anyone could have hoped for. It may seem like I've deserted you, but I'm here. I'm watching out for you, and—" I lean in close, my words a solemn oath. "I *promise* I will make this right. So you focus on getting better, and I'll do whatever's needed to keep you safe."

For a moment, a brief, hovering moment, she turns her head toward my voice, goose bumps rising on her skin. Did she hear me? But when she stands with a wince and shuffles past me to close the window, I realize it was only the breeze.

"Goodbye, Tills," I whisper.

In a flash I travel back to the magnolia tree, where Reed is waiting for me, hauntingly beautiful and ready to enact our revenge.

CHAPTER 25

Reed

We decide to start at the corner of Montgomery and Elm and walk toward Franklin. Tessa checks the left side of the street for Carl's car. I check the right. If he's parked it in a garage we won't see it, but this is all we have to go on. By the time we reach Franklin it's 4:15 p.m., and no sign of Carl or his car.

"Now what?" Tessa asks.

"Do it again?" I shrug, checking the phone. I hate seeing time slip away unnecessarily.

"How about you start back on Elm, I'll start here, and we'll meet in the middle? We can cover ground quicker that way."

"Okay." I cup her cheek in my hand, and she leans into my touch.

"Be careful out there," she says, pressing a kiss to my palm. Before I can breathe a word, she's gone, leaving a vacuum behind her.

I wander past the drugstore and the Starbucks, dodging people on the sidewalk. Eventually I get to the residential section, and the traffic thins out except for the occasional dog walker or UPS delivery truck. There's a curve ahead in the road, a summer breeze rustling the leaves of the ancient oaks lining the block. I swear I hear my name on the wind, a light caress. For a moment it reminds me of the whispers of the smoke people, but when I hear it again, louder this time, I recognize Tessa's voice. She sounds like she's in trouble.

I race ahead to the corner and find both Tessa and Carl on the sidewalk about halfway down the block, shaking and doubled over. In a heartbeat, I cast myself beside her.

She reaches for me. "He pulled up to get something from his house and I barreled through him, twice. I did what we practiced. I told him I was here for revenge and asked how he'd like to die." Tessa grabs my arm, still unable to stand up fully. "I think he heard me, Reed. It's working."

"Who is this?" Carl's eyes are wild as he scans the surroundings. "Stay the hell away from me." He stumbles toward his car, restarts the engine, and begins to pull out of the driveway.

"Do something!" Tessa urges.

Without thinking, I project myself further down the street, right in Carl's line of sight if he could see me. Since he can't, that gives me the upper hand. I've never tried to intercept someone moving so fast before, but I brace myself as his car heads my way, lining myself up with the driver's side.

There's a rush of wind and sound, it comes on fast, but I allow the vehicle to pass through me—even as every impulse inside me screams to jump out of the way. I stay rooted in place, a tree against raging floodwaters. Before I know it, Carl and I are occupying the same space. I halt the flow and sink right into his body. I hold there, using all my strength, riding along with him, inside his head, as he speeds down the road.

This is my chance. I flood his mind with flash after flash of his crime: picking berries in the greenhouse, curling up outside the kitchen once he realized what he'd done, running away as we drew our last dying gasps. *We see you, Carl*, I say in my most threatening voice. *We know what you did . . . because we're watching you. If you lay one finger on Tilly, or anyone else, we will haunt you until your dying day.*

Then I'm out, on the street on my hands and knees, gasping for air. Every fiber in me is repulsed from being inside him. It's as if my body, wracked by convulsions, is trying to leach a poisonous toxin. It took all my strength to hang on that long, to shove my memories into him instead of the reverse.

I lift my head to find his car's slowed down. He's swerved into the other lane but hasn't stopped. He's getting away, getting closer to Tilly with every passing second.

Tessa tries the same trick I did, projecting herself ahead of the car to intercept Carl as he drives. The onslaught. That's what we're calling it. Go big or go home. It's a risk to spend so many of our remaining days at once, but we need to scare him so thoroughly that he backs off for good.

In the distance Tessa falls, writhing and groaning. Her efforts helped, though, because Carl's completely lost control of the vehicle. He careens off the road and crashes into one of the oak trees. Smoke spirals up from the hood of his car.

I project myself forward, appearing beside Tessa.

Carl stumbles out of his car, limping toward a branch on the ground. He brandishes it like a weapon, swinging it wildly. "Stay away from me. Keep out of my head." He pivots, yelling in all directions.

I surprise him, stepping in from the side. *Boo, Carl. We're not staying away until you stay away from our greenhouse. Stay away from Tilly. If you touch her, if you so much as look at her again, we'll gut you.* It's all I can manage before I collapse back on the ground. These attempts are getting harder. I'm losing strength.

But then Tessa, relentless, charges through him again. Carl cries out in agony over whatever she's saying to him. Though it's not long before she's down on the asphalt gasping for breath.

Carl staggers backward, crashing against his car, his eyes panicked, darting in every direction.

Tessa crawls my way. "Did you see?"

"See what?" I shiver.

"His plans. He's going to burn down her house tonight . . . with Tilly and her parents inside. He has gasoline in his basement." A sob flies from her lips.

"*What?*" I start scrambling, pushing myself off the ground to go after him again, but it's no use—my body is spent.

Carl wanders into the middle of the street. "Is that all you've got?" he roars. "I know who this is. You two nerds can't scare me. *Your* greenhouse? Is that where you're hanging out these days? I have news for you: I bought gasoline to use on Tilly's place, but I think I'll use it on that old mansion first." He stumbles off toward his home.

Tessa's face is tense with worry. "He's completely delusional."

Shit. "I screwed up." I was so focused on frightening him I forgot to protect us. "He saw my memories of the van der Born place, he knows it's our home base, that we can't leave for long." Oh God. What have I done?

"What happens if he burns the mansion down? What happens to our door?" Tessa staggers back, her voice growing increasingly frantic.

I can't be responsible for trapping Tessa here for eternity, left to wander the fields lost and forgotten, forever blaming me for holding her back, for blowing our plans. She'd hate me all over again.

"We have to stop him," I say as Tessa offers me a hand up.

At the end of the block, Carl stumbles up the driveway to a pale-yellow two-story home, one of those places with rocks out front instead of a lawn. Lacy pink curtains flutter in the windows, their color sun-bleached from years of neglect, while boxes of fake flowers hang half-forgotten from the kitchen sill. Nothing about the place says "college student psycho killer." "This is where he lives?"

"It's his childhood home," Tessa informs me. "I saw in his mind. He inherited it a couple years ago. I know where he's headed, too. He keeps the gasoline in some canisters downstairs."

Tessa and I arrive as Carl is fishing the key from his back pocket. He claimed he's not scared of us, but his hands are shaking so badly he can barely turn the lock.

Carl shoves his shoulder against the doorframe and tumbles inside. "I know you're there. You're not invited in." He scrambles forward, careening down the hall.

"Does he think we're vampires?" Tessa mumbles.

He left the front door open in his panic, not that it would deter us. We step over the threshold, unafraid, watching as he makes his way toward the kitchen.

"We're gonna have ourselves a fun bonfire tonight," he howls, a wolf baying at the moon, as he flings the basement door open.

My thoughts are all-consuming: protect Tilly and her family, save the van der Born estate, save our door. I already lost Tessa her life by grabbing Carl's poisoned drink; I can't take away her chance at the afterlife, too.

I don't calculate my move. I'm high on adrenaline, shaky and determined, as I charge Carl from behind—anything to keep him away from that gasoline. The room pulses and vibrates as I slide into his mind. *You sick psycho. You think you're safe here? I won't let you alone for a minute. You'll be haunted for eternity. I will peel your mind back layer by layer until there's nothing left, until they haul you off broken and crying to a padded room.* I flood Carl with terrorizing images of him curled up and alone, rocking back and forth in an asylum as his mind fractures. *You. Cannot. Escape. Me.*

Carl buckles over, hands pressed to his ears. "Fucking leave me alone!"

Then I'm coughing and gasping on the floor by Tessa's feet, face pinched tight as my body spasms. Carl, half retching, trips over himself and tumbles forward. It all happens in slow motion: Carl's body somersaults down the wooden steps, face up, feet up, over and over, a circus act gone horribly wrong.

I gasp in horror at the loud crack that reverberates off the walls when his head collides with the cement floor.

"Oh my God," Tessa whispers, fear twisting her features.

Carl's eyes are fixed on the ceiling, staring blankly. Blood begins to pool under his skull, soaking his crimson hair.

"I—I was trying to scare him," I choke out. "It was an accident. I never . . ." I trail off, trying to absorb the horror of the moment, of what this makes me. "I didn't mean . . ."

Tessa slowly helps me to my feet, and we take the stairs together.

We're no killers. Please just let him be roughed up.

But as we reach the cold basement floor and Carl's motionless body, we see it. Glowing and pulsing, sandwiched between the boiler and an old metal shelf stacked with ancient paint cans—Carl's door.

CHAPTER 26

Reed

"Oh shit." I buckle to the floor, head between my legs. "I just killed somebody."

"It was an accident." Tessa turns away, trying very hard not to stare at Carl's mangled body. Or maybe she doesn't want to face me and what I've done. Can I blame her?

I can hardly wrap my mind around it myself. Another life snuffed out by Reed Walker. Another death on my conscience. I press my forehead to the cold cement floor, unable to catch my breath. "He fell because of me. If I hadn't passed through him in that moment, if I hadn't tried to get inside his head, then maybe . . . he would have . . ."

"He would have what? Run downstairs to grab some gasoline to raze our mansion to the ground, or come after Tilly and her family to burn them while they slept? We didn't have a choice."

Tessa reaches for me, but I pull out of her grip to stand. I feel dirty, like a weed infestation, as if my crimes could bloom and contaminate her, too.

"I got inside his head and distracted him at that moment." Carl's lifeless body is bent at odd angles on the floor, but I force myself to look at him. "It's my fault that someone else is dead, even if that someone is a low-life creeper like Carl." I wipe my eyes. *Look. Look at what you did. This is who you are. You are a menace to society, even when you're dead. You cannot be trusted. You're a horrible person.*

"You better not be shedding a tear over that psycho," Tessa says.

"Excuse me?" I whip around, piercing her gaze. Does she not understand what happened? Can't she tell I'm drowning? "You really don't get it, do you? His death is on *me* now. Just like yours is. Just like—" *My father's.* I can't even say it. I shake my head, all warmth gone. "Do you have any idea how much this has been weighing on me? What I did to you. To us." I'm incandescently pissed. "It's so easy for you to lecture me or shrug this off, because you don't have to carry the weight of those deaths on your conscience *forever.*"

She stares, stunned. "I'm not shrugging anything off. And if you've been consumed with guilt over my death, it's the first I'm hearing about it."

That stings. I've been suffocating inside, but she's never asked or wondered. Never noticed. "Then you haven't been looking very closely."

"I get that my own death was an accident. I mean, yeah, am I ticked off you grabbed some random drink instead of making one yourself, and stole my whole future from me? Yeah. That does make me mad."

"Ha. I knew it!" I point my finger at her angrily. "You've been holding—"

"But," she cuts me off, her voice rising to overtake mine, "I've FOR-GIV-EN you." She claps out each syllable.

"That's sure what it sounds like," I scoff.

"Aaagh," she growls. "Taking Carl out, that was the *right* thing to do. I think that's why we've remained here at all—to protect Tilly from him. Well, guess what? We did that. We stopped him."

"*We*?" I spit out. "*I'm* the one who did it." I thump my chest. If these deaths are my fault, I may as well get the credit. I'm the one who has to pay for them. "Tilly's not even my friend."

She jerks back. "And I'm supposed to be . . . *what*? Thankful? This was all some favor for me or something? Is that what you're saying?"

And there she is. *This* is the Tessa I know. Rigid. Full of accusations. She stands in front of me, face livid, hands fisted at her sides.

"No. It's not some favor I'm doing for you. Jesus fucking Christ. But you know what, now that you mention it, I wouldn't mind some appreciation. Maybe a little sympathy. It's only my goddamn soul I'm sacrificing here."

"I thought you didn't believe in all that."

I bark out a sharp and condescending laugh, take two steps away, then swing around. "All I ask is for a thank-you, and you can't even do that. You're so stubborn sometimes, Tessa, it drives me crazy. If this is all so easy, then you do it. Let's see how you feel taking someone else's life."

She blinks back tears. But in this moment, I'm glad to see it. I need her to understand.

"This was a mistake."

"I thought you said killing him was a good thing."

"No, not Carl. *Us.* You and me." She waves her hand between us. "I don't know what we were thinking. We were probably scared and needed company, but we should have known . . . it was always going to end like this."

"End?" I stagger backward, seeing her as if for the first time. "That's not what I'm saying." We're fighting, sure, but that doesn't mean we end things because they get hard. Can she really discard us like that?

"These last few weeks feel like a fever dream that we're only now waking up from. We've argued and sniped at each other for years, Reed. This is what we know. It's the habit we'll always fall into."

I cross the room so I'm inches from her face. "Is that right?" We glare at each other. "This is what you want, then? To end things?" My mouth pulls tight in a thin line. My body vibrates with frustration. But there's something else behind it I can't place. A confusing array of feelings somersault through me.

Anger.

Desire.

Remorse.

Everything has gone sideways so fast. I don't know what to think anymore. So I do something I never thought I would: I breathe my worst secret into the world.

"When I was nine years old, I called my dad to pick me up from a sleepover. I told him I couldn't sleep, but really, I was scared, and I think he knew it." Tessa looks taken aback, unsure where I'm going with this. But she holds her ground, breathing hard, waiting to see what I'll say. "It was stormy out and he was worried about the roads. But I begged him. I didn't even say goodbye when we hung up, only *Hurry*." Tessa eyes me warily as my voice drops to a whisper. "But he never came. He spun out on black ice. I was so focused on wanting to be home, so focused on *myself*, that I forced him to drive through the storm. I killed him."

"Reed—"

"I did that. I took his life from him, like I took yours. And Carl's. That's what I do. I steal people's chances. I annihilate their dreams."

"That's not on you."

"But it is. I have no idea what's waiting for me over there." I nod at the door. "But I doubt it's anything good."

"I understand why you're freaking out. I'm freaked out, too." She steps closer, resting a hand on my arm. Her head tilts up until our eyes connect—hers hazel, flecked with gold.

I want nothing more than to get lost in those eyes, but she crossed a line before and I'm not sure I can find my way back. I'm not sure I'd deserve it even if I could.

"What happened to you is heartbreaking. But you were a kid, Reed, and your father *loved* you. That was an accident. All these deaths were accidents. And with Carl, we're not talking about Mother Theresa here. He was going to *kill* Tilly."

I sigh and step out of her grasp. Has she not been listening?

Tessa pursues me. "You're not thinking straight, but if you take a second to breathe, you'll see this for the win it is. Carl can't pick things up now. He can't burn anyone alive. We saved Tilly.

You saved her." A tide of relief falls over Tessa, her shoulders slumping as the air gusts out of her. "I've been so distracted by all this." She gestures, indicating the room. "But you *saved* her, Reed. It's over."

My jaw twitches. Has it only ever been about Tilly? Am I a means to an end? But before I can ask more, the flickering of Carl's door catches my eye. For the first time I really look at his golden countdown timer, and the numbers are so much higher than ours. "Is it really . . . a *win*?"

Tessa follows my gaze, and her mouth drops.

"He has 13,304,562 seconds." I press my temples, running the calculation in my head. "That's just over five months."

She staggers back. "Why does he get so long?"

"Maybe for a redemption arc." I huff out a breath.

"I highly doubt that." The clock ticks back another slot. "So, he gets five more months than us. We'll be long gone, but he'll be here getting into who knows what kind of trouble. She's not safe. All our efforts . . . all this fighting, and Tilly's still not safe."

Whatever Tessa and I had feels so tenuous, like it could crumble in front of our eyes. And now Tilly's in danger again. Has this all been for nothing? But there's no time to wail at the universe about how life and death aren't fair, because Carl's still out there, and he needs to be stopped.

That thought sparks something in me, a memory of that first misty morning waking up in the ballroom, police scattered around the grounds. "Where's Carl?"

Tessa turns behind her, where he lies dead on the floor.

"No, not his actual body. His ghost. He's got to be somewhere in this house."

“Oh crap.” Tessa starts for the stairs and I follow.

But before we get too far, there’s a shuffling noise behind us from the back corner of the basement. I turn as a shadowy figure rises beside a rack of fraying towels next to an old washer and dryer.

My heart thunders in a panic. Tessa freezes beside me.

He’s here.

CHAPTER 27

Tessa

There's a flash of red hair as Carl steps into a small pool of light from one of the hanging basement bulbs. "What the—" he says, when his gaze lands on us. "No way." He staggers back in shock. "You can't . . . no." He runs his hands over his face like we're some kind of hallucination he can scrub away.

But when his eyes snap to mine, I only nod in response. A deep chill creeps along my skin from his icy stare. There's no warmth to be found, only calculating animal instinct.

"You're not r-real," he stammers, paler than normal.

My eyes dart to Reed, unsure of our next move. How do you break it to someone that they're dead? Or, worse, that you're responsible? "Yeah, so uh . . . this might come as a bit of a shock . . ." I edge a step closer, nails digging into my palms as I attempt to project a calm I'm not feeling.

Carl pushes past us into the room but halts when he notices his door. "What the hell is this?" Before he can really take it in, he pivots and comes face-to-face with his own corpse. I hear the breath gust out of him, his back rigid, as he stares.

At least my body was under a tarp and I only saw my shoes at first; I can't imagine what it's like to watch yourself bleed out.

"Stop making me see shit." He rounds on us, hurling the accusation. "Get out of my head!"

"We're not doing anything to you." Reed chances a step closer, hands up as if calming a snarling animal.

"You died, Carl." I join Reed. "That's why you can see yourself . . . why you can see us."

I'm afraid he's going to cry, or scream, but as his eyes roam first over his corpse, then the canisters of gasoline tucked along the shelf, he throws his head back and roars with laughter. Totally unhinged.

Reed shoots a nervous glance my way as an uneasy feeling prickles up the back of my neck. Carl's reactions always surprise me, which means I can't predict him, and if I can't predict what he'll do, then how can I stop him?

Carl spins to face us, still cackling. "You thought you were getting rid of me, but I always planned to die with her." He waves at the gasoline cans. "My very own murder-suicide pact. But this is so much better." His eyes sparkle with malice. "Now, I can haunt her every breath. I can pull her into this world with me." He saunters over to a dark corner in the back of the basement, a smug smile on his face. It's only then I realize he's created some kind of psychotic stalker altar to Tilly. We never noticed before, too caught up in our argument.

I gasp, and Reed tenses beside me as Carl runs his fingers possessively over the photos he's tacked there.

"Don't you dare." My voice is steeped in menace, ears roaring. There are images of Tilly running laps at school, as if he snuck onto the grounds to take them. There's Tilly caught in silhouette through her bedroom window, and with her arm wrapped around me on one of our coffee dates. There's even a couple recent photos through her mom's shop window of Tilly chatting with Santiago. Carl's scratched out my face and Santiago's face with a red X. My body vibrates with fury. Waves of anger roll off Reed, too, as he worries about his friend.

How did we not see these before? Reed and I were so infuriatingly lost in each other.

Carl watches the blood pool beside his body and laughs before marching up to us. He's so close I can see his acne scars. Everything in me wants to recoil, but I hold my ground and Reed does, too. "I'm going to be the most terrifying fucking poltergeist this town has ever seen." A sick smile spreads slowly across his face. "You two will regret this so badly. I'm never leaving her alone now."

Reed doesn't break eye contact with Carl, but he reaches down to squeeze my hand. I startle at the contact, then wrap my fingers firmly around his. All our hurtful words to each other are still ringing in my ears. But some things transcend arguments, and facing a psychopath is one of them. Though if Reed's gesture is meant to reassure me, it doesn't work.

We've made things so much worse. We haven't solved

anything. All we've managed to do is pull a vindictive monster into this realm with us.

Carl is so focused on us, he doesn't notice the door flicker behind him. I hear a sharp intake of breath and know that Reed has seen it, too. When he turns to me, eyes full of fiery determination, it's clear we're thinking the same thing. Forget everything that happened between us.

We need to push Carl through that portal. We eliminate him the only way we know how. I don't care what's waiting for him on the other side. He can't stay here.

"Now!" Reed yells, and we both lunge before Carl can react. As we shove him backward, he smirks at first, cocky as ever, like he assumes he's untouchable. We can push him all we want; it will do little good. But when he whips his head around to catch the door looming closer, dissolving momentarily into an empty chasm—a yawning mouth ready to swallow him whole—beads of sweat form on his brow.

He tries to get a foothold to shove against us, but we've got the upper hand. Reed is much taller than him, and that gives us leverage. Realization dawns over Carl's face: He's going to lose.

For a brief glimmer I see it, his real and palpable fear.

So long, asshole.

But at the last moment, Carl ducks and rolls to the side, halting our momentum. He shuffles to his feet and makes a break for the stairs. Reed and I stumble.

My knee slams into the hard cement floor. "Stop him!"

Reed launches himself across the room and grabs the banister. He pulls his body onto the stairwell, blocking the kitchen entrance, standing firm in Carl's path.

"Get out of my way," Carl seethes.

"That's not going to happen." Reed begins pushing him down the stairs. One step. Shove. Two steps. Shove. Carl's foot slips and he tumbles backward, a replay of his own death, only to land beside his corpse. He stares into his own lifeless eyes, shudders, and rolls to his feet, scanning the room for another exit.

There are a couple small rectangular windows at ground level. Outside the sun slips behind some clouds, plunging the lawn in shadow. But since the windows are sealed, they offer no escape. Carl can't physically affect them now.

He spins to face me, likely assuming I'm an easier match than Reed.

"You're going to let me walk up those stairs, because if you don't, your little girlfriend is going through that door." He lunges, grabbing my wrist, and begins dragging me toward the portal and its golden countdown clock.

The gateway warps and buckles, the fabric of space-time bending and bubbling like a mirage. As if it senses someone's about to enter, the buzzing gets louder, drowning out the hum of the lights and the whir of the fan. It overtakes the room, an insatiable hunger.

I try to wriggle free, but Carl only holds on tighter, pulling me toward him. This is how it's going to end for me. I'll be lost who knows where, alone, and unable to help Tilly—or to ever fix things with Reed. Hazy memories of YouTube self-defense videos swim through my head. Twist my wrist. Use the element of surprise. My brain skips from thought to thought so fast it's hard to land on a plan. All I know is that the door is looming closer, and although I claw at Carl's arms to break loose, I can't escape his grip.

Rather than jumping over the banister, Reed dissolves through it and lands on the floor. He inches closer, trying to position himself to intercept us, hands twitching, looking for his moment. Carl pauses his tugging and his eyes narrow, temporarily stunned by Reed's ability to move through solid structures. This is my chance. I plant my feet against Carl and shove backward hard, knocking us both to the floor.

In an instant, Reed is on him, a savage sound ripping from his chest. I've never seen him like this: There's no regret for what happened to Carl before. All that's left is a kind of brutal ferocity. He wants Carl wiped clean from the earth.

They roll across the floor, their movement so fast it's hard to see who has the upper hand. At one point Carl has his hands around Reed's throat. At another moment Reed is throwing a series of punches. The basement lights begin to flicker. The washing machine turns on and off out of nowhere. There's big supernatural energy swirling around the room as they fight, and it's somehow seeping into the natural world.

When Carl's back on top, going for Reed's throat again, I throw myself against him, knocking him to the ground. Reed staggers up, clutching his windpipe, gasping for air. Before I can scramble toward him, Carl shoves me backward with such force my head hits the wall behind me. In an instant Carl's back on his feet. With Reed still distracted, trying to catch his breath, Carl slams into him.

Time slows, distills, until there's only: Reed losing his balance, stumbling backward, a shocked expression on his face.

Carl beaming, triumphant. The golden door dissolving again into a dark and desolate abyss.

For just a second, Reed's eyes meet mine, as if he's unsure how his life has brought him to this moment. "Tessa," he breathes—a hope for salvation, a prayer. Everything unsaid hangs thick in the air between us. We *should* be together. I didn't mean what I said before. *I need him.*

But I'm too far away. I cannot stop this train wreck from happening. Because in the next heartbeat, Reed is sucked through. The golden outline shrinks back in on itself and vanishes, the portal sealed.

And just like that, the boy I love is gone.

CHAPTER 28

Tessa

I race to the wall, screaming "REED!" I run my fingers along the seams, pounding on the bricks, trying to find some crack, some fissure, some way to break through. He can't be gone. Not like this. Not after all those hurtful things I said. Why was I so cruel? Of course he was freaking out; he felt responsible for his father's death. But did I see the signs? Did I listen? No. I snapped at him. Like I always do.

I pinch my eyes tight, unable to shake the pleading look on Reed's face. He needed my help. And I did nothing.

I've saved no one.

My failures keep stacking up, one upon the other. The weight of them becomes a force so suffocating, I don't know how to go on. If I could launch myself though the door after Reed, I would.

I bang against the wall again, until my hands are raw and

swollen. "Reed, come back!" Tears stream down my cheeks. "Can you hear me, I'm right here!" *Bang, bang, bang.* "I'm sorry. I didn't mean what I said before. Please come back!"

But it's no use. I sink to the floor in despair, dropping my head on my knees. What fate have I condemned him to? What lurks behind Carl's door? I can't put my finger on it: It looked the same as Hal's, but something felt *off* about it. When Hal stepped into his great unknown, it was welcoming. This time, it felt like a threat.

Across the room, Carl watches me with interest, a cat eyeing a shiny new toy, as if he's imagining the fun he can have torturing Tilly and me.

"Boo-hoo," he says. "Your precious golden boy is gone. That's what you get for coming after me. You want to weep over him, be my guest. Personally, I don't see the appeal." He saunters backward toward the stairs, arms stretched wide. "Me? I'm a fucking god now. I was always invisible, always ridiculed and passed over in life. But not anymore."

"Are you kidding me? You're more invisible now than you ever were before," I snarl. "That's what it means to be a ghost."

Carl *tsk*s. "Such a temper. But don't worry, I don't plan to stay invisible. I plan to make my mark here." He walks up the stairs, only pausing when his eyes are level with one of the basement windows. Several potted plants are tucked along the sill. "Do you know what that is?" He arches an eyebrow in wait. "No? It's *Dionaea muscipula*, the unassuming but deadly Venus flytrap." He runs his finger along the bumpy ridges of the nearest plant.

That's right. I forgot he was obsessed with those.

"You see, *Tessa*"—he bites out my name—"the world is made

up of prey, victims ripe for the plucking, and those with more . . . predatory urges." He flashes me his teeth. "Now, some carnivores are ostentatious, all claws and fangs. But there are others, just as deadly, who set their traps quietly and lie in wait. Like this *Dionaea muscipula* here. You have to admire the patience." He laughs softly. "Tilly will be mine, or she'll die. Or both. Because what I have, what I've cultivated, is persistence, and deadly patience." And with that, he waltzes up the final steps, heading no doubt for Tilly's house to begin his campaign of terror, and I have no clue what to do or how to stop him.

So instead I shiver on the cold cement floor, broken, paralyzed with grief, and utterly alone.

I languish in Carl's basement, feeling hopeless. How long has it been? I check the phone. Five p.m. I don't bother calculating how many days remain. I don't care anymore. Reed promised we'd go through our door together. I know I never promised the same, but it doesn't feel right to leave without him. It doesn't feel right to be without him at all. I need him.

For a brief moment, when Carl fell, I actually thought I could have it all, both Tilly and Reed. Tilly would be free from harm, able to live her life as she pleased. Reed and I could get our happily ever after and leave together hand in hand. But now he's gone. How do I do any of this without him?

I curl up in a ball on the floor as waves of guilt overtake me. Carl won't know the trick to reappear places, so he'll have to travel on foot to Tilly's house. That affords me some time, but he'll likely get there soon. I know she needs my help. I should go to her now, but I feel trapped, overcome by my failures. Who am I to change anything? Help anyone? All I do is make things worse.

All my second-place trophies swim before my eyes, taunting me with the reminder that I'm never quite good enough. It should have been Reed who stayed. He'd know what to do. But Tilly's stuck with me.

I hug my knees tighter to my chest, wanting nothing more than to disappear. This is one test I don't know how to pass. There's no book to study, no answer key, no prescribed way to get from point A to point B.

It's just me, alone, with all my shortcomings. I can't overpower Carl as a ghost, can't beat him in a fistfight. My last remaining shot is to come at Carl as a fade. I'm tempted to jump-start the process, transport myself back to the hospital and run though people left and right. End it all in a blaze of glory and await the transformation.

But then I think of my dad. I'm not sure why my brain has settled on him in this hour of self-pity, but it occurs to me that he's someone who's faced his fair share of setbacks in life. He lost his wife; he almost lost custody of me; he lost his job; for a while he wasn't sure if he could afford to keep our home. But he still picked himself up day after day, dusted himself off in the face of his failures, and tried again. That's the man I saw and loved. The man who tried, not the man who failed. So, why can't I give myself the same grace? I sit back up, lean against the bricks behind me, and close my eyes.

We are not our failures. I am who I am in spite of them—or

maybe because of them. I don't need to be afraid all the time of not being the best. A thing is still worth doing even if you don't get the number-one spot. Besides, life can be lonely from that vantage point. What's worth fighting for isn't some tally on the point board, it's the things we care about and the people we love. And I love Tilly with my whole heart.

And, without a doubt, I love Reed, too. If I wondered before, I know it now, down to my bones. My stomach flutters thinking of his whispered promises in the bedroom and him bathed in starlight on the mansion roof as we lamented the lives we could've had. He's so unbelievably beautiful, smart, and thoughtful. I want to shout my feelings through the wall, in case he's listening on the other side. Anything to cover up the deep ache of losing him.

What was it Hal said? *Bravery isn't always rushing off to fight the dragon. Sometimes, it's picking yourself up after crippling loss.*

I've lost my life, I've lost my college dreams and future, I've lost the boy I love, but so help me, I won't lose Tilly.

She needs me. And Reed would want me to do all I could for her, no matter what happened between us. I stand up and wipe the tears from my eyes, steeling myself for what's next.

We may come into this world alone and leave it alone, but before I go, I'm shoving Carl out first.

CHAPTER 29

Tessa

I imagine the magnolia tree on Tilly's lawn. *I'm coming, Tills.*

When I arrive, it's getting close to 5:30 p.m. Her parents won't be home for another hour. Tilly's on her own.

I'd hoped to find Carl on the lawn; I was counting on it, in fact. I'd allowed myself to go to pieces back in his basement partly because I assumed he'd be stuck out here. But as the lights flicker in her bedroom and Tilly cries out, I know Carl's made it inside.

Which means he figured out how to cross through doors. Did he get the idea watching Reed pass through the banister back in his basement? If Carl's already conquered that skill, who knows what else he's discovered?

I pray I'm not too late.

I hold the image of Tilly's bedroom in my mind, her

pale-blue comforter and twinkle lights, and in a moment I'm there. Immediately, I know I should have come sooner. Tilly's cowering in the corner and Carl's on his hands and knees on the rug, breathing hard. He's clearly been tormenting her.

But no more. I step forward, fists clenched at my sides.

He grins, victorious. "Here to take part in the fun, are you?"

Tilly scrambles to a lamp that's fallen off her bedside table. She stands, wielding it like a weapon. "Stay away from me, Carl." Her voice shakes like she's fighting back tears.

"What have you been doing to her?" I growl.

"Oh, we've been having all kinds of conversations. And I'm not doing anything you and your boyfriend didn't do. I must admit, it's fun making her watch the replay of my death over and over, and yours. She loved seeing that. Not to mention her car rolling in that accident. I've got lots of little gifts to share." He dusts himself off, standing up. "But now, I think I'll show her what I'm planning next."

I reach for him, but he slips out of my grasp and straight into Tilly again. She comes in and out of focus as the space around her buckles and bends, crackling like static on an old TV. They're both here and not here. "No!" Tilly screams in agony. She's fallen to the floor, hands covering her ears. "That's never going to happen." She grapples for her lamp again, swinging it wildly. It crashes into the wall behind her, shattering into countless pieces. Blood trickles down her palm.

I've no real plan; all I know is I need him out, right now. I've never tried to cross into someone while there's another ghost in there. It seems crowded, but I don't care. I lunge for Tilly.

The overhead light explodes, sparks raining down. I can feel

Carl trying to keep a foothold in her mind, but he's weak from his repeated attempts and I shove him out.

All's quiet for a moment—a ship cast temporarily into the eye of the storm, blue skies and calm sails—but only for a breath. I need to pass through her, but I don't want to take a greater toll on her body. So before I go, I reach out with my mind and flood her with happy memories of our time together: laughing on my bedroom rug eating Takis Fuego, writing our travel itineraries, vintage shopping at Second Place, watching fireflies dart overhead as we camp out in her backyard, dreaming of our future. Anything I can think of to make her feel safe and loved.

"Tessa?" she gasps. "Is that you?"

Yes, I think at her. *It's me, Tills. I'm here. I'm not going to let him hurt you anymore.* Then my body rejects the crossing. I can't hold out any longer. I drop to the floor, curled in the fetal position, as waves of nausea sweep over me.

Tilly falls beside her broken lamp, wincing from the pain of her collarbone.

"You might slow me down," Carl says from across the room, breathing hard. "But you can't stop me."

"Why?" I demand. "Why Tilly? She doesn't want anything to do with you. Leave her alone." I push onto my hands but can't stand yet; my legs are too weak.

Tilly feels around on the floor for something else to use as a weapon.

"Because it's our destiny to be together, and she knows that deep down. Why else would she have gone out with me?" Carl stalks closer, a predator looking for his moment to pounce.

Keep his focus on me. That's all I've got. Hold his attention and keep him talking, until I can think of a way out of this mess. "Uh . . . because she didn't realize you were a fucking psychopath at the time. And as I recall, it only lasted a few weeks, so get over it."

"That's what you think, but it lasted a lot longer than that."

"You stalking her does not make it a relationship."

He growls. I've hit a sore spot. "She's going to regret every missed call, every snide comment. I'll break her until she's crawling back to apologize." He lunges for Tilly, but I grab his leg and he crashes to the floor. Carl tries to kick me loose, but I scramble forward and scratch his face. He howls with rage and shoves me off him, but I keep coming. Hands, teeth, hair, spit, it's a blur as I throw myself at him, anything to keep him away from terrorizing her.

Something strange starts to happen. The bedroom door opens, then slams closed again. Tilly edges closer to it, unsure. The lights flicker, while music plays from somewhere. Her laptop? Tilly's pillow, sweater, and journal rise from her bed into the air and circle around the room. It's a full-fledged haunting.

I'm not doing any of this, and from the confused expression on Carl's face, I don't think he is, either. There are just big energies at play in here. *Keep going, something's working*, I think as we roll across the floor, locked in battle.

"Tessa," Tilly calls, standing flush against the wall, staring in horror at the objects swirling around the room. "Tessa, if you're here, if you're trying to stop him—and as impossible as it is to believe, I think that's what you're doing—I just want to say thank you, and I love you. I believe in you."

I'm so exhausted, with no idea how to make this end. But

Tilly knows I'm here. Tilly's rooting for me just like I'm rooting for her. Carl has freed himself from my grip at last, but I can tell our tussle has taken it out of him, on top of his multiple passes through her. He staggers against her desk, clutching his side. When he sees I'm still incapacitated on the floor, his eyes land on Tilly and narrow. "Payback time, bitch." He struggles to walk but plows ahead anyway, straight for her.

I do the only thing that comes to mind: I roll toward him and grab his ankle. I reach out with my mind and imagine a place we can go, somewhere far from Tilly. I close my eyes and project myself there and hope to hell he comes with me.

When I come to, I'm shivering on the icy concrete of Carl's basement floor. The room swims in and out of focus, from the pockmarked ceiling to the rack of old towels. Even his prized collection of Venus flytraps remains untouched on the windowsill, patiently awaiting their next meal. There's a moan to my left, and when I tilt my head, I find Carl beside me, with his corpse beyond us, a reminder of all the violence that brought us to this moment.

I did it. This was the first place that came to my mind. I wasn't sure if I could take someone with me when I traveled. It was a shot in the dark, but it seems to have worked—the last remaining trick I had up my sleeve.

Little by little, my strength returns, but barely. Being by the site of Carl's death must be helping; we're gaining energy from whatever strange power source surges in these places.

"How did you do that?" Carl groans.

I push myself up, and that's when something gold catches my eye. I freeze as the floor falls out from under me, reality spinning on its axis. It can't be . . .

Carl's door is back.

His countdown clock is still ticking. How?

Has Reed returned? Did he find a way to escape? I run over to the threshold, careful not to step too close. "Reed? Are you there?" It's silent, save the deep hum reverberating off the walls again. "Reed!" I turn to shout up the stairwell, in case he's in the house.

"He's not here." Carl shuffles to his feet. "You watched him get sucked through like I did. You don't return from something like that."

I don't want to listen to Carl, but doubt creeps in. If Reed came back and we were gone, he'd go to Tilly's. I know it. He'd figure that's where Carl would go. But he didn't show up there. That is, if a person can cross back over at all. Maybe the portal swallowed him up, and now it's ready to take Carl, too.

With a sinking feeling, I realize it's not going to be that easy. Hoping for something isn't enough. Reed won't magically appear because I want him to. The world doesn't work that way. We have our shot here and then we go, that's the deal. That's the grand bargain. Finish your business then decide: Stay or go. There are no take-backsies.

Carl steps closer, and I wonder if he's trying to position himself subtly to send me through. It's certainly what I'm thinking. But neither of us has enough energy yet for the attempt, too drained from our fight at Tilly's.

"You're going to tell me how you did that neat little trick of yours, zapping us back here. In fact, you're going to share all your secrets with me. Or you and I both know where you'll end up."

"I don't think so," I say, buying time as we slowly edge around each other, the dance of fencers readying for a match. Behind Carl are his carnivorous plants, but it's what's behind those, out the small rectangular windows, that catches my eye. It's a familiar sight: mist swirling and gathering on the lawn, ominously rolling up against the house. I edge myself closer to the stairs as a plan begins to take shape.

The smoke people are attracted to the sites of recent deaths. They gather in wait, whispers on the wind. They desperately want inside.

I take off up the stairs.

Carl laughs behind me. "Afraid I'll tug you through? That's right, run away. You can't escape for long. You forget, I know where you live."

The front door is still open from when we chased Carl home. Was that just this afternoon? The mist presses against my ankles, gathers out on the street, wanting a touch, wanting a taste. I used to fear them. But all they want is a way out. I want a way out, too. Besides, the real monster's downstairs.

"Hey, you, smoke people," I shout at the tide of mist coalescing down the block, billowing up the driveway, pressing tightly against the windows of Carl's childhood home. "You want a taste of this?" I throw my arms open wide. "Come on in. Fresh meat!"

CHAPTER 30

Tessa

Bodies form out of the ether, slowly filling in the details with limbs and long-fingered hands all belonging to the dead and forgotten. "This way." I beckon from the doorway, waving them forward. "Step right up." If it's an invitation they need, then it's an invitation they'll get. The first creatures hover toward the door, with twenty or so more gathering behind, rising out of vapor, one after the other.

The smoke darkens, dips, and swirls around their bodies to transform into shadowy memories of suits, gowns, hospital robes, their last living imprints on earth. *Like me*, I think, looking down at my repurposed lace dress. But their faces remain a void, as if over time they've forgotten what they look like and let decay take over. For the first time I see them for what they are. Hungry, but not for blood—for meaning, for a chance to remember, for a chance to feel whole again.

The first creatures press together, angling to get through the narrow doorway. I step back, leading my quarry farther into the house. I walk backward down a long wood-paneled hallway, through a yellow kitchen with cracked linoleum floors, chipped-paint cupboards, and empty beer cans on the counter.

The fades push closer, as if the pull from the door below and its promise of escape draws them near. I gasp when I recognize one. With her black-bustled dress and long satin gloves, it's the woman from the mansion gate. A brooch on her neck glints in the overhead light with the initials BvdB.

Is that why she wanted inside the mansion so badly? Could this be Brielle van der Born herself? Was it her home?

But there's no time to wonder as I round the corner to the basement stairs, pausing only briefly to let them catch up. Though the fades may not need me anymore. There's an agitation, a rattling energy, as clawed hands with ancient fingernails reach forward, yearning, moaning, each of them struggling to arrive first. I take the stairs two at a time, landing on the floor only long enough to hear Carl jerk back in surprise and say, "What is this?"

But I don't answer; I don't want to call attention to myself. I grab hold of the banister and swing under the stairwell, tucking inside the small empty section below the lowest steps.

Not that the smoke creatures care; the door is in their sights now. They surge forward, arms outstretched, a frothing undulating mass. Before Carl can do more than throw his hands up in protest and scream, they're carrying him forward, an overflowing river of bodies, a current too strong to break. Carl searches me out by the stairwell as he's shoved along, the door looming closer. Fear flashes behind his eyes. He waves in a panic, shouting for my help, "Tessa!"

Just like Reed's final words. So much hope carried on my name, but this time it echoes hollow in the room. He's begging me to stop the madness.

But I don't. As if I even could. Instead, I step out of my cubby, raise my hand in the air, spin it around, and flip him off. It's the last thing he'll ever see.

I win, asshole. You'll never hurt Tilly or anyone else again.

The gateway opens, larger than I've ever seen it, expanding to take up the entire basement wall. The fades rush the gap, bodies tumbling inside, dragging Carl with them, pulling him forever out of this world.

The door snaps shut, the golden outline vanishing.

I lean back with a deep sigh.

He's gone.

It's finally over.

Without the presence of the door, the several fades that couldn't pass the threshold in time dissolve into mist. I'm alone. At least, it seems, Brielle made it through. Good for her.

I can't bring myself to check the phone. Hal said any time we betray our presence to the living we lose time off the clock. The lights flickering and objects flying around Tilly's house must have docked more days. I'm sure my time is almost up. And if it isn't, what's the point? This day has taken such a toll, I'm at a complete loss for what to do.

I sink to the floor, staring in wonder at the wall, which moments ago had cracked open to suck Carl and those creatures through. Now, it's lined with shelves of aging paint cans, tattered towels, and faded linens. If Reed had any chance to escape, Carl's departure was probably his moment. But he didn't return. The pain of that admission cleaves me in two. He's well and truly gone now.

I bury my head in my hands, ready to go to pieces, then snap forward when someone knocks at the basement door.

"Hey, Carl, it's Alvin. Your neighbor. I saw your car down the road and wanted to check on you. You down here?"

I turn as a middle-aged man, hair graying at his temples, plants a foot on the first creaky stair. "Your door was open, I hope it's okay that—" He gasps and almost loses his footing when his eyes land on Carl's broken body, spread across the floor. "Oh my God." He runs down the remaining stairs while dialing 911.

So, there it is. The police will come. They'll find Carl. They'll see his wall of stalker photos—those disturbing images of Tilly, me, and even Santiago. A hit list, perhaps. If they poke around and start asking questions, they'll discover Carl was at the party and learn what he's been studying. This might be just what's needed to connect the cases.

But I don't wait to find out. I can't take any more death—any reminders of all that happened here and all I've lost because of it. But I can't face the van der Born estate without Reed, either. So I close my eyes and go to the only place I can think of. The place I've missed most in the entire world.

I imagine the green shag carpet my parents never ripped out, the sagging couch with Grandma's quilt we'd tuck over us for movie nights, the family portraits hung over the mantel of Jillian and me at every awkward age, and in an instant . . . I'm home.

Home.

A deep sigh escapes my lips as a warmth spreads through my limbs. The word has such a different meaning now. Home used to be a place to sleep, do homework around the kitchen table, breeze in and out of with my busy schedule, but now I see it for what it actually was—a treasure. I never realized how much I cherished this little corner of the world until it was ripped from me.

It's quiet, save the ticking of the grandfather clock in the hallway and the laughter of the neighborhood kids at the end of the cul-de-sac. I couldn't go inside before, face all that I'd lost and my father's grief, but I guess once you conquer an actual monster, confronting your inner demons doesn't feel as impossible.

The temptation is high to sink into my dad's recliner and drink in the memories of our life here. But for now, I keep moving.

I wander past the kitchen, where I spied my father through the window breaking down as he washed dishes. His plates are laid neatly in the rack now. Somehow there's comfort in the small fact that he's taking care of himself. I need to know he'll be all right, or I don't know if I can leave.

The pull of my room is strong. I want nothing more than to curl up on my bed and miss them, the people who made up my too-short life. But rather than project myself there, I amble down the hallway, letting my eyes land on every framed photo and family memento. There's seven-year-old me, mouth stuffed with cake, lips ringed in chocolate, eyes sparkling. There's the crocheted owl I made my dad when I was twelve, which he first thought was a shoe. We laughed so hard at that, he said he had to keep it forever. There's the photo of Jillian and her date before prom with me photobombing. And the last one with my mom holding me as a newborn, my tiny hand wrapped around her finger.

As I make my way down the hall, something occurs to me that I never realized before. There's no report card tacked to the wall. No A+ essay, framed college admission letter, or certificate of achievement. All those things I thought made up my worth weren't what made me loved by my family. It was *me* they loved, not my accomplishments. Where I saw success or failure, they saw me. This is who I'm leaving behind for them. Not the scholarship winner or the salutatorian. But all the versions of myself—especially the deep and private ones only the people closest to us ever witness.

At last, standing outside my bedroom door, I take a shaky breath and pass through. I'm greeted by my sewing machine and dress form, my bolts of fabric in the bin by the window, and my wall collage with images of Kathmandu and the Himalayas.

It's evening now. The room is cast in a rosy hue, the sun's rays streaming in through gauzy curtains. A sadness falls over me as I realize this is a space my dad has left untouched. Even the trash by my desk hasn't been emptied. I still spy my crumpled graduation speech notes tossed in the bin. Though it wasn't that long ago, the room seems like a time capsule now, a museum piece. *See here, folks, this is how people used to live.* It's as if it belongs to another girl, in another life.

In the center, piled high with pillows, is my bed. It was a good bed, the right amount of smoosh. Tucked in neatly at the corners is the quilted bedspread my mom sewed during her guilt-filled years after the divorce. I know I haven't always been fair to her. She made mistakes, sure, but she wanted to repair them, and that's something. Perhaps this bedspread was her way of saying all the things she couldn't bring herself to say in person. *I hear you, Mom*, I think, as I curl up and imagine breathing in the scent of her.

My eyes close. Not to sleep, but as close as I can get. I wish I could dream away the pain, loss, and worry swirling in my head.

If Reed really is still trapped inside that portal, then I've flooded it with Carl and a bunch of fades. Do all doors lead to the same place? And if not, what fate have I subjected him to? I was trying to protect Tilly, but would he understand it like that? Would he forgive me?

And what do I do now? I suppose I no longer need to stay behind. Tilly's safe. But I'm not ready to leave this world. Why can't I quietly haunt my old house?

I don't even have Hal anymore. I don't have anyone. Who will hold *my* hand when it's time to cross over? I've never felt more alone in my not-life.

I imagine what my days would be like if I somehow didn't fade away. Would I hover over my dad as he did his morning crossword? Follow Jillian around the NICU saving babies? Actually, that sounds pretty sweet. I could raise my hand in my old classes and get annoyed when I wasn't called on. Or haunt the student government meetings and make the lights flicker when I disagreed with their choices.

But then I think of school dances, and having no one to dance with, or family dinners on Friday nights, except the table's only set for two. It's all a mirage, a half-life, or no life at all. And don't I deserve more than that?

As the waves of self-pity become almost too much to bear, I hear something down the hall. My dad's low voice is mixed with someone else's. And they're getting closer. The door rattles, and my father swings it open to stand on the threshold. He sighs deeply before flicking on the light. "Haven't spent much time in here since . . . well, you know."

I sit on the edge of the bed as he steps farther into the room, leaving space for Tilly to follow behind. They're here. They're both really here. My heart starts pounding, my breaths quickening.

"Tessa's been on my mind a lot lately. You could say, even more than usual." Tilly's talking to him, but her eyes scan the room. I'd have thought she'd be home recuperating from her ordeal, but with the way she's glancing around, like she's looking for something, or someone . . . I wonder if she suspects I'm here. Maybe she wanted to thank me, to let me know she's all right. My heart clenches around the thought that even when she's scared and in pain, Tilly's still looking out for me.

"That so?" says my dad. "Tessa's been on my mind a lot, too. Well, she's always on my mind, but uh . . . lately . . . I've actually been thinking of you both. That's why I asked you to stop by." He walks over to my desk and stands with a small bundle of something at his back.

Tilly follows him over, tilting her head curiously.

Like he's bestowing a gift on a young child on Christmas

morning, my dad steps aside to reveal our travel books. A large smile spreads over Tilly's face. There's our *Lonely Planet* guide to Nepal, *The Backpacker's Best Trekking and Hostel Routes in the Himalayas*, and our travel journal where we scribbled down our itineraries, hopes, and dreams.

"Oh." Tilly pats them gingerly, as if they're precious cargo. "Thanks." With her good arm, she flips open the journal on top of the stack. Her shaking fingers trace the pages as her eyes brim with tears. "It's so hard to see Tessa's loopy, perfect handwriting. All these silly thoughts and scribbles feel so important now."

"You should see my desk. I've got a collection of every sticky note she wrote reminding me to take my pills or buy milk. I couldn't bring myself to part with them."

I didn't know he'd do that. I sniffle, wiping the tears pooling in my eyes. For all his tough exterior, Doug Sinclair always was a sentimental sap.

He reaches into his back pocket, pulling out an envelope. "I am . . . uh . . . ready to part with this, though." He hands it to her.

"What is this?" Tilly asks.

I wander over to look, too, my curiosity piqued. What in the world is he giving her? Did he write her a letter?

"Tessa didn't know, but I've been saving up for that trip of yours. I wanted to give her a little nest egg for it as a college graduation present. Now, I thought I had four more years to save—" His voice cracks, but he pushes through. "So it's not much . . . but I want you to have it."

Tilly opens the envelope, running her thumb over the bills

inside. "There's close to seven hundred dollars here. I can't accept that."

"Sure you can."

She presses the envelope back into his hands. "You have so much going on here. I think you should keep the money. Use it for yourself."

"The thing is, it's never been my money. I always thought of it as hers. And I know she'd want you to have it."

"I would," I whisper.

"Go to Nepal. Or go somewhere else. Just promise me you'll use it when you graduate with that journalism degree of yours and celebrate in some way. I've always been so proud of you girls. You've both worked so hard, and you deserve it." He pats her shoulder proudly. "One day you'll be on my TV anchoring CNN."

"Oh stop," Tilly teases, using our favorite catchphrase.

"No . . . you stop," my dad and I echo at the same time. He cracks a small smile. And I can't help it—I do, too.

"Thank you." Tilly hugs the envelope to her chest. "Thanks to you and Tessa both." Her gaze darts around the room again, like she can feel I'm close.

"It's nice to talk about her." My dad's eyes fill with tears. As do Tilly's.

They're both catching up to me because I'm a hot sobbing mess. We stand in my childhood bedroom, the living and the dead, weeping side by side. If only they knew.

There's a knock on the door, and Jillian pokes her head in. Though she's still in her nurse's scrubs, her long black curls cascade perfectly around her face, because leave it to Jillian to look glamorous after a tiring day. "There you are. I've been searching the whole house for you. Everything okay?"

"Yeah, yeah. We're good," my dad says, pulling himself back together.

"Are you ready for Friday night family dinner? I picked up some pizza from Reggio's on the way over. I got enough for Sarah, too."

"That smells great. You want to stay, Tilly, grab a slice?"

"Oh, I would, but my friend Santiago's waiting for me outside in the car. We promised my mom we'd head home to help make lasagna." I peek out the window and notice the car parked out front, and my heart explodes with happiness for her. Maybe they really are friends, or maybe something more. Tilly, finally making a solid choice where boys are concerned. I can't think of anyone better to help her do some healing.

"You ever want a good recipe, I know the guy to ask." Jillian smacks our dad on the back.

"Who's Sarah?" Tilly asks, which I'm thankful for since I'm super curious.

"Oh, picked up on that, did you?" My dad smiles.

"Sarah is my dad's secret hot veterinarian girlfriend."

"What?" Tilly and I both spit out at the same time.

"Oh yeah, he's been dating her for a while, keeping it on the down-low from Tessa and me, but I figured it out." She gives his shoulder a playful punch.

"Way to go, Mr. Sinclair." Tilly nods approvingly.

For the first time I feel like he's going to be okay. Maybe not now, maybe not for a long while. But he'll get there. They all will.

My dad shrugs. "I thought about ending it after everything that happened, but Sarah's a widow, and honestly, it's been nice to have someone who gets it."

They all nod silently for a second, that normal lull in the conversation suddenly filled with the absence of me. Only I'm here. Sort of. I wish I could reach out and hug them. Instead, I love them as much as I can, in the way that I can, standing right here beside them.

But it doesn't feel like my world anymore. It's theirs. My dad's to find love, Jillian's to find happiness, and Tilly's to find adventure.

And as for me, I suppose I have to find my own fate. It's waiting for me back at the van der Born estate. "Goodbye," I whisper to them all as they turn off the light and shut the door—their voices and laughter carrying them down the hall.

I close my eyes, readying myself for whatever comes next, and imagine the mansion gate.

It's time to write the final chapter of my own story.

CHAPTER 31

Tessa

I could have appeared upstairs by the golden door—I know that's where I'm headed—but nostalgia tugs at my heart. I take the long route, meandering along the overgrown trail, full of echoes from the night of the party with my classmates running and laughing through the bushes. Above me is the gray roof and that nook beside the northernmost turret where Reed and I watched the shooting stars.

Memories slip out from every corner. Our moms laying the wreath together on the porch steps. Our friends arriving on the lawn for the séance. And always, there's Reed. We're sock skating in the ballroom, rolling with laughter on the circular bed upstairs, lying quietly side by side through a storm. When I dissolve through the entrance, instead of focusing on the impressive compass rose inlaid on the floor, my eyes dart to the stairs where Reed held and kissed me through the night, hoping, wondering if we could be great together. And we were.

Somehow in such a brief span of time, the van der Born estate has transformed from a dusty, empty house full of cobwebs into a refuge. Just as the boy inside it transformed from my rival into my friend.

The ache for him is overpowering and all-consuming: for the things I never said to him, and for those I did that I regret—our last moments always hovering at the edge of my mind.

Reluctantly, I march upstairs to meet my fate. The golden timer has less than an hour remaining. I'm cutting it close. Hal would scold me, but I suppose it's good I've left it this long. In a secret corner of my mind, I hoped this would give Reed more time to arrive back here, if he somehow managed to escape wherever he went.

But the house is empty. The only sounds are the branches rubbing against the glass of the upper windows and a whistling draft blowing through the walls.

This is going to be for me to face alone.

It isn't the end, I realize. Reed's out there somewhere, like I am. This door was meant for us both. We're linked, he and I. And if we're linked on this plane, then perhaps I can find him on the other side, tug on that cord between us. I vow not to stop searching until I know he's safe.

With my mind made up, I take a steadying breath and stare down the countdown clock.

I'm coming, Reed . . .

CHAPTER 32

Reed

I rub my eyes, gulping for air as my muscles spasm. I was drowning . . . or was it falling? Just moments before. Tugged under, I threw all my will against that tide—against a current beckoning me to murky depths, quarters unknown—as I forced my way to the surface.

Tessa. I was reaching for her, pulling my mind up, up, up.

Her terror-stricken face was pleading with me. She needed help. For what I can't remember, but it was enough to heed her call.

Tessa, with her hand outstretched, even though we both knew it was an impossible distance.

I slowly come to, feeling the weight of my body again. The ground is mushy, unsteady under my back, while above me is a surreal and cloudless bright-orange sky. Is that a bat?

Where am I? This feels like a dream, and I can't tell if it's the good kind.

I roll onto my hands and knees, shaking my head, clearing out the cobwebs. My disordered thoughts shuffle into place. There was a basement. And Tessa was in trouble. And I was sucked backward, sucked through a door. I watched as it sealed up behind me, until all that was left was her face, twisted in panic, her eyes, twin pinpricks of light, begging me to stay, and then . . . nothing. Nowhere.

I must be on the other side now.

I blink, taking in my surroundings for the first time. The squishy ground beneath me is actually grass, rising between my fingers. My fist tightens around a clump. I'm outside. In a grassy field or . . .

I make my way unsteadily to my feet.

A cemetery?

Around me in all directions are gravestones as far as the eye can see.

The other side is . . . *a cemetery*?

I'm surrounded by aisles of the lost. There are stones crumbling with age, their dates barely visible from centuries past, while others, freshly dug, are bedecked with wilting flowers. I spin in a slow circle. It's entirely empty. All that remains are the dead and forgotten.

And I'm one of them.

The air gusts out of me when I realize *exactly* where I'm standing.

My own plot.

HERE LIES
REED WALKER

BRILLIANT MIND, KIND HEART
VALEDICTORIAN, TRAILBLAZER

YOU INSPIRED US ALL

I can hardly think. I can barely breathe. I mean, of course I have a grave, but I haven't dwelled on it. Somehow this makes it so much more real. There *is* a Reed Walker . . . some version of Reed Walker lying underground somewhere. But that's not the only version of me.

So why am I here?

Am I supposed to hang out in this cemetery now? 'Cause that sounds like a great fucking time. Tessa once said that maybe we pass through the door only to take on a series of tests. Maybe that's what this is, a test of some kind. But I don't know what to do. Or whether it's better to stay or go. I'm used to tests I know how to pass, but this . . . is something else. I run my hand through my hair. My brain can't handle this level of metaphysics right now.

Unless . . . this is my punishment? Maybe I'm supposed to remain here with the dead, confronting all the lives I stole through my carelessness. I need to own the hurt and pain I caused in the world.

I deserve that.

Something shuffles on the periphery, catching my eye. I startle when a hazy figure emerges from the pines dotting the hillside. A woman. Walking this way.

Could it be?

But as she comes closer, brushing her long dark curls away from her face, I stagger back, heart in a vise.

It's . . .

Mom.

Is *she* dead, too? *When did . . . ? How . . . ?* I can't add the pieces up. Why would she be here so soon?

"Mom." I step closer. "It's me."

When she pauses at my gravestone, my heart thrums in my throat, waiting for her to speak, to wrap me in her arms. But her eyes drift past me as though I'm not here. My words are carried off on the breeze. Instead, she bends over my grave, hair falling across her face as she collects old flowers and sweeps some fallen leaves aside.

I hover behind her, watching the degree of tenderness she places into each small task.

So . . . what is this, then, a vision I'm supposed to see? Is it a detour before whatever comes next? Because that's some serious Ghost of Christmas Past shit. Except *I'm* the ghost. And . . . I already feel like a crap son for everything I've put her through.

My mom wraps her sweater tight around her as the wind picks up.

Tears prick my eyes. The regret. The longing to hug her. It feels like it could knock me to the floor.

After tucking the old bouquet into a bag at her side, she neatly places some fresh roses against the headstone, her fingers running along the grooves, tracing over the dates.

If only I could tell her. She could take some comfort in knowing I'm okay. I take another step closer as she gingerly rises to her feet.

She pauses, her head turning slightly to the side. Can she sense I'm close? I don't know. I watch as she pulls her sweater tighter around her frame.

"So, baby. Here we are again." My heart almost stops when she speaks. She's talking to *me*. She glances around nervously, as if embarrassed to put her thoughts into words. "I've been thinking recently about our years in Denver. And those wonderful parties we'd throw after your dad opened the music studio. We'd get together with some friends in the evening, bring a big pitcher of sangria, hand out instruments, and jam. Though I'd always ask for the shaker eggs. That's about all I was good for." She laughs quietly. "But you, Reed. You were so talented. Your father would clap out these intricate, complicated rhythms and you could repeat them just like that." She snaps her fingers. "You could get so lost in each other. He could see all that talent in you. All that potential. We both could . . ." Her voice breaks. "He loved you so much, Reed. I know you beat yourself up over the years about everything that happened with him and the accident that night. And I think I understand that now in a deeper way because I've been doing the same with you. Blaming myself. I should have kept you home from the party. Or I should have come to get you, made sure you were okay. There are a thousand versions of that night that play out in my mind, a thousand versions where I made a different choice and saved you. But these things aren't our fault. Tragedies happen." She leans over the gravestone and sobs. "It's not our fault."

"Mom." I reach out a hand as I step toward her, unsure how to help, how to absolve her of her guilt. It *isn't* her fault.

And it's not mine, either.

Maybe it never was.

"I'm still trying to tell myself that, anyway. Perhaps one day I'll believe it." She wipes her eyes, while the first stars blink through the vanishing sunset. The fluorescent orange sky is fading. A sliver of moon rises over the treetops, the light catching in her hair.

This strange liminal plane where I've arrived begins to take more shape.

Or maybe . . .

The thought hits me like an Alex Pereira left hook.

Maybe this isn't some in-between place. Maybe you can't travel through someone else's door.

I stagger back, my pulse quickening. Because if that's the case, then I'm not somewhere else, I'm *here.*

And if I truly am back in this time, in this reality, then that means Tessa's out here, too.

Relief floods through me. We haven't been torn apart after all.

My mom stoops to pick up her bag. And even though I need to find Tessa, longing twists in my stomach as my mother turns and steps away. But as if she senses my need, she pauses and swings back around. "Oh, I'm leaving Steven."

My mouth falls open.

What?

"It's something I probably should have done a long time ago. I know you were never a fan. I just . . . thought the stability would be good for us. And it's not that he's a bad person, he just has his priorities, and I have mine, and I don't think those two will ever align." She sighs.

That's one way of putting it.

I glance around, worried my time is running out, but uncertainty creeps in.

I must have reset to the cemetery for a reason. Is there something here I'm supposed to see? Something I'm supposed to understand?

"In fact, I'm taking some time off work. I can't focus. I need to do some healing. Your uncle Javier and aunt Paula invited me to stay with them in Seville this summer. I'm going to use your ticket. I always got along with Marco's family. I don't know why we didn't see them more." She smiles. "And your cousin Carla has insisted I join her on the coast, too. So maybe I'll even learn to kitesurf for you."

I walk up so that I'm standing beside her. She places her hand on top of the gravestone. "I'll see you tomorrow, Reed."

Tomorrow. The word ricochets through me.

I won't get a tomorrow. At least not here. Maybe I'll never see her again. But I hope that's not the case.

I lift my hand and place it gently over hers, whisper soft. Not passing through her but connecting in the smallest way. The only way I have to let her know I'm here.

My mother gasps. The wind picks up, leaves swirling in eddies around our feet.

"Goodbye, Mom," I whisper. "I love you."

"I love you," she says back, almost like she can hear me.

Then she shivers, grabs her bag, and walks briskly away.

The sun dips low on the horizon, the gravestones casting long shadows across the grass, like so many fingers directing her toward the exit. Get out while you can. Don't tread here.

I shouldn't be here, either. Tessa could be in trouble. I reach into my pocket, but it's empty. Tessa has the phone.

I have no idea how much time we have left. All I know is I need to find her. I promised we'd leave together. Who knows what happens to our door if one of us crosses before the other?

Fog rolls in over the gravesites as an owl takes flight overhead. Whispers surround me on all sides, a lament carried on the wind.

They're coming for me.

Bodies appear out of the mist—rolling upward into great hulking forms, decaying fingers beckoning me to them. Oh God, my time's up. *Good work, genius. You stayed too long.* And Tessa's probably left. She's smart. She'd know not to push it this close to the countdown.

Please let her still be here.

I won't give the smoke people their chance to claim me. Not yet. I send myself back to the mansion.

If Tessa hasn't crossed over, and there's still a chance, then I'll wait for her by the door.

I'll wait until the very last second.

CHAPTER 33

Tessa

The door flickers in front of me—an offer or a warning. Time is running out.

I gird myself. *Enough. You can't stand here forever. Be brave. Go find Reed.* I'm about to step forward when something brushes against my shoulder. I startle, then stare dumbfounded at the boy beside me, black hair tucked behind his ears, adorable dimple denting his cheek.

He's here. He didn't leave me.

Reed shakes his head in relief, smiling from ear to ear, but then starts shivering as if adrenaline has caught up with him. He doubles over, hands on his knees, but raises one finger in the air while he catches his breath.

I can hardly contain my excitement. I'm lightheaded, giddy with it; a bubbly effervescence flows through my veins. When he stands his expression is glorious, a match to my own. "How could . . . Is it really you?" I stammer.

Rather than explain himself, he makes a big show of examining the countdown timer etched in light, head tilted to the side, just as cocky and sure-footed as ever. "I was hoping to rework it like the sign at school, but . . . it's numbers." He taps his chin. "So, I think I'll go with my word scramble idea from before of *neighborhood hellraiser.* That feels pretty on point." He turns and slips me a sly, knowing smile.

I fling my arms around him, hugging him close. He's solid. He's here. I could hold him forever, but I pull back to check him over; he doesn't appear harmed in any way. "How did you get here?"

"I don't know. The last thing I remember is seeing the horrified look on your face as I was sucked backward. When I woke up . . ." He waves at the door. "I thought I was on the other side."

"So you've been around the whole time?" I smack him.

"Ouch." He laughs. "I forgot how feisty you are." He reaches for my hands, possibly to hold them and possibly to prevent me from thwacking him again. "I guess you can't travel through someone else's door." He shrugs. "I don't know how long I was out, but when I finally came to, I wasn't in the ballroom like before. I was at my gravesite."

"What?"

"Yeah . . . and my mom was there." He looks at me significantly.

"Whoa."

"I know. But I really needed that." He places his hand over

his heart. "All I can think is maybe you reset to wherever your actual body is, like how we arrived here that first night."

I nod slowly. "That makes sense. It's either that, or the door *knew* somehow—knew you needed to say goodbye." There's still so much about this place we don't understand.

He looks wistfully out the window. "Whatever the reason, I'm glad I got the chance."

"I saw my dad, too. But . . ." I indicate the giant glowing portal in front of us. "I thought you were gone. I was ready to launch myself across space and time to find you."

"You'd do that for me?"

"I'd do anything for you."

Without a moment's hesitation, he cups my face in his hands and brings his lips to mine. We're kissing, urgent and deep, clinging to each other, all the fear, all the worry, all the loss poured into this moment between us.

Tilly's safe. Reed's safe. We're safe.

I pull away. There's something I need to say. "Hal was right. People are trying to do the best they can. I judged you too quickly. I've judged a lot of people too quickly: Brandon, Jenny, Santiago, but especially you. I'm so sorry for before. Of course you were upset about what happened. I should have listened to you and instead—"

"You don't need to apologize." He stops me, stepping closer, tucking my hands back in his. "I'm the one who should apologize. I was freaking out, but you were right. He's dangerous. And we are better off with him dead." He glances over my shoulder at the countdown timer. "But with only twenty-one minutes left, is there any chance we can still take him?"

I can't help my smirk. "Well, while you were having your little nap, I eradicated that asshole from the face of the planet. You might have beat me in high school, but I'm thinking I win the afterlife."

"Always so competitive," he says, laughter dancing behind his eyes. But there's something else mixed with it. Respect? "So, how'd you get rid of him?"

"I called the smoke people into his house, and they surged and carried him through his door."

"Wow." He looks shocked. "That was actually a really good idea."

"I know." I blow on my nails and playfully rub them against my dress, throwing him a wry smile.

"I sure am lucky to have died with the smartest girl in school."

"I didn't do so bad myself."

"So . . ." His eyes drift back to the golden portal glittering in front of us. "I guess it's time, then."

I nod. It's still terrifying, facing the unknown, leaving the world and everyone we love behind, but I have Reed now. Whatever comes next, we can handle it. Together.

Without a second thought, Reed marches ahead of me with his long strides, toward the door.

"Nuh-uh-uh. Just what do you think you're doing?"

"Um . . . walking through the door, like we agreed," he states matter-of-factly.

"And you think you get to go first?" I scoff. "Because, what? You were valedictorian?"

He shrugs, like yeah, duh.

I roll my eyes. "You only got eight-tenths of a point higher than me, Reed."

"Shouldn't the title come with some perks?"

I stare, stunned.

"Then again, I suppose saving the world from the scourge that is Creepy Carl should bump your grade point average a bit, like some added extra credit or something."

It's possible my mouth drops even wider.

A slow smile spreads across his face. He's been joking this whole time.

I shake my head, eyes alight.

"It's always been too easy to get under your skin." He's absolutely beaming now.

It occurs to me that what I used to think was spite is really his way of pushing me, challenging me to be the best version of myself that I can be. It's hard to even reconcile him with the guy who made fun of my graduation speech back in econ, or at least with who I assumed that guy to be. Now I understand. Reed doesn't placate me or go easy on me, but I don't mind. I'm up to the challenge. He raises the bar, but I raise it right back.

How ironic that it took my dying to learn how to live better. "I want to be the person you've always known I can be."

"Me too," he says, more seriously. "For you."

"Maybe we'll get the chance to change, to do better, with whatever comes next." I gesture toward the door.

He looks deep into my eyes and nods, an unspoken oath passing between us: Whatever's next, we'll keep striving, keep pushing to be our best selves—for each other. "So, together then?" He reaches out his hand.

"Together." I place my palm in his.

"What was that quote Hal liked from *Peter Pan*?" he asks.

"To die will be an awfully big adventure."

Reed turns to stare down our door and its infinite possibilities. "Are you ready for our next adventure?"

I realize I am—ready as I'll ever be, anyway. I gaze at Reed Walker, first my nemesis, then my ghost frenemy, and now so much more. There's no one else I'd rather embark on this next chapter with.

"Let's do it," I say, my resolve hardening.

With a deep breath, we inch closer to the precipice, hearts racing as the door dissolves before us into a vast, shimmering promise. It reminds me of the night sky we watched together from the roof: mysterious but full of potential.

He gives my hand a fortifying squeeze.

We walk up to the threshold, and step thr—

Acknowledgments

I've fantasized writing my acknowledgments for years. And now that the moment is before me, it feels like an almost impossible task. How do I capture—heart splayed across the page—the immense gratitude I have for all the people who have helped make this dream come true? Words cannot do you all justice, but I hope you'll take mine to heart anyway, meager as they are. I mean each and every one.

First, a huge and heartfelt thanks to my agent, Uwe Stender. You are both the loveliest human and a fantastic partner in this endeavor. I'm so glad to have you in my corner!

I'm throwing all the confetti for my editors extraordinaire, Emilia Sowersby and Kate Meltzer. Thank you for seeing the potential in me and in this story. I will be forever grateful for your suggestion to make this dual POV. I've loved bringing Reed's voice into the mix. You are both so brilliant and are absolute joys to work with. How did I get so lucky?

It takes a village to publish a book, and I owe so much

gratitude for all the support, guidance, and hours of dedication I've received from the teams at Roaring Brook Press and Macmillan.

Thank you, Abby Granata, for your remarkable eye for design, and Jacqueline Li, for illustrating the cover of my dreams. I can't stop looking at it! Thank you for all your incredible work Connie Hsu, Allison Verost, and Jennifer Healey. You've helped make Roaring Brook Press the perfect imprint to call home. A special thanks as well to production manager Elizabeth Peskin, whose steady guidance helped turn this manuscript into the beautiful book you hold in your hands. And to my incredible production editor Kristen Stedman, copyeditor Melanie Sanders, and proofreaders Stacey Sakal and Jaime Herbeck, your eagle eyes never ceased to amaze me. I owe you a round of margaritas for the challenges of keeping all the timelines straight! A night out on me!

Every book needs a dynamic team behind it handling publicity and marketing. Molly Ellis, Sara Elroubi, and Gabriella Salpeter, thank you for all your hard work in championing this sweet and haunting story. Oodles of appreciation as well for editorial intern Bailey Knaub, and Triada intern Shobhadevi Singh, for your help and cheering throughout. And a special thanks to sensitivity reader Dori Lumpkin, for your thoughtful feedback. It means a lot to have had your eyes on Tessa and Reed's journey.

To Jenn Bennett, Jenni Howell, Elle Gonzalez Rose, Elle Tesch, Molly O'Sullivan, Katie Gilbert, and Jennifer Dugan, who so generously gave of their time to read and blurb this book, thank you from the bottom of my heart for offering such kind words and support. I've loved watching all of your trailblazing author journeys and will happily consume anything you write.

To my phenomenal critique partners: Erin King, Vania Stoyanova, and Emma Baker, your fingerprints are all through these pages, and I mean it from the bottom of my heart when I say I could not do this without you. I adore each of you and feel so lucky to count you as friends. Thank you for reading so many drafts, for the long Zoom brainstorms, and for the celebratory (and occasionally panicked) DMs. I'm so blessed to have you all in my life!

I was a lucky winner of the Revise & Resub contest in 2023 and want to thank the entire RevPit community for being so welcoming. But I owe a special debt of gratitude to the lovely Caroline M. Tell for being *You're Dead to Me, Reed Walker*'s first yes. Your insights were so thoughtful and helped this story grow in a myriad of beautiful ways. And to my incredibly talented RevPit cohort, our Discord chats and late-night writing sessions are some of my favorite places to be. Misa Dessalines, Kimberley Lynn Hanson, Elizabeth Soule, Nicole Loose Miller, Megan Ye, and Melody Thio, your friendship means the world to me. Thank you for reading early versions and revised chapters and for being an all-around supportive home for me. I love you all.

My other writing home has been a group of dynamic and fierce writers I've worked with for years (we really do need a group name!). I love consuming your words and thank you endlessly for being with me from the beginning. Your notes and feedback have shaped this book and me as a writer in so many ways. Huge thanks to Lindsey Danis, Adrienne Robillard, and Renee Pettit.

To my ride-or-die besties, Stephanie Brady, Karen Brenes,

and Andrea Ames, your support and encouragement have kept me going these many years. But, Andrea, I need to doubly thank you. You read my very first draft of this book (when I'd only gotten half of it down) and then read it again later. Thank you for always being willing to jump into my stories.

I'd be remiss if I didn't give a special shout-out to my fellow 2026 debuts! It's been an absolute privilege to get to know you all. I'm in awe of your words and your generosity. And to the NYC contingent, I can't wait to be front and center at your signings!

To Matthew Williamson, my brother from another mother. You are, and always will be, family to me. There's a reason I go to you first with every story I dream up. You are whip-smart with structure and I love brainstorming with you. And to my dear and longtime friend Anna Khaja, thank you for letting me pepper you with questions over a late-night meal in Williamsburg. I'm so proud of us both! And I have a feeling Mrs. Russell would be, too!

To Richard Prock, I tip my hat to you, sir, for your impeccable UFC knowledge, friendship, and all-around awesomeness. And to my doormen, Santiago Mejia and Tony Torres, and doorwoman, Sam Sinanaj, your checkups on how my writing was going and encouragement during my scribbling sessions on the roof always buoyed my spirits.

To my friends, extended family, and coworkers who have checked up on me when I was huddling in my writing cave and celebrated the victories large and small along the way, thank you!!! Your excitement for this book and wild journey I've been on was just the fuel I needed to keep striving.

And finally, to my family:

Rain, I'll never forget sitting in the Brooklyn Botanic Garden and having a long chat with you over the phone while furiously trying to capture all your fantastic insights. Thank you for reading and for being your amazing self!

Eowyn, River, and Jeannie, your support has meant everything to me over the years. And Shashie, Ila, and Tony, I can't tell you how tickled I was that you printed out an early version of *You're Dead to Me* to read at home. It warms my heart to be able to share this part of myself with you!

To Odmaa, Byambaa, Teje, Gigi, Ideree, Hali, and Tselmeg, thank you for all your love and support! I've been so touched. And to the youngest members of our family, we'll make readers out of you yet!

To my father, Jeffrey Falt, and stepmom, Oyungerel Tsedevdamba, thank you for all your encouragement and for leading the charge by showing me how it's done. Go check out their incredible books, all! But Dad, especially, I have so many fond memories of you hovering close and lending me your thoughts when I got stuck with my own writing as a teen. I really believe I'm the writer I am today because of your passion for words and stories. (I mean, who else's parents can quote "Kubla Khan" or "The Rime of the Ancient Mariner" or recite the end to Darwin's *On the Origin of Species*, I ask you?) Thank you for reading E. E. Cummings and T. S. Eliot poems at the dinner table and instilling in us a love for the written word.

To my mom, Linda Falt, both generous in spirit and large of heart. You didn't get to be here for this, but I can imagine you clear as day, rocking in your chair or curled up in bed and holding my book like so many others you'd pore over. You really loved a good story. And I love that you got to be part of my story, now and always. Jeg elsker dig!

To my sister and best friend, Erica Smilevski, I love you and your big, beautiful heart. You have been my "mostly companion." We've holed up countless times with this book at every stage. Honestly, I cannot thank you enough for your belief in me, your love of this wacky tale, and your endless help. Your decisiveness is truly a thing of beauty. I am in your fan club eternally.

To Zdravko, Thaddeus, and Aria, thank you for cheering me on throughout!!! Having you here in this little corner of NYC with us makes life so fun. Thaddeus, I've always loved brainstorming stories together. You made my first fan art, and it makes my heart swell whenever I look at your depictions of Tessa, Reed, and Tilly! I'll be the first in line when your book comes out one day! And the first to cheer future diplomat Aria when she negotiates world peace!

To Jonas, the love of my life and my anchor. We met when we were nineteen and have been holding on for dear life ever since. Thank you for being so supportive with this endeavor of mine to squirrel away at all hours and live in my imagination. You've read, brainstormed, talked me through worries, held my hand, and been my greatest champion. No one makes me feel more like home. I love you endlessly.

To my extraordinary kids, Taia and Sierra, both incredible artists in their own right. I hope my journey can show you that life is limitless. It's okay if the path meanders at times, because each stop along the way expands and fortifies us into becoming the people we are. May my sometimes-circuitous route show you that you can make a choice and make another, that your dreams are always worth pursuing, and that your voice and perspective are needed in the world. I can't wait to see where your own roads lead. I love you with all my heart. And hey, I made a thing! Diggy diggy diggy doo!

And lastly, dear reader, if you have followed me through all this gushing, might I throw a little your way, too? Thank you to all the readers, book bloggers, booksellers, librarians, and to anyone who has held and championed this book. We need stories in the world, told by humans, that reflect the very essence of the human experience back to us. My plea to you all is to please keep supporting the writing and art created by *actual* human beings. And know that when you do, you step into a long and flowing conversation reaching back through generations of writers, across languages and cultures, our words connecting us to one another in this elusive mystery of existing. We get our fleeting moment to strut and fret our "hour upon the stage." I'm so glad to have spent some of mine with you, sharing Tessa and Reed's story.

On to the next adventure!